WHAT
THE
SILENCE
HOLDS

WHAT THE SILENCE HOLDS

MATTHEW DYER

Published by Quiet Current Press

An imprint of **Stratum Sphere LLC**

Texas, United States

ISBN: 978-1-970775-01-3

Library of Congress Control Number: 2025924727

Cover design, typography, and interior layout by Matthew Dyer.

Printed in the United States of America

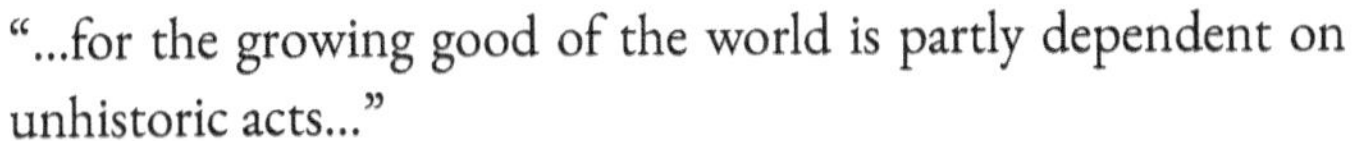

"...for the growing good of the world is partly dependent on unhistoric acts..."
— George Eliot, *Middlemarch* 1872

THE SPACE BETWEEN

It wasn't a place you found on the way to anywhere. Highways curved past it like water around stone, leaving the town settled quietly in the bend of old routes and older habits. The welcome sign stood at the edge of the main road, its paint weather-soft and leaning slightly, as if even it had grown tired of introductions. Past it, the streets folded inward—maple-lined and uneven, cracked where roots had pushed through years of resurfacing. On maps it was barely a thumbprint, but to those who lived there, it was an entire geography of small routines. A place where the air smelled faintly of roasted coffee in the mornings, and porch lights flicked on a little earlier than they needed to each night.

The square sat at its modest heart, its uneven brick paths never quite lining up the same way twice. The courthouse clock kept imperfect time, chiming a few minutes late on good days and never agreed with the church bells down the block. Across from it stood the post office, its brass boxes dulled to a honeyed patina, the flag lifted straight in the morning light. The grocery anchored the corner, with its single automatic door that opened a beat too late, its carts with one wheel that always wobbled left. And beside it the diner with cracked vinyl booths, its windows fogged from breakfast through last call, the smell of bacon grease and fruit pies seeping into the sidewalk outside.

On Saturdays, the farmers' market spilled across the lawn, tables sagging under the weight of tomatoes, wildflower honey, and pickles that all claimed to be "the best in the county." Children chased each other between tables while older men argued kindly about rainfall and the right way to start seedlings, and no one ever really won.

A narrow street curved away from the square toward the coffee shop and bookstore—a two-story brick space where light caught in the windows and steam fogged the glass each winter morning. From the sidewalk, you could hear the scrape of chairs, the clatter of mugs, the low hiss of milk steaming. It smelled of espresso and paper and sugar, a blend that seemed to settle into the wood itself. Some came for caffeine, others for quiet. Most for both.

The street continued past smaller storefronts stitched together by happenstance as much as anything planned. There was the hardware store with its bins of screws and paint samples faded to gentle pastels, the faint scent of cedar oil and dust clinging to the air. The barbershop came next, two chairs with cracked leather cushions and a television bolted into the corner, muttering weather reports no one fully heard. Around the corner, the laundromat hummed at all hours, its mural of mountains faded to watercolor ghosts. There was a record shop that played more silence than sound, and a florist whose small talk was half the sale.

On the next block stood the volunteer firehouse, its doors open on summer evenings to let the air through. A weathered siren perched on the roof, and when it sounded, half the town paused mid-sentence. A block beyond that, a single-story building with blinds half-drawn and a radio murmuring from within housed the sheriff's office. Its door was rarely locked before dark, and the deputy often left his hat on the railing. People still waved when they passed, not out of obligation, but because it was what people did here.

At one end of town stood the elementary school; an aged red-brick building with narrow hallways and a playground of metal slides and tire swings that burned hot in the sun. The air there smelled faintly of rust, cut grass, and sunscreen. Children's voices carried farther than they should have, bouncing off the walls of the nearby gymnasium.

Across town, near the open fields, sat the newer high school; a ponderous building, low-slung and square, its walls still smelling faintly of paint and rain-soaked asphalt. The football field stretched behind it, bleachers bleached silver by years of sun and wind. On Friday nights, the lights glowed like a second dawn, bright enough to draw every moth in the county. Families filled the stands wrapped in blankets, voices rising in the cold air. The marching band played a beat behind itself, the drums echoing across the rooftops like thunder; the announcer called names over the loudspeaker like a litany. Even those who didn't care about the score still came for the ceremony of it, because it was the kind of night that reminded people who they belonged to. By Monday morning, the field stood empty again, the white yard lines already softening under dew.

The park rested near the center of it all with a pond that mirrored the sky in imperfect fragments, a bandstand that served more as a home to starlings than to music, swings that creaked even when empty. On still evenings, light pooled between the trees like something poured carefully and left to settle. Couples walked the gravel path in slow circles, dogs trailing behind, and children tried to skip stones across the water's skin. Families picnicked under sycamores in spring; in winter, the pond froze in uneven patches that caught the orange of streetlights. Ducks lingered longer than they should, skating clumsily over ice that never quite held.

Neighborhoods spread outward like fingers. The older homes nestled closest to town, porches with paint chipped and peeling from years of exposure, driveways patched with gravel, and the faint smell of laundry drifting on the wind. Newer developments pressed against the highway, tidy and quiet, their symmetries slowly giving way to time. Between the two lay the town's pulse, not fast, but steady.

If you followed the old railway spur past the grain silos, you'd reach the water tower, its paint flaking in long curls. Teenagers had once climbed it to carve initials, though no one bothered painting over them anymore. Beyond it stretched only low hills and the idea of distance. The road curved there, narrow and stubborn, as if deciding whether to leave or turn back.

Still, life went on in its quiet ways. The bell above the library door stuck on humid days. The church on Cedar Street rang for weddings and funerals, sometimes in the same week. In the diner, coffee refills came without asking, and advice came even quicker. The newspaper printed obituaries in the same font it used for birthdays.

At night, the train passed without stopping, its whistle cutting a clean line through the dark, serving as a reminder of what connected this place to others, and what didn't. Streetlights hummed above cracked sidewalks; through open windows came the clatter of dishes, a radio murmuring, the sound of lives folded neatly into themselves. The quiet wasn't empty, rather it was a kind of company.

It was a town that didn't try to be remarkable. It simply existed—in the scrape of chair legs, the smell of bread cooling behind a counter, the way fog lifted off the pond just after dawn. Its map was drawn not in streets, but in gestures: hands opening doors, voices calling across yards, the quiet faith that tomorrow would arrive much like today.

And if you stood at the edge of Main Street at dawn, when the light came slow over the rooftops, you could almost hear it breathing. It was a living thing, a town between roads, between yesterday and tomorrow, steady in its unremarkable grace. A quiet proof that some things are beautiful not despite their impermanence, but because of it.

1

GRAVEL AND GRAVITAS

Jonah watched from across the street as Mr. Beverly jiggled his key in the lock, then paused to listen for the click of the deadbolt latching before pulling it free. On the porch, the older man paused and waited for the light to flicker into its incandescent brilliance. His breath hung in the air like the incarnation of words that had only been thoughts. He stepped off the porch and onto the grass, producing a soft crunch as his thick-soled boots made their way across the snow-covered yard. At the sidewalk, he turned around to observe his footprints and let out a laugh. From where Jonah stood across the street, he could hear him muttering to himself, "Carry on, Lord. Carry on."

Mr. Beverly glanced over, and for a brief moment, their eyes met. Jonah hurried to look away, hoping to avoid the inevitable conversation.

"Good morning, Mr. Ashford," the man greeted him warmly. "It's mighty early still; what has you up at this hour?"

Jonah tried to pretend he couldn't hear him, but Mr. Beverly kept looking at him expectantly. After a moment, he answered succinctly, "Couldn't sleep."

"Well, I can tell by the gravel in your voice that you've been trying." He smiled, as if at some shared joke between them, then continued, "Tell me, if you don't sleep, how do you know if your day is beginning or ending?"

"Guess I don't," Jonah replied, his breath fogging as he shifted his weight, scuffing at the snow with his boot. "What about you?"

"What's that, now?"

"I said 'What about you?' How do you know?" His voice came out sharper than he meant, defensive.

"Always beginning, Mr. Ashford." He smiled. "It's always beginning." He gave a small nod, lifted a hand in farewell, and started down the sidewalk.

Jonah watched him go, the old man's words settling in the cold air around him. "Yeah," he muttered to no one. "Good talk."

He stood there for a moment, watching Mr. Beverly's figure disappear around the corner, his words echoing in the cold air. Always beginning. The phrase clung to him, equal parts irritating and intriguing. Jonah pulled his coat tighter and turned back toward the house, the porch light casting his shadow long across the snow.

He reached for the doorknob, paused, then stepped back inside.

The warmth inside was more theoretical than physical, but it helped. His breath stayed visible as he rubbed his hands together. The house exhaled around him—dim and drafty, walls that clicked and hummed from old plumbing and older wiring. The kitchen light spread a dull yellow square across the hallway carpet.

His father sat at the table, hands wrapped around a coffee mug stained more than glazed. He hunched over a newspaper with corners worn from too much folding. Beside it sat his leather-bound planner—the kind with color-coded tabs and ruled margins filled with goals that, Jonah suspected, were more aspirational than actionable.

"Forget something?" his father asked, eyes still on the paper.

"No," Jonah said, shrugging out of his coat and hanging it on the hook. "Just cold."

His father flipped a page, adjusted the planner's ring spine so it lay flat again.

"Coffee's fresh."

"Thanks," Jonah said. "I'll get some at work."

The clock on the wall ticked—loud, mechanical.

"You working all day?"

"Yeah."

He nodded. That was it.

Another pause. Another silence they didn't need to fill.

2

DUST AND DAWN

Jonah walked out the front door, letting it shut behind him with a defined thud, pulling it again until the latch caught with a sharp click. The wind had picked up—not howling, just insistent, like it was trying to get his attention. He bundled his coat tighter around himself, but the chill morning air seemed determined to find every seam, every loose thread. The wind tugged at the stitching as if it meant to unravel him.

His worn soles scraped against the pavement in a steady rhythm, broken only by the occasional stutter when he caught an uneven section of sidewalk. A bead of sweat rolled down his forehead, despite the winter air biting at his lungs. His hands trembled slightly as he wiped it away—too much caffeine yesterday, or not enough sleep. Probably both. The first tendrils of light were just cresting the horizon as he reached the corner, just enough to bleed the black into slate. Streetlamps still hummed, casting long shadows across the road.

Frost feathered the edges of mailboxes and windshield wipers, curling in delicate whorls like forgotten handwriting. Somewhere behind a closed window, a dog barked twice and fell quiet. He could smell the faintest curl of chimney smoke, wood and ash layered into the air like memory.

He paused when he noticed the footprints in the snow. Mr. Beverly's, probably—no one else on the block walked that early. But the man himself was nowhere in sight. There was a strange quiet in the absence, like the stage lights were still hot but the actor had exited.

Jonah kept walking, replaying the morning's exchange—not the words, necessarily, but the look. Mr. Beverly always had that look, like he was mid-sentence with God and everyone else was an interruption. But this morning had felt different. More focused. Less vague and floaty, more... aimed.

Always beginning.

The phrase clung to him, an irritation lodged where he couldn't shake it free. Like a pebble in his shoe.

He reached the corner and turned. The shop was three blocks down, past a row of homes half-awake with porch lights and the faint clatter of a snow shovel scraping rhythmically against concrete—pause, scrape, pause—like someone clearing their thoughts as much as the sidewalk.

Christmas lights blinked halfheartedly from one front window, still up weeks past New Year's. A paper wreath sagged on another door. A plastic tricycle lay tipped on its side at the edge of one yard, half-buried in snow.

It was easier to think of Mr. Beverly as a small-town relic—part sidewalk preacher, part local sage. But every once in a while, the man said something that stuck too well. Those were the mornings Jonah wished he'd just stayed inside.

Lost in thought, he almost walked past it.

The Grind & Bind sat quietly, a crooked wooden sign above the door bearing its name in hand-painted script—coffee and books stitched together like the place itself. The building had once been a law office or real estate firm or something equally forgettable. Now it leaned slightly left if you stood across the street and squinted. Patty said that gave it character. Brian called it "aesthetic." Ms. Wallace called it "structurally sound."

Jonah didn't call it anything. He just unlocked the door.

The key stuck slightly in the lock. It always did. He jiggled it with a practiced twist, then nudged the door open. The bell overhead gave a low, reluctant chime.

Inside, the familiar scent wrapped around him: roasted beans, aging paper, and the faint trace of lemon sugar from yesterday's scones. The kind of smell that made people nostalgic, even if they weren't sure what for.

He flicked on the lights. They clicked to life one by one—pendant fixtures over the café counter, track lights above the book displays, and a softer, golden glow upstairs that spilled down through the open space at the center of the second floor. The hanging ferns in the front window, Ms. Wallace's pride, cast long, trembling shadows across the floorboards. The metal spiral staircase toward the back gleamed faintly. Shelves lined the walls even near the café—early risers often plucked books to skim while sipping, sometimes re-shelving, sometimes not. Comfortable chairs and patchwork couches were arranged into intimate reading nooks that gave the space a lived-in warmth. One of the armchairs wobbled slightly, and Jonah made a mental note to shim it later.

Near the register, a sticky note had fluttered to the ground. He picked it up—Ms. Wallace's handwriting, a scrawled reminder about decaf labels.

Below it, in different ink, was added

Review lease documents.

He stared at it for a moment, then pressed it flat and stuck it back to the cabinet. The surface was slightly tacky with syrup from yesterday's rush.

He moved through the motions—flipping on lights, starting the grinder, prepping the till, checking the thermostat. The ovens came next; he twisted the dials and heard the low whoosh of gas catching, their pilot lights clicking to life with small blue flames that danced. He felt the first breath of warmth beginning to build in the kitchen space behind the counter.

From the walk-in cooler, he pulled trays of scone dough that Patty had portioned the night before—neat triangles studded with dried cranberries and orange zest, their surfaces still pale and waiting. Beside them sat bowls of muffin batter, covered tight. Patty swore the cinnamon batter baked lighter after a night's rest, the brown butter deepening as it waited. He spooned it into paper-lined tins, each portion falling with a satisfying plop, then slid the trays into the preheating ovens. The timer's tick joined the shop's morning symphony.

Wiping tables, restocking napkins, filling the display cases with yesterday's remaining cookies. His body moved without thought. That was fine by him. The familiar routine steadied his hands, gave his restless mind a surface to hold on to.

He paused once to adjust the rubber mat near the counter, noting where it had started to curl. Another mental note. Then he crossed over to the bookshelves near the front and picked up a display sign that had started to lean. A thumbtack had worked itself loose. He refastened it. No one else would've noticed.

The silence wasn't empty—it was layered. The hum of compressors, the ticking of a heat vent as it cycled on, the faint creak of the upstairs banister as the building settled in for the day. He wiped down a countertop that didn't really need it, just to hear the cloth squeak and feel something respond.

He liked the opening shifts. There was peace in them. The town wasn't quite awake enough to make demands. The quiet hum of the fridges, the hiss of steam, the way the shop breathed around him—it gave him something to belong to, even if just until the next wave of people wandered in needing caffeine and small talk.

The first timer chimed softly, and he pulled the muffins from the oven, with their tops golden and slightly cracked, releasing clouds of sweet steam that mingled with the coffee's bitter edge. The scones would need another few minutes, their edges just beginning to blush with color. He set the muffins on cooling racks, the metal singing softly as it contracted.

Brian arrived at 6:15, breaking the reverie of the routine. Early, but not predictably so. Just enough to keep the morning off-balance.

"The caffeineator general has arrived," he called, tossing his jacket over a stool and stretching like he'd just finished a marathon.

"You're early," Jonah said.

"Time is a social construct, my man. I'm living in the future." Brian replied.

He tied his apron around his waist—badly—and arranged the fresh pastries in the display case with surprising care, each muffin positioned to catch the light. The glass fogged slightly from their residual warmth, and he wiped it clean with a cloth before stepping back to admire his work. "Perfect," he murmured, then began rummaging through the back shelf in search of his "experimental flavor journal," and finding it tucked behind some bags of spent espresso grounds.

"You sleep?" Brian asked without looking up.

"Not really."

"Same. I was up watching dolphins run cons on each other. Whole ocean mafia."

Jonah let the silence stretch. Anything he said would only feed it.

Brian kept going, unfazed. "Sleep's overrated anyway. Half the good ideas show up when you're too tired to fight them. Like, maybe exhaustion is just…clarity in disguise."

Jonah glanced over, a small smile tugging at his mouth. "That might be the deepest thing you've said before sunrise."

Brian lifted a finger, scribbling what Jonah could only assume was some new recipe idea into his journal. "I contain multitudes, man." He always said that. Probably thought it was Whitman. Jonah had stopped correcting him months ago.

The morning moved in slow, steady beats—regulars drifting in like snowflakes. A retired teacher who read the obituaries first, a postal worker with a hushed voice and a flask in her jacket, a young mom juggling two kids and a laptop bag. The retired teacher lingered longer than usual at the counter, mentioning something about "changes coming to the neighborhood" before Brian distracted her with questions about her crossword puzzle. She left with a still-warm cranberry scone wrapped in wax paper, steam ghosting from the small tears in the packaging. Brian had something to say to each of them. Jonah mostly listened, fighting the urge to rub his eyes when the overhead lights started to feel too bright.

They played music from the approved rotation—instrumental jazz, soft indie, that one lo-fi playlist that sounded like someone spilled coffee on a piano. Patty hated the playlist; Brian queued it anyway.

She walked in just before ten, purse slung over one shoulder like it was loaded for battle.

Patty was the kind of woman who ran the place without making a show of it. Short, fast-moving, and clearly caffeinated, she didn't believe in wasted motion or unnecessary kindness. But she knew her people. And she knew Jonah.

"You restock the cinnamon yet?" she asked, not quite looking at him as she hung her coat and pulled on her apron.
"Yep."
"And the almond milk?"
"Fridge. Back left."
"Trash emptied?"
"Done."

She gave him a nod—the closest thing to a compliment he'd get before noon. Her eyes lingered on his face a moment longer than felt comfortable, the way they did when she was deciding whether to say something else.

Brian looked up with mock solemnity. "The day shift commander has entered the arena."

Patty eyed the counter. "Arena's short on cups again."

He lifted a hand. "Ah, that's simply strategic rationing."

"More likely simple forgetfulness."

"Or," he countered, "a test of customer loyalty. If they stay without cups, they're true believers."

Patty gave him a flat look. "Or they walk down the street to the diner."

Brian tried again, grinning. "Less waste, smaller carbon footprint—eco-warrior status unlocked."

"Nice try." She shifted her gaze to the small handwashing sink next to the mini-fridge. "Eco-warriors don't leave whipped cream cans in the sink."

Brian clutched his chest with theatrical defeat as he shuffled toward the supply shelf. "And so ends my reign of terror."

Patty turned to Jonah with a satisfied smile. "Place actually looks pretty clean."

"Just keep an eye on Brian. He's feeling experimental again."

She paused, then nudged a cinnamon scone toward him with a

look that said nothing and meant everything: GOOD JOB, KID.

He broke off a corner and gave her a half-smile. She watched just long enough to be sure he ate it before turning away. They didn't need to say much.

***

The lunch rush brought the usual crowd, but also Mr. Fielding from the hardware store, who mentioned that their landlord had been asking questions about the businesses on the block. Patty's jaw tightened slightly when she overheard, but she said nothing. Jonah didn't press, but the words lodged somewhere behind his ribs, low and unsettled. Questions like that usually came before decisions, and decisions rarely showed up alone.

He clocked out around two. The sun had finally risen high enough to burn through the cloud cover, making everything look colder than it was. He walked home in silence, boots crunching new patterns over the ones he'd made that morning. It felt arduous, his body finally registering the accumulated fatigue of another sleepless night.

The air had lost its bite, but the wind still moved like a whispering presence, brushing past fences and through bare branches overhead. Someone was grilling in the distance— maybe charred onions or mesquite chicken—and the smell hit him as oddly out of place, strangely comforting.

The house was still empty. He wasn't surprised. His dad worked strange hours—or maybe he just didn't want to be home when Jonah was. It was hard to tell.

Inside, the air was still and faintly stale, like a book left open too long. He set his bag down, took off his boots, and started dinner. Nothing fancy. A skillet of seasoned ground beef and onions, some boxed rice, steamed vegetables from the freezer. He found himself cooking more than needed, the way his mother used to when she was worried about something. He portioned the extra into a container for his father and left it in the fridge. It was a small gesture that felt both caring and distant.

He ate in silence. Washed his plate. Dried it.

His room was quiet except for the hum of the baseboard heater and the soft creak of old wood under settling walls. He grabbed a book—one he'd started three times and never finished—and lay back on the bed.

He read two pages before setting it on his chest and staring at the ceiling. The words had blurred together anyway, his tired eyes refusing to focus.

'*Always beginning,*' Mr. Beverly had said.

Maybe he meant that every moment offered a chance to start over. Or maybe he meant that nothing ever really ended, just kept cycling through the same patterns.

The shop would open tomorrow, the same customers would order the same drinks, and Jonah would go through the same motions, fixing the same small problems that broke again the next day.

He didn't know what it meant. The book lay heavy on his chest. Outside, a car door slammed. The pattern would repeat tomorrow. The certainty of it was the worst part.

3

CRUMBS AND CURRENTS

The alarm clicked on before it buzzed. Jonah had already been awake, lying still with the covers pulled tight across his chest, trying to convince himself that warmth was a good enough reason to stay put.

But the house had other plans. It greeted the morning with a series of complaints, the sound of something old but still holding. Jonah had grown used to it. Familiar, but never quite silent, never quite still. He could hear the faint whoosh of the furnace kicking on, then the metallic tick-tick-tick of the ducts waking up. Somewhere in the walls, the pipes groaned in solidarity. The house had its own way of waking: reluctant, but practiced.

He got dressed in the half-light and made coffee in the dark. It tasted burned and familiar. He cradled the mug in both hands, letting the steam soften the edge of morning. The first sip was always too hot. That was part of the ritual too.

At Grind & Bind, the snow still clung to the curbs and corners, hardened overnight into gritty ridges traced with salt. The bell over the door had a new rattle, probably loose from the wind the night before. Jonah made a mental note to fix it —added it to the growing list in his head. The sidewalk had a glaze of packed grit and crushed ice. He shuffled a bit of it away with his boot before unlocking the door, not out of necessity, just habit.

He unlocked the door and stepped inside. The warmth wasn't just from the heating—it was the insulation of comfort, the smell of coffee and old paper. The lights clicked on one by one, illuminating the familiar sprawl that started near the café counter, and beyond that, the hushed canyons of bookshelves that meandered deeper into the building.

The front half was a café through and through—chalkboard menus, two pastry cases, mismatched chairs chosen for charm rather than ergonomics. One had a faded cushion that still bore the outline of a coffee spill no amount of scrubbing could erase. But just beyond the espresso bar stood several low rows of bookshelves, cozy armchairs, and a spiral staircase of black-painted iron winding upward to the second floor. It was wide enough to carry boxes—Jonah knew this from routine—and had a satisfying groan on the third step from the bottom. He glanced toward it now, not expecting—but half-hoping—to see Herb already up there grumbling about shelving order. Herb had been there since the beginning. He often said he was practically part of the furniture, a claim nobody disputed, though they noted the furniture never grumbled about Dewey Decimal misclassifications. But the upper floor was still dark.

Upstairs held more of the collection: classic fiction, oversized art books, obscure travel guides. More seating too—window benches, study nooks, a wide table often covered in old book jackets and half-finished puzzles. Herb spent most of his time up there, deep in some obscure mystery novel or rearranging history books by obscure thematic links. He was rarely seen downstairs except during his coffee runs—black as night, always in a real mug, and usually punctuated by a muttered critique of someone else's shelving logic. Nobody took offense. Herb had been around forever, and his grumbles were just part of the rhythm of the place—half noise, half affection, all Herb.

Jonah had started his shift with a shim to the wobbly table near the magazines—his second attempt this week. It wasn't perfect, but better. He re-secured the loose outlet by the pastries with a flathead from the utility drawer. One of the lights above the self-serve station flickered too often. He'd fix that tomorrow. Every day, the place offered up some new ache to mend.

Brian stumbled in, right on time, which meant he'd probably overslept and sprinted to work. One sock was blue, one was gray. He was slightly out of breath.

"Don't tell Patty," Brian said, wrestling with his jacket sleeve. "I'll pay my debt in emotional labor."

Jonah smirked, not looking up. Brian's version of penance rarely aligned with reality, but it was always entertaining. "She'll smell the fear," he replied.

Brian nodded solemnly. "She always does."

A brief pause. Then the rhythm resumed: grinding beans, wiping counters, checking the float in the register. The ordinary choreography of opening a place that never truly closed.

They opened. They brewed. They counted. Jonah existed.

It was almost ten when the door chimed again, and Amanda breezed in like a one-girl parade.

"Jonah!" she sang, arms raised like she'd just been handed a Tony Award. "Your favorite customer returns, tragically caffeine-deprived and emotionally fragile. Save me before I spiral."

"Mandelion," he nodded, pretending not to smile.

She dropped her backpack by her mom's usual stool and leaned across the counter like she owned the place.

"You'll never guess what I got cast as."

"Hamlet."

"Nope."

"Juliet."

"Nope."

"A tree."

"Close. Mother Willow. The emotionally repressed matriarch with a drinking problem."

"Sounds uplifting."

"She dies in Act Two."

"A tragedy for the ages."

Amanda grinned and grabbed a day-old muffin from the discount basket. She unwrapped it with dramatic flair, then took a bite and immediately regretted it.

"Ugh. This tastes like regret and raisins."

"You picked it."

"I have no one to blame but myself," she sighed. "A lesson for life."

She glanced around the shop, half-watching customers, half-watching Jonah. Her eyes lingered too long, like always. It wasn't uncomfortable, exactly, just... noticeable. Like a breeze you only feel once it's gone.

A couple at the back whispered over a shared paperback. The espresso machine hissed softly, as if eavesdropping. Outside, the sun finally broke through cloud cover, throwing gold rectangles across the floorboards.

"You're going to come to the show?" she asked, chewing deliberately.

"When is it?"

"Next month. I'll remind you every day until then."

"I'm sure you will."

She grinned. "You make dependable look almost cool."

He smirked. "Almost is a very generous qualifier. Being dependable isn't really much of a party trick."

"No," she replied, softer now. "But it does make a person feel special."

Patty arrived ten minutes early, which meant something had gone wrong or she was feeling generous. She gave Amanda a once-over.

"Don't you have class?" she asked.

"Free period. I'm sustaining myself spiritually."

"On day-old muffins?"

"And Jonah's moral support."

Patty gave Jonah a suspicious glance.

"Don't worry," he said. "She's eating responsibly and undermining my boundaries in equal measure."

Patty snorted. "Long as she's not undermining me."

"Inconceivable," Jonah assured her.

"Hmph, I don't think that means what you think it means," Amanda chimed in with a puckish grin.

She sighed, crumpled her muffin wrapper with unnecessary flair, and slung her backpack over one shoulder.

"See you later."

Jonah muttered—just loud enough for her to hear—"As you wish."

She paused in the doorway, glancing back with a grin that said she'd caught it. Then she disappeared into the cold. The door protested as it closed behind her, rattling in the frame. A gust of air crept around Jonah's ankles before retreating.

By eleven, the rush had died down. Amanda had gone back to school. Brian was somewhere in the back pretending to reorganize the supply shelf. Patty had claimed the register, giving Jonah leave to escape for a moment. He glanced toward the stairs just as Herb shuffled down, cradling his usual mug like a sacred relic. He paused by the mystery section, scowling faintly as he nudged a spine half an inch to the left.

"Alphabetical, not autobiographical," he muttered, mostly to himself. Followed by "Still got coffee?" voice still low and already halfway into a sigh. It was rhetorical. If there wasn't any, he'd complain louder. If there was, he'd still act like there wasn't enough.

Jonah answered anyway, "Fresh pot's on the left. Should be hot."

Herb gave a grunt of approval and crossed behind the counter without ceremony. He poured with practiced precision, then sniffed the steam like he was appraising something far more consequential than beans and water.

"Still better than the swill they serve at town hall," he muttered.

Jonah didn't ask when he'd last been to town hall. He just nodded as Herb retreated up the spiral staircase, mug in hand, mumbling about genre mislabeling and the death of critical thinking. The groan of the third step followed a beat later—familiar, inevitable.

He lingered at the front, cloth in hand, wiping a counter that didn't really need it, watching the wind push drifts across the sidewalk. The street was quiet again, the kind of quiet that held space.

A jogger passed by, their breath a visible ribbon. The wind picked up, gently nudging an old flyer off the utility pole across the street. It danced once before falling.

And then the door opened.

She stepped in like someone who didn't entirely want to be seen—coat zipped, scarf high, eyes scanning quickly but carefully. Her boots left no squeak on the floor, just a hush of snow melt. She hesitated near the display table, then walked up to the counter.

Jonah didn't know her. That was the first thing.

In a town this size, new faces stood out like a fresh coat of paint. Hers was alert, reserved. Eyes taking in the room without giving much away.

She looked at him, not past him. That was the second thing.

"What's good?" she asked, voice calm, low, a little hoarse—like she hadn't spoken yet today.

"Depends. Coffee or books?"

She considered. "Let's start with coffee. Books take longer."

"Light roast's hot. The dark one's from this morning, but still holding strong."

She pulled her scarf down just enough to smirk. "Then light roast it is."

Jonah poured her a cup.

A timer chimed softly from the kitchen, and Jonah excused himself to pull a batch of blueberry muffins from the oven. They'd risen perfectly, tops golden and just beginning to crack, releasing puffs of sweet steam. When he returned to the counter, the woman was watching him with curious eyes.

"You bake everything here?" she asked.

"Most of it. Patty does the fancy stuff—the layer cakes, anything with frosting that needs to look professional. But the daily things..." He shrugged. "Someone has to."

"Smells like someone who knows what they're doing."

He set one of the warm muffins beside her coffee. "House rule. First-time customers get to judge the baker."

She broke it open, steam curling from the center, and took a bite. Her eyes closed briefly. "The baker passes."

She took her coffee and the muffin and sat by the window—Mr. Beverly's table. He wasn't in today.

A single leaf—damp, tattered—clung to the outside glass beside her. A remnant of autumn, freed by the midday thaw.

She opened a journal but didn't write. Just sat. Eyes occasionally flicking to the door. Or to him.

Brian reappeared, saw her, and immediately mouthed 'who is that?' with exaggerated eyebrow lifts.

Jonah ignored him.

Patty didn't seem to notice the shift in the room. But Jonah did. And he wasn't sure he liked it.

The woman finished her coffee, tucked the journal under one arm, and slipped out as quietly as she'd arrived.

Jonah didn't see her look back. But somehow, he felt it anyway. There was the ghost of a question on his tongue, but the moment passed, and so did she. He told himself it didn't mean anything. He didn't quite believe it.

***

That night, Jonah cooked again. Pasta, this time. Left half in the fridge, covered, marked with a note. Same pen. Same handwriting. Same space.

It read:

PASTA WITH SAUCE. NOT SPICY.

It felt unnecessary, but he wrote it anyway, like he always did.

His dad still wasn't home when Jonah went to bed.

He read a few chapters of a detective novel Herb had pressed into his hand last week. It was good. Grim. Honest.

He thought about the woman at the shop. Thought about Amanda's stage voice. About Mr. Beverly's silence today.

He thought about the phrase still echoing quietly in his head.

Always beginning.

He turned off the light. The dark didn't answer, but the words lingered in the silence, a promise he couldn't quite trust.

SILHOUETTES AND SILENCES

The sky outside was soft with snowlight—gray and gentle, the kind that hangs after snow has already fallen.

Downstairs was quiet. Jonah's father had already left; the coffee pot was half-full, the kitchen chair still slightly turned from where he'd last sat. A newspaper lay folded beside it, crossword half-finished, steam still lifting from the forgotten mug. Jonah poured himself a travel cup and took it with him on the walk. The streets were slushy and indifferent. He kept to the edge of the sidewalk where the melt hadn't yet refrozen —his boots hissed softly in the wet, his breath trailing behind him like a loose thread.

He made it to The Grind & Bind without incident.

The shop greeted him like it always did—warm, quiet, and already smelling like someone else's morning. Faint traces of cinnamon and espresso clung to the air, as if the walls themselves had absorbed years of conversations. He started his usual routine. Lights, machines, pastries. The flick of switches, the thrum of the refrigerator motor kicking on, the hiss of the steam wand warming up—it was like winding up a familiar clock. He moved toward the back prep table and tied on an apron, the cotton still creased from yesterday. Baking always came first—before the register, before the grinder, even before the lights some mornings. His mother used to say that flour in your fingernails meant you were starting the day with care, not haste. He didn't remember when it stopped being her habit and became his, but the motions had long since settled into his bones. He hadn't even gotten the register booted when the bell over the door chimed.

"Hope you've got caffeine," she said, tugging off her gloves. "I tried to journal this morning and ended up writing a grocery list that somehow turned into a crisis."

She said it like a regular. Like they did this every Wednesday. But something in her expression didn't quite match the cadence.

Jonah turned.

She stood in the doorway, backlit by the morning gray, which made it hard to see her face at first. Just a silhouette in a knit hat and a leather jacket worn soft at the elbows. A thick book was tucked under her arm.

"Uh… we're not technically open yet," he said, failing to sound authoritative.

She stepped inside anyway, peeling off her gloves with practiced precision.

"Technically," she repeated, eyes sweeping the shop. "But you're here. The coffee's clearly on. I'm happy to pretend if you are."

Jonah didn't answer right away. It wasn't the words that caught him; she said it lightly, but it landed deeper than he expected. He shifted behind the counter, unsure what she was reading and how much she already understood. He didn't know what to say. He was too busy trying to determine if he should be annoyed, amused, or concerned.

"You new in town?" he asked, finally.

She flashed a grin. "That obvious?"

He didn't answer. She walked up to the counter and set her book down like it was a flag and she was staking claim.

"Friends call me Gen."
    "Are we friends?" He wasn't sure if he was joking.

She raised an eyebrow. "Not yet."

He stared at her. She stared back.

Then he reached for a mug.

"I'll take that as a 'yes, we're serving strangers before open.'"
    "Only the suspicious ones," he muttered.
    She smirked. "Lucky me."

He poured in the brewed coffee and pushed the mug across the counter toward her. She lifted it to her lips, inhaled deeply, then gave a theatrical sigh. "Okay, yeah. I can work with this."

She walked toward the window counter and perched on a stool like it was built for her. Her book thudded open, pages spread like wings.

Jonah hovered for a second behind the counter, unsure if he was supposed to go back to his tasks or wait for something else. He stepped out from behind the counter and made his way toward the door, emphatically flipping the sign to indicate the shop was open.

She didn't look up.

He busied himself with the pastry case, re-centering things that didn't need centering. The glass panel caught a faint reflection of his face—blurred, smudged by fingerprints and time. The croissants looked too perfect this morning, like they were mocking him. He noticed a wobble in one of the café tables nearby and made a mental note to shim it later. That kind of thing annoyed him more than it should.

"So," she said casually, eyes still on the book, "what's the story here?"

"With the pastries?"

"With the shop."

He glanced up. "It's a bookstore. And a coffee shop."

She gave him a look. "Yeah, no kidding. But it feels like a place that has a story. Like, someone opened it after a heartbreak or a sabbatical in Greece or something."

He raised an eyebrow. "Or maybe someone just wanted to sell books and coffee."

She smiled into her cup. "Sure. But that's boring."

"Sometimes boring's underrated."

"No, it's safe," she corrected, finally looking up. "Boring is what people say when they're afraid to admit they're stuck."

He didn't answer.

A long sip, then: "Do you own it?"

He laughed. "No. I just run the morning shift, sometimes the closing shift if it needs coverage."

"Shame," she said, flipping a page in her book without looking. "You've got the look for it. And the whole 'quietly judging the clientele' vibe."

A faint smile touched his lips despite himself. He turned toward the back counter without replying. Her presence felt like static—pleasant, but distracting. It tickled the corners of his focus, made every task feel slightly misaligned. His thoughts kept sliding sideways. He found himself adjusting the same bag of beans twice. He tried to focus on the espresso grinder's hum, the clock ticking above the shelf, anything else.

She stayed.

Not long enough to be rude. Just long enough to feel inevitable.

She sipped from her mug, eyes half on the street outside, half on him.

He moved behind the counter, pretending to adjust inventory labels that hadn't changed in months. He scanned the shelves behind the bar, checking for gaps in the bean jars and syrups, tightening a loose hinge on the small under-sink cabinet while he was at it. The hinge squealed faintly, and he winced at the noise—too sharp for this soft-lit morning.

She let the silence settle this time, not filling it with commentary or cleverness. Just sitting there, like the room was hers, like it always had been.

Finally, he asked, "What was the name again?"
    She looked up. "Hmm?"
    "You said earlier—Gen?"
    "Yep."
    "Short for something?"
    Her smile thinned just a bit. "Yeah."

She didn't follow up.

He raised an eyebrow. "You gonna make me guess?"
    "I'd be disappointed if you didn't."
    He leaned on the counter. "Genevieve. Genna. Genny-from-the-block."
    Her grin returned. "Cute, but no. Too French, too '90s, too J-Lo."

She waited a beat, then shrugged.

"Genesis."

He blinked. "For real?"

"Unfortunately," she said, though she didn't look unfortunate, just hesitant. "My mother's idea. Big on symbolism, obviously."

He looked at her again, as if the name had changed her posture, her silhouette, something beneath the surface.

"Huh. Obviously." His voice trailed as he pretended to rearrange items on the counter.

Genesis.

The name hung in the space between them—heavier than it had a right to be. Jonah felt the corners of his thoughts fold in around it. Beginning. It wasn't just a name—it was a trigger. A mirror held up to Mr. Beverly's early morning wisdom. *'The weight of names,'* he'd said once, during one of their porch conversations. *'They don't always fit when we're young. But sometimes we grow into them.'*

He didn't say anything. He didn't have to.

She was already watching him differently now, like she knew the name had hit harder than he meant to show.

He straightened and reached for the towel on the espresso bar.

"You planning to stay in town long, Genesis?"

She raised an eyebrow. "You planning to start using the full name now?"

"Just testing the weight of it."

She smirked. "I like to keep people guessing."

"Looks like you're doing a pretty good job."

She didn't reply. Just lifted her mug and toasted the empty room like she'd just won something.

The shop picked up slowly, like a train resisting its first pull forward.

The bell chimed. Two regulars shuffled in, both mid-60s, both ordering their usual with the wordless efficiency of people who didn't believe in new things. Jonah served them with practiced ease, already reaching for their favorite pastries before they asked. They took their seats at the same corner table they always claimed, arguing softly about crossword clues and whether or not the heat was turned too high. From upstairs, a chair leg scraped, then quiet. Most likely Herb moving books the way wind moves leaves.

A young couple came in next, stopping to browse the staff recommendation shelf on the book side. The guy asked Jonah if they had any Madeleine L'Engle beyond *A Wrinkle in Time*.

Jonah nodded toward the staircase. "Upstairs. Far wall, right side. Look for the green spine—Patty made a display."

The girl smiled. "Thanks. This place is kind of a dream."

Jonah just nodded. He wasn't great with compliments.

Genesis didn't move for a while. Later, as she sketched by the window, she paused to watch Jonah knead tomorrow's bread dough—a simple white loaf they'd serve sliced thick with soup. His movements were rhythmic, meditative, pressing and folding with patient strength.

"I've never stayed anywhere long enough to learn something like that," she said quietly.

Jonah looked up, startled. He hadn't noticed her approaching the counter. It was unlike him to miss something like that. "It's just repetition, really. Muscle memory," he replied, his hands still working the dough.

"No," she said, pencil hovering over her page. "It seems like there must be more to it than that." The pencil started moving again. "Otherwise, why wouldn't you just use one of those industrial mixers?"

Something in her voice made him pause. She was drawing his hands, he realized. The way they moved with certainty through something that required patience.

"I've been in seven towns in three years," she added, almost as an afterthought. "Always moving before I had to learn the rhythm of anything."

After a while, she set her pencil down and opened her book. She read for a bit, or at least pretended to. Occasionally, she looked up at customers like she was deciding if she pitied them or wanted to join them. The window light had shifted by then, angled sharper through the glass. A thin trail of snowmelt streaked across the floor by the door, tracking the prints of earlier arrivals. Eventually, she drained her mug and stood.

"Well," she said, slinging her book and sketchpad under her arm, "not sure if this was fate, boredom, or simply a caffeine shortage. Either way, thanks for the fix."

He nodded. "Anytime."

She hesitated by the door, turning slightly.

"I'll probably be back."

"I'll definitely still be here."

"Will you?" she asked. She held his gaze for a second more

than was comfortable, then gave a small, unreadable shrug. "We'll see."

Then she was gone.

The bell chimed, and the silence she left behind felt louder than it should've. Even the hum of the cooler and the occasional clink of a spoon in a mug felt too bright in her absence.

The next few hours passed in a blur of orders and small talk, but his focus was elsewhere. He unevenly tamped a shot of espresso, something he hadn't done since first learning to be a barista. A local teen was asking for a book on Norse mythology for a school project. A woman was debating between three types of herbal tea while her toddler tried to chew a paperback. He gently swapped the soggy book for a plastic-covered board book from the display bin, earning a toothy grin and a grateful smile from the mom.

She lingered at the counter while her kid flipped through the new book upside down.

"This place always this cozy?" she asked, adjusting the knit scarf around her neck.

"Usually," Jonah said. "More so on Saturdays."

"Why Saturdays?"

He nodded toward a sign near the register. "We do children's story hour in the mornings. The local librarian, or sometimes even someone from the shop, reads picture books in the corner nook."

The woman raised an eyebrow. "The grumpy old man with the hair like a scarecrow? Is he one of the ones reading?"

Jonah cracked a rare smile. "Sometimes. We rotate."

She laughed. "I kind of hope it is him. It feels like it'd be memorable either way."

Jonah glanced toward the kid, now completely absorbed in poking a pop-up frog on the page. "We try to keep it relaxed. No registration or anything. Just show up."

"I might," she said, tucking the board book under her arm. "He's never sat still for a whole book before, but maybe the magic's in the space."

Jonah shrugged, almost bashful. "Could be."

She gave a final, warm smile. "Thanks, really."

"Anytime," he said, echoing the morning.

He watched them go, the toddler stomping once in the slush at the threshold before disappearing into the bright cold. The bell over the door gave a softer chime on their exit, as if the shop had exhaled.

The quiet returned, but it wasn't empty. It carried the residue of voices, of motion, of something gently disrupted and still settling back into place. Jonah moved to wipe down the counter, but his hand paused on the towel.

A name drifted back to him—uninvited, but insistent.

Genesis.

Not just the syllables, but the shape of her standing there in the morning light. The way she had claimed space without demanding it. How she had somehow left the room both quieter and louder by her absence.

It wasn't the words that stuck with him. It was the space she left behind, and the shape of it.

5

GRAIN AND GHOSTS

The snow had firmed overnight, crusting along the edges where boots hadn't touched. Jonah stepped around his own footprints from the day before—shallower now, a little blurred—and made his way to the shop. The morning air was brittle, every breath like biting into an icicle. He exhaled a plume of white into the quiet street and adjusted the strap of his satchel. Across the road, frost clung to telephone wires like spun sugar. Somewhere distant, a snowplow scraped along asphalt, the sound too faint to break the hush of his neighborhood.

Inside the Grind & Bind, the bell over the door gave its usual groan, metal on metal, like it resented being disturbed. The shop smelled like warmth: fresh espresso, hints of clove and cinnamon from the pastries, and the deeper, muskier scent of old books. Jonah took a moment to breathe it in. It hit him in layers, like stepping into a remembered childhood room. The windows fogged lightly at the corners, tracing blurred halos around the reflections of streetlamps still glowing outside. He stamped the snow from his boots on the mat, leaving wet tracks that would dry by midmorning.

The floorboards creaked familiarly beneath his boots as he moved to the back, flicking on the row of pendant lights that hung low over the counter. A few of them buzzed for a second before stabilizing. He made a note to check the wiring on the middle one—it had been flickering lately. Another task for the list. A faint metallic hum rose from the espresso machine as it cycled awake, steam hissing in quiet pulses. Jonah reached absently for the rag beneath the counter and wiped down the prep area, fingers moving with practiced memory.

He started the shift alone. Brian was late. Unusual, but not unprecedented.

Jonah went through the opening routine at a slightly slower pace, not from laziness, but from the kind of deliberate focus that tried to outpace a racing mind. He restocked the pastry case, shimmed the loose leg on the sugar caddy table with a torn coaster, and adjusted the humidifier under the fiction section's central shelf. The books had been curling at the edges again. He paused a moment beneath the spiral staircase, watching a beam of morning light stretch slowly across the floorboards, illuminating specks of dust that danced.

Patty arrived early—again. She didn't comment on the extra muffins he'd already laid out or the fact that he'd cleaned the back prep table without being asked. She just raised an eyebrow, sipped from her battered thermos, and took over the register.

"You're extra cheerful today," she said, dry as ever.

"I'm always cheerful."

"Right. You have such a sunny disposition as you stand and brood in silence."

He stifled a laugh that he couldn't quite keep from escaping. Even Patty smiled at her own amusement.

Brian came in ten minutes later with a half-apology and two very mismatched socks. Jonah let it go. He was too distracted to lecture. Brian shed his coat like it offended him, flinging it toward a hook and missing entirely. It slumped to the floor behind the register, unnoticed.

The morning built slowly. A couple of regulars filtered in— the elderly woman who always asked for help finding her glasses while they were on her head, and the middle-aged man who swore he had read every book on the bottom left shelf of the sci-fi section. Jonah helped him track down a novella he swore had a red cover and something about time travel and tuba players. They found it, eventually; a blue cover, and no tuba players.

Herb muttered as he walked past, not to Jonah, but to the

scrawny cactus on the shelf next to him. "Demoted," he grumbled, rotating its pot a quarter of an inch.

A high school couple claimed the loveseat in the back, whispering over a shared latte and drawing hearts in the condensation on the window. Someone had brought a dog—a tiny, jittery thing in a cable-knit sweater—and tied it outside. Jonah caught it staring mournfully through the glass every time the door opened. As the morning rush trickled to a lull, Jonah filled a small ceramic bowl with warm water from behind the counter. He stepped outside, the chill catching at his collar, and knelt beside the shivering pup. The dog backed away a step, then sniffed the bowl and drank gratefully, tail giving a cautious wag. Jonah reached out and gave it a gentle scruff behind the ears, fingers brushing against the softness of knit and fur. The dog leaned into it with a sigh; the little head pressed hard into his hand, a quick, honest weight. "Hang in there," Jonah murmured.

As he stood, the cold biting through his sleeves, he caught a glimpse of someone inside—a woman at the corner table, half-hidden behind a screen. She looked away quickly, her hands stilling on the keyboard. Jonah felt the flicker of it, brief, but unsettling. He wasn't used to being the one noticed. The moment tugged at him, not quite a connection, but something quieter, like being seen without warning. He gave the dog one last scratch and stood, the warmth from the exchange quickly fading.

Back inside, he went straight to the sink, washed his hands under warm water, and toweled them dry with a practiced flick. The bell over the door jangled faintly behind him, though no one came or left.

Around ten-thirty, the bell chimed and Mr. Beverly appeared.

He walked slower these days—deliberate, careful, like the world had gotten just a little heavier and he was still deciding whether to carry it or let it pass by. Jonah had seen that walk before in grieving neighbors, in silent church pews. Mr. Beverly wore the same old brown coat, the one with frayed elbows and a missing button, and carried a small, cloth-bound book in his gloved hands.

"Mr. Ashford," he said warmly, tipping his hat like they were on some 19th-century street corner.

"Morning," Jonah replied. "Didn't see you yesterday."

"I was watching the snow," he said, as if that explained everything.

"Must've been good snow."

He smiled. "It was trying its best."

Jonah poured him his usual—black, no fuss—and slid it across the counter. Mr. Beverly didn't take his regular seat by the window. Instead, he chose a smaller table nestled between the nonfiction section and the spiral staircase, a quiet spot where the overhead light dimmed naturally. His movements were careful, almost ceremonial, as he removed his gloves and placed the book in front of him like a relic. The steam from his cup rose in a slow spiral, catching the yellow glow of the pendant lights above.

He flipped through his little cloth book but didn't seem to read. He'd glance up occasionally, eyes drifting around the shop like he was waiting for someone who hadn't arrived yet.

"Something bothering you?" Jonah asked finally, when he brought over a scone on the house.

"Not at all," Mr. Beverly said. "Just thinking."

"Dangerous habit."

"The only one I can afford these days."

He took a long sip of his coffee, then added, "How's your reading going?"

Jonah shrugged. "Slow. I've started four books this week."

"And finished?"

"Zero."

"Mm." Mr. Beverly tapped the spine of his notebook. "Sometimes we don't need to finish. Just to start."

Jonah raised an eyebrow. "Is that more prophecy, or just old man poetry?"

"Hard to tell the difference, sometimes, isn't it?" he said with a wink. Then after a beat, he added, "There's a novel I always find myself coming back to—*Calder Hale's Ledger.* Not flashy. Just... honest."

Jonah tilted his head. "Don't think I've seen it."

"It must be out of print now. Ms. Wallace might still have a copy or two upstairs—gray cloth binding, simple blue lettering." Mr. Beverly's gaze drifted toward the staircase like he could see it there. "It's about a bookkeeper on a farm estate who writes down everyone else's stories and can't quite tell his own. Nothing much happens, but somehow it stays with you anyway."

Jonah gave a half-smile. "Sounds a little too familiar."

"That's the trick of it," Mr. Beverly said. "It's the kind of story that notices you back."

Jonah didn't write it down, but he wouldn't forget it. He could already imagine the cover in his hands, soft and weathered at the edges, like something left behind on purpose.

He straightened the sugar jar so its label faced out and wiped a ring he hadn't noticed until now.

Mr. Beverly stood a few minutes later, leaving behind a few crumbs, a dollar more than needed, and the faint smell of cedar.

Later that day, Amanda popped in after school, snowflakes tangled in her hair and a self-important bounce in her step, a gust of motion and color against the shop's quiet. Her coat was unzipped, scarf trailing, cheeks flushed from the cold. She gave a little wave toward the back.

"Hey, Mom," she called, dropping her backpack into a chair with the theatrical gravity of a stage entrance. Her voice registered a few degrees louder than the day had been so far.

Patty looked up from the register with a smile, exasperated but genuine.

Amanda walked up to the counter.

"Got a minute?" she asked Jonah.

"For you?" He glanced over to Patty who gave an almost indiscernible nod.

"Great! Bring coffee."

They sat in the corner for ten minutes while she ran lines. Her voice was bright, confident, full of mock gravitas and dramatic flubs. Jonah corrected a few cues. She corrected him back. At one point, she dropped her script, and Jonah bent down to pick it up at the same time. Their heads almost collided. She laughed louder than necessary. Jonah exhaled a quiet breath that might've been a laugh, or just relief.

In between cues, Amanda asked about the new books Ms. Wallace had shelved upstairs. Jonah promised to check the latest shipment and put a few aside for her mom.

As he stood, stretching his legs and collecting the coffee mugs, he glanced around the room—just habit. The college-aged woman from earlier was still at her table near the front, now doodling absentmindedly in the margin of a notebook. She didn't look up this time, but Jonah noticed her pen pause briefly when his eyes passed over her. He looked away before it could become a thing.

The door swung open then, but no one stepped inside. It was just the cold air following someone who had already passed by. Jonah glanced up and caught a glimpse through the front window. She was walking past with her coat collar turned up and a sketchbook clutched to her side. No stopping in for coffee today. Not even a pause. Just a quick glance through the glass, unreadable. Something caught in Jonah's chest, then passed, like the small jolt of a step missed on a familiar staircase.

He didn't move, though he felt as if something were pulling at him. He watched the space she'd left behind. The door eased shut behind the ghost of her presence, letting out a low creak as it caught.

Then, suddenly, Amanda asked: "Who was that girl?"

She stared at him, the script forgotten in her lap.

"What girl?"

She raised an impertinent eyebrow.

He hesitated. "Her name's Gen."

Amanda tilted her head. "She looked at you like you were some sort of math problem she didn't know the formula for."

"Hm, I didn't notice."

Amanda blinked slowly. Then said, with perfect deadpan precision:

"I did."

———

That night when he got home, Jonah started fixing the back fence. It didn't really need fixing—just a few loose boards and a gate that squeaked louder than it needed to. But his hands needed something to do.

The wood was old, dry, and splintering in places. He ran his fingers across the grain—felt the uneven ridges, the shallow valleys worn smooth by time and weather. It was the kind of surface that told its own story. Not broken. Just shaped by what had passed over it. A squirrel darted along the fence line, startled by the creak of the gate. Jonah watched it disappear into the shadows beneath the hedge, tail twitching.

He lined up the first board, held it steady, and drove a nail in with three sharp blows.

The sound was too loud in the quiet yard. The wood, old and dry, split along the grain.

He stared at the plank. The grain curved at an angle—not symmetrical, not perfect, just... growing however it needed to. He traced one swirl with the edge of his thumb, following it until it disappeared beneath the next board.

Everything leaves a mark.

He set the hammer down and leaned back on his heels. The wind stirred the trees above, soft and directionless. A branch overhead groaned quietly, dropping a single curled leaf that drifted down and caught on the corner of his sleeve.

He should've kept working. But he didn't. He stood there, watching the lines in the wood like they meant something.

Then he left the gate halfway open.

That night, he couldn't read. The words slid past him like water over glass. He lay in bed, listening to the heater click on and off and the quiet shuffle of pipes in the walls. The room smelled faintly of dry air and wood polish. The ceiling creaked occasionally, like the house was adjusting its posture.

The room hadn't changed. Nothing had changed.

Except him. Maybe.

Or maybe something had moved through and left its shape behind.

He closed his eyes and saw weathered pine split along the grain lines, the faint smudge of a face behind glass, and a name he'd been trying not to say all day.

FRACTURES AND FORECASTS

Yesterday's snow had frozen into an invisible skin of ice. Jonah didn't see it until his boot slid out from under him on the sidewalk. He slipped twice on the way to the shop. He didn't fall. Just staggered, cursed under his breath, and kept going, boots scraping for traction that wasn't there.

Storefronts looked frostbitten, their glass hazed with condensation and old tape marks from holiday displays long since peeled away.

The Grind & Bind was warm when he arrived. Not just heated —warm. It felt like people had already been inside, like voices had echoed in the walls and sunk into the floorboards. The scent hit him first—coffee grounds and burnt sugar, with a ghost of clove from the day-old pastries. The kind of warmth that had nothing to do with thermostats.

But when he stepped through the door, the lights were still off.

Strange.

Patty was already at the counter when he flipped the switch. Her posture was off—shoulders tight, one hand braced on the edge like it was holding her up. In her other hand, she was holding a letter.

"Morning," she said, not looking up.

He raised an eyebrow. "Did someone forget to lock up yesterday?"

"Nope." She handed him the envelope. It was already torn open, creased once across the middle. "It's from the property management company. Ms. Wallace got the original, I guess. She forwarded it."

He read it twice. It didn't help.

"Rent's going up?"

Patty nodded. "By a lot."

"But they just renewed last year."

"They said the market shifted. New appraisal." She flicked the paper with a finger. "Something about 'Opportunity zone potential.'" She said the phrase like it was something she'd scraped off her shoe.

Jonah stared at the letter. The phrasing was polite, corporate, and completely impersonal. It didn't care that their espresso machine was held together with prayers and food-grade tape. Or that Ms. Wallace had started the place with a second mortgage and a dream about slow literature.

It just cared about numbers.

He folded the letter again and placed it gently on the counter. He ran a fingertip along the counter's edge, where a syrup ring had half-dried into a tacky crescent. Some problems stayed small. Others didn't.

"Ms. Wallace knows?"

"She does," Patty said, arms crossed. "And she said she's considering options."

"Options?"

"She didn't elaborate."

That word sat wrong with him. Options usually meant cutting losses.

He made the coffee a little stronger that morning. Ground the beans a little finer, like the act of measuring something precise could restore balance to the morning. The first pull from the machine sputtered slightly—he adjusted the portafilter, wiped the counter twice, then moved on. The rhythm helped. A little.

Brian showed up late, but didn't joke about it this time. Just muttered a "sorry" and got to work. That concerned Jonah more than anything. He was about to ask if everything was okay, but decided to give him some space. Brian was a talker; he'd bring it up when it was time.

The morning rush came and went. Regulars trickled in, then out. Amanda dropped by and pretended not to notice anything was wrong. She adjusted the same stack of flyers three times before inquiring about the espresso machine's condition, as if it possessed emotions of its own. She wasn't good at pretending. She fidgeted with a muffin wrapper in an obvious attempt to keep her hands busy and her mouth quiet, glanced once toward the back office door, and left without her usual pirouette. Even her goodbye felt like an echo.

Even Herb noticed the shift.

"You all look like someone canceled Christmas," he grumbled, blowing on his coffee. "What happened? We out of cinnamon again?"

"Something like that," Jonah said.

Herb squinted. "Don't lie to a man who drinks his coffee black. We can smell guilt."

Jonah didn't answer.

And Herb didn't push. He lingered a bit longer than usual, pretending to read the same page of his paperback three times before finally grunting and heading toward the back stacks. His footsteps were the only ones that didn't squeak on the warped wood near the romance section.

Genesis came in later. Just past noon. No announcement. No commentary. No smirk. Just the wind following her in and the sound of her boots melting snow on the mat. She walked to the counter, jacket unzipped, cheeks reddening from the cold. Her hair was loose—wind-swept, curling slightly at the ends.

"You good?" she asked, watching him too closely.

"Yeah, I'm fine."

"That was convincing. You know, you deflect prettier than most people. I almost believed it, but your delivery lacked conviction."

"Guess I need more practice," he muttered, setting a mug on the bar. The words hit deeper than he let show, like she'd opened a door he hadn't meant to leave unlocked.

She glanced at the steam rising from the coffee, then back at him. "Something's wrong."

"Shop stuff."

"That specific, huh?"

He didn't answer.

She tilted her head, more curious than offended. "You don't talk much when things matter, do you?"

He shrugged. "Not sure there's anything to say."

"There's always something to say."

Jonah met her eyes for a moment too long, then broke the stare and busied himself with a nearby towel. She took the hint. Or decided not to press.

She lifted the mug and took a sip. "Well, you make good coffee. Even when you're clearly avoiding something."

"I'm not avoiding," he said too quickly. "Just don't see the point in talking a thing to death."

"In my experience," she said, her tone deceptively light, "ignoring a thing doesn't make it disappear. It just teaches it how to hide."

He didn't respond.

Genesis looked at him a moment longer, then gave a small, almost imperceptible nod—like she'd cataloged something about him and filed it away.

She turned and walked to the window seat. Mr. Beverly's seat. Again.

This time, she didn't open a book. Just sat. Sipped. Looked out at the street like she was waiting for the rest of the scene to catch up. A shadow moved across her face from the reflection of a passing car. She blinked slowly, not at the car, but at whatever she was tracing in her thoughts.

A couple wandered in a few minutes later, half-covered in scarves and snowflakes, peering around like they hadn't quite made up their minds about what kind of place this was. Jonah greeted them with a gentle nod and asked if they were looking for something specific.

"Something light," the man said. "But not silly."

"Surprising," said the woman. "A little weird, maybe."

Jonah paused, then pointed them toward a shelf just left of the staircase. "Ray Bradbury's a safe bet. *Dandelion Wine* is gentler. *The Martian Chronicles* gets weird in the best way."

They both smiled. "Perfect," said the woman, and they wandered off arm-in-arm.

Genesis watched the interaction with a tilt of her head. Jonah caught her eye, and she looked away.

She didn't stay long. When she left, she didn't say goodbye. Her mug sat half-full, a fingerprint on the rim catching the light. He left it where it was, waiting until the steam curled away, hoping she might come back to claim it. Eventually, he cleared the mug, pouring out the tepid remnants and rinsing it slowly, swirling his thumb over the smudged fingerprint. He hesitated, like cleaning the mug was erasing something. He finished washing and placed it upside down on the drying rack like it still held weight.

Later, Jonah found himself reorganizing the fiction section. Not because it needed it, but because he needed something to fix. He passed the secondhand book cart near the front window—still stocked with the same dog-eared paperbacks his mom had always insisted belonged in circulation, not retirement. He hadn't moved them in months. He got as far as the S's before realizing he was just holding a copy of *The Sound and the Fury* and staring into space.

He'd read it in high school. Pretended he understood it. Mr. Matheson had told him not to fake it. Told him it was okay not to get it yet. That some books were meant to be re-read when people were older.

He still didn't get it.

He shelved it sideways and walked away.

The garage still smelled like motor oil and dust. Cold light filtered in through a clouded windowpane, dust swirling in its beam like unsettled thoughts. A cracked radio sat on the shelf above the workbench, silent, though someone had scrawled the word "tunes" on it in faded Sharpie years ago.

Jonah leaned against the workbench, arms folded, watching his father tinker with an old snowblower that hadn't worked in three winters. The hum of a nearby space heater that barely took the bite out of the air.

"You want help?" Jonah asked.

His father didn't look up. "You know anything about carburetors?"

"Nope."

"Then no."

A silence. Then Jonah said, "The shop's in trouble."

Still no eye contact.

"They might raise the rent. Too high to stay."

The wrench clicked against the bolt. Finally, his dad sighed. "That the bookstore? Coffee place?"

"Yeah."

His father wiped his hands on a rag. "It's a job, Jonah."

"It's more than that."

His dad gave him a long look, then turned back to the machine.

"You always were your mother's boy," he muttered, not looking up from the engine. "Always trying to save things that can't be fixed."

Jonah felt the words land like gravel in his chest.

"She used to sit on the porch with a book until it was too dark to see. Swore the story was better if you had to squint."

That was the closest thing to tenderness he'd said in months.

Jonah didn't respond.

He just stood there, quiet, as the wind rattled the old windows.

That night, he couldn't stop thinking about the letter. The phrase that stood out:

> We understand that rising costs may create challenges for some tenants.

Some tenants. Like they were optional. Like they didn't matter.

He thought about saying something to Ms. Wallace. Asking if she had a plan. But she wasn't around. No one really knew where she went on her off days.

And Genesis... well. She hadn't come back after that coffee. Just sat. Just left.

Like she could feel the shop bracing for something, and didn't want to watch it fall.

He made dinner. Ate half. Left the rest in the fridge, covered.

He lingered at the kitchen sink afterward, staring out the window into the backyard. The porch light flickered twice before going dark entirely. He didn't bother fixing it.

The house was silent when he went to bed.

And colder than usual.

7

COUNTERS AND CONFESSIONS

The letter stayed on the counter all week. Folded neatly, never discussed, but always visible. Like a menu no one ordered from. Like a storm warning after the sky had already broken.

Jonah found himself baking more than usual. Not because they needed the inventory, but because the measuring and mixing steadied his hands when his thoughts wouldn't settle. Tuesday brought burnt scones—he'd forgotten them while staring at the rent letter. The smell hit first, sharp and bitter, clinging to the air like disappointment. They were blackened at the edges, hard enough to knock against the tray. Wednesday's muffins came out dense, the baking powder expired without his noticing. They sat squat and heavy in the pan, refusing to rise. A quiet protest in pastry form. By Saturday morning, he was checking and double-checking everything, finding solace in precision when the world felt unreliable.

Genesis noticed. She arrived as he was pulling a perfect batch of cinnamon rolls from the oven, their spirals golden and even, the kitchen fragrant with brown butter and spice.

"Better today?" she asked, settling at her usual spot.

"Getting there." He drizzled glaze over the rolls with careful strokes. "Baking doesn't lie. If you're distracted, it shows."

"And today?"

He set one on a plate, still warm. "Today, I paid attention."

The shop felt tighter. The walls didn't move, but something in the air did. Brian talked less. Patty worked like she was trying to beat the clock, even when there wasn't one. Jonah felt it in the back of his jaw, the tightness that came when something went unsaid too long. The whole place felt oversteeped. Like the smell of dark roast that clung too long to a forgotten filter—bitter, metallic, and hard to scrub away.

At the far end of the shop, a semicircle of beanbags and mismatched cushions had been pulled together around the low reading chair near the window alcove. The weekly children's story time was in full swing—Ms. Curlee from the library perched on the edge of the seat, glasses on a chain and a picture book propped wide in her lap. Her voice lifted and dipped with practiced rhythm, giving a gruff squirrel and a confused owl distinct personalities as a group of children listened, slack-jawed and fidgety. One girl was upside down on a cushion, her legs bicycling in the air as she whispered the story's ending to herself ahead of time.

Parents clustered at nearby tables with half-drunk coffees, murmuring to one another or flipping aimlessly through magazines. Every so often, a child giggled at a page turn or raised their hand with a question that had nothing to do with the plot.

Herb had stationed himself nearby under the pretense of shelving returns, though he hadn't moved in ten minutes. His eyes followed Ms. Curlee more than the books, one hand absently stroking the spine of a detective novel as she gave a particularly theatrical reading of the owl's confused dialogue. Jonah caught the look and smirked to himself without comment.

Jonah had refilled the hot water carafe twice already. He could hear the rustle of pages and the soft pat-pat of stocking feet darting between tables. Usually, the energy from story time buoyed the shop. Today it just made him feel like everything delicate was happening somewhere else—far enough to seem out of reach, but close enough to hear it.

The register drawer stuck that morning. Twice. Patty gave it a thump and muttered something about mercury in retrograde, but neither of them laughed. Even the espresso grinder sounded louder than usual, whining high as it spun through its cycle. Jonah shook the grounds bin out too hard, and flecks of spent espresso sprayed across the prep counter. He wiped them off one at a time, more slowly than needed, letting the small motions anchor him.

Customers noticed too—some asked if everything was okay. Most didn't.

Jonah told them it was fine. He said it like he believed it. He even added an extra flourish to the latte art—a ghost of a leaf, a lopsided heart—as if performance could hold the place together.

One customer complimented the design without looking up from their paperback. Another spilled sugar across the counter and walked away without brushing it aside.

The morning wore on. Someone knocked over the suggestion box, but no one stopped to pick it up. Jonah did, eventually, and found only one note inside:

"More window seats. Less indie jazz."

He read it twice. He didn't know if he wanted to laugh or cry. It wasn't the suggestion that got to him, but how easy it was to pretend nothing else needed fixing. He flipped the paper between his fingers a few times before tucking it behind the register. The box itself had a fresh chip in the corner now. He rubbed his thumb over the edge of the chip, then looked around the shop like he might find a spare answer tucked between the napkins or syrup pumps.

Around noon, the bell over the door rang.

Ms. Wallace.

She rarely came during business hours. Usually, she appeared in the quiet moments—after closing, before dawn, in that liminal space where bookshelves creaked like they were whispering to themselves.

But today, she came in with purpose.

She wore a navy coat that looked like it had belonged to someone more formal. A scarf she never unwrapped. A folder in her hands, overstuffed and starting to fray at the edges. Paperclips hung from the sides like loose stitching. She looked like she belonged in a boardroom, not here among mismatched mugs. Her heels clicked softly on the floorboards as she crossed the threshold. Jonah noticed a sliver of snow still clinging to the cuff of her pants, melting in quiet streaks onto the mat.

Patty glanced up from the register. "Hey."
Ms. Wallace nodded. "Just checking in."

She moved behind the counter like she still belonged there. She did.

Even when she didn't speak much, the space shifted around her—like an instrument being tuned just by her presence.

She opened the folder. Papers, contracts, printouts—things too sharp for this space.

The clatter of the paperclips as she shifted the stack echoed louder than it should've. Jonah adjusted the tamp on a puck of espresso, watching her sidelong, the corners of his mouth set tight.

Jonah was wiping down the espresso bar when he asked, casually, "Any word on the rent?"

She didn't look up. "I'm still weighing options."

That phrase again.

"Still?" he said, unable to stop the edge creeping in. His hand tightened around the rag he was holding, twisting it once before setting it down.

She paused. "It's only been a few days."

"Feels longer."

She didn't respond. Just turned a page slowly, her fingers careful at the edges, like she didn't want to leave fingerprints on what came next.

Jonah tried to keep his voice even. "If we need to organize something—fundraiser, press, whatever—I can help."

"I know."

"But are we?"

"I don't know yet."

He nodded. He wasn't sure why the answer felt like a shove.

A few customers filtered in. He barely noticed. Patty handled them with mechanical grace. Brian reappeared from the back, then seemed to sense the weight in the room and vanished again. Someone at the back coughed. A teaspoon scraped along the inside of a ceramic cup. Jonah watched the steam curl up from a forgotten mug beside the sink, the warmth thinning too fast to be of use. Somewhere near the shelves, a child laughed, then was hushed quickly by a parent.

"So you're just going to let them raise it? Let them push you out?"

She finally looked up.

"Jonah," she said gently. "That's not what I said."

"But it's what you're doing."

Her expression didn't change, but her eyes narrowed.

"I've run this place for seventeen years. I know what I'm doing."

Jonah shifted, like something too heavy was leaning against him. He shouldn't say it. He knew it wouldn't help. But the words were already lining up in his mouth to force themselves past his teeth.

"Then maybe act like it."

The words were out before he could stop them. Hard. Unfair. Too sharp for the room.

The kind of words that echoed.

Brian glanced over, his mouth half-open like he wanted to defuse it and couldn't. Patty didn't look up, but her pen stopped its frantic scratching. The silence that followed was absolute. A mug clinked in the dish rack, and no one moved to quiet it.

Ms. Wallace set her papers down and met his gaze. Her voice didn't rise. It didn't have to.

"You think this place matters more to you than to me?" she asked, calm but steady. "You think I haven't already asked myself if it's worth fighting for?"

Jonah opened his mouth. Closed it again. His throat was dry.

"I know it matters to you," she said. "But don't mistake your fear for my indifference."

She picked up her folder.

"I built this place from nothing. You found your way into it."

She didn't say it with cruelty. Just precision. And that's what made it sting.

She turned and walked into the office without another word. The door clicked softly shut behind her, muffling the sound of the room exhaling.

Jonah stood behind the counter for a long time after she left. His hands moved—wiping, sorting, pretending—but his thoughts didn't follow.

They sat in place, replaying the words he'd thrown like a bottle across the room.

He hadn't meant to say any of it. Not like that.

He wasn't angry at her. Not really.

He was scared. Of the silence. Of the change. Of the fact that the shop—the smell, the light, the rhythm—was the one thing that had stayed the same while everything else around him cracked or shifted or disappeared.

He hadn't realized how much he needed it until the ground underneath it started to shift. He thought he'd been trapped here. Turns out, he was holding on.

The hiss of the milk steamer startled him out of his thoughts. He turned it off, realizing he hadn't meant to activate it at all.

He stared at his hands. The bar towel was still in one, crumpled, damp at the edges. It left a faint print on the steel as he set it down.

The rest of the day passed like snowmelt—slow, cold, leaving small puddles no one wanted to step in.

That evening, Jonah stayed late to sweep. The place didn't need it. But he did.

He moved the broom with slow strokes, dragging it across floors that had already been clean for hours. He paused under the display shelf, stooping to pick up a penny and an empty tea sleeve someone had dropped days ago. Little things. Forgotten.

The front window reflected just enough light to show him what he looked like. He barely recognized the expression. Hollow.

He turned the sign to "Closed." The bell's single parting chime was swallowed by the emptiness. Then, nothing. Just the silence, and the cold air waiting outside.

8

LEVITY AND LEMONS

The door clicked shut behind him, and the shop exhaled the way it always did—soft and warm and faintly sweet. The scent of coffee grounds, old books, and yesterday's muffins hung in the air like a memory that hadn't yet moved on.

Jonah flipped the sign, then paused a moment at the threshold. He didn't know why, exactly. He just stood there and let the stillness settle before stepping forward. Maybe it was habit. Maybe it was respect. Maybe it was guilt, or just the quiet asking to be felt.

Everything seemed slightly off. The light over the counter buzzed faintly—same as always. The espresso machine let out its usual early-morning grumble. But the air felt different. Not colder, not heavy—just... aware. Like the shop knew something had shifted and was trying to figure out what came next. The lights were a little too bright. The floor creaked in different places. The air carried yesterday's words like dust kicked up and left suspended.

The pendant light above the counter flickered—the same one he'd noticed last week. He made a note to check the wiring later, then let it be, the shop still holding its early-morning hush.

On the corner of the counter, a faint ring marked where someone had left a mug. Jonah wiped it clean, the motion quieting something in him, then set the cloth aside.

He moved through the open as always: counters first, then grinders, then the neat line of mugs waiting to be filled.

On the office door, a note had been taped slightly off-center:

I'll be in tomorrow evening. Let's talk then. —W

No emotion. No punctuation beyond the period. But she'd signed it with her initial. Ms. Wallace didn't usually do that. Her handwriting was neat and firm, but the slant was softer than usual. That, too, felt like something. He stared at it, his thumb grazing a stray edge of tape as if it might offer more context. It didn't.

Patty arrived early. Not dramatically so—just enough to be noticed. She shook the snow from her coat as she stepped inside, nodding once without a word. She surveyed the shop, her gaze landing on the peace lily by the register.

"You're looking peaky," she stated, and poured the last of her water into its pot before Jonah could say anything.

She moved past him and disappeared into the back, boots thudding in the quiet.

Jonah didn't call after her.

A few minutes later, she came out with her thermos refilled and leaned against the counter, watching him mop the last stretch by the pastry case.

"You missed a spot near the back," she said, then took a sip. "Not that I'm complaining. Just don't want someone breaking a hip."

Jonah wrung out the mop and kept his focus on the floor. "Noted."

Patty let the silence hang a beat. "You didn't have to come in early."

"I know."

Another sip. She nodded, just once. "Alright," then added, "You get some sleep last night?"

"Enough."

"Enough to deal with customers, or enough you want me to leave you alone?"

Jonah glanced over. "The former, I think. But I don't know, I'm pretty tired." He managed a small smile.

Patty tossed a clean towel at him on her way past. "Try not to wear yourself out before the rush."

He cracked a tired smile. "Sorry. For yesterday."

She studied him for a long moment, then nodded slowly. "You said it to her, but it hit all of us."

"Yeah. That wasn't my intent."

They stood in a pause that felt like shared ground. Behind them, the espresso machine hissed like it had something to say.

"We've all had bad days, Jonah," she said. "And we all love this place. We just... don't always show it the same."

Another pause.

"Next time," she added, "try yelling at that infernal espresso machine instead. It deserves it more."

He chuckled. "Noted."

That was as close to forgiveness as Patty gave. And it was enough.

The tension that had coiled behind his ribs all morning unwound slightly—not gone, but no longer braced for impact. He pulled two espresso shots and let the scent of them wrap around the moment like punctuation.

The morning steadied itself. Light slanted through the windows, catching in the steam from the machines. Outside, someone's dog barked once and then quieted. Tires hissed over the wet road. The world was awake now, but the shop remained its own little pocket—suspended just slightly out of time. Jonah kept moving, but more gently now—like he was tuning an instrument instead of bracing for a fight.

Mid-morning brought a lull. A couple came in asking if they carried local authors. Jonah pointed them toward the small shelf near the fireplace, where self-published poetry chapbooks nestled beside cookbooks with too much character.

A middle-aged woman lingered near the counter, flipping through a paperback with a bright blue cover.

"Is this any good?" she asked, tapping the book.

Jonah scanned the title: *The Waves* by Virginia Woolf.

He hadn't read it but remembered Herb ranting about it last week.

"It's divisive," he said. "Beautiful writing, not a lot of plot. Herb says it's like meditating while someone describes waves for 300 pages. If you like atmosphere, it's your kind of thing."

She smiled. "I like atmosphere."

"Then you'll like this one. Just don't expect everything to make sense."

She bought it. She left a tip in the jar with the note that said,

'BOOKS DON'T BITE, BUT THE ESPRESSO MIGHT.'

One of Brian's more eccentric contributions.

Jonah turned the note slightly to face outward. It made the jar feel less like a demand and more like a dare.

Snow tapped softly against the front window now, more flurry than fall. Outside, the world kept moving. Inside, the shop seemed to pause again—just long enough.

He wiped down a shelf, rearranged a crooked display stand. Near the register, a child had left behind a crayon drawing last week—half sun, half coffee cup. Jonah straightened it where it had curled at the corner, smoothing it flat with the palm of his hand. Something about the slowness of it all felt earned.

Amanda arrived just past what should've been lunch, scarf wrapped to her chin, hair tucked under a beanie with cartoon lemons on it. She looked more like herself again—tired but focused.

She didn't bounce. She just walked in, dropped her bag next to the stool, and slid into her seat like gravity had gotten stronger.

"Hey," she said quietly. "You okay?"

Jonah glanced up. "I'm fine."

"Well, I'm convinced."

Patty looked up from the register. "She's getting too good at that."

"Like a little carbon copy," Jonah muttered.

"Hi, Mom," Amanda said without turning.

"Did you eat?" Patty asked.

"Granola bar and a vending machine mistake."

Patty sighed. "Try again."

Amanda turned to Jonah. "I'll take a muffin. Not the sad kind."

He handed her a blueberry one. "Here, a happy muffin."

She bit into it, made a face, then smiled. "Perfectly acceptable. Just what I needed."

"I heard about the rent," she said after a moment, her voice low.

He looked up.

"I didn't get it from Mom," she clarified. "I just... pay attention."

Jonah nodded.

"You all will figure it out," she said. "And if you don't, I'll riot."
    "You don't even know how to riot."
    "Of course I do. I'm in theater."

She paused. Then, more gently:

"I know this place is more than a job to you. You don't have to say it. I already know."
    "Thanks."

She stood, brushed off crumbs, and grabbed her bag.

"Take care of it. And yourself."

As she turned toward the door, Jonah called softly:

"Hey—Mandelion."

She turned. Smiling.

"Thanks."
    She grinned wider. "I'm a flower, Jonah. Even in this blistering winter."

And off she went—boots squeaking across the mat, scarf trailing behind her. Her scent of cold air and citrus lingered a little longer than expected. Jonah returned to the register with a muffin crumb still balanced on his sleeve. He didn't brush it off. The beanie she'd left behind once, the one with embroidered cats, still hung from the coat rack in the back. He hadn't returned it. Neither had she asked.

Outside, the sky had brightened without getting any warmer. The kind of afternoon that looked softer than it felt.

Genesis arrived mid-afternoon. Her cheeks were flushed, and her scarf hung loosely. She stepped inside, blinked at the warmth, and let the door fall shut behind her.

There were customers at three of the tables: an older man reading Don Quixote, a woman grading papers, and a pair of teens sharing headphones and giggles.

Genesis scanned the room, then made her way to the counter.

"You're still here," she said.

He offered a dry look. "The shop hasn't fallen yet."

"You looked like you were thinking about pushing yesterday."

"Tempting, sometimes. But not now."

She smiled, then added more softly, "Just wanted to check."

He poured her a cup—already in hand before she asked. She took it with a nod of quiet gratitude.

They spoke for a while, in the way people do when neither one wants to say too much but both are glad to be there.

When he told her about the rent, the outburst, the guilt, she didn't try to solve it.

"You don't owe this place your entire self," she said. "But if it's shaped you, then it's already taken a piece. Maybe you're just trying to make sure it's a piece you offered willingly."

They stood in the hush between customer orders, words drifting like dust in sunlight.

"I like this version of you," she said.

He frowned. "Version?"

"The one who talks like his chest might open if he breathes too deeply."

That stayed with him long after she returned to her quiet corner. The scraping of her chair across the floor echoing a sense of finality.

He wiped the counter a little slower, thoughts circling without landing. It didn't feel like clarity, but it felt less like drowning.

Her coffee sat mostly untouched. Still warm. Like she was waiting for something she hadn't decided to say yet.

The light shifted toward gold, bending through the front windows in long, slow angles. Jonah brewed another pot without thinking. The rhythm was starting to return. The afternoon passed without much urgency. A few orders. A few thank-yous. A teenage boy asked if they had a book on chess openings. Jonah didn't, but pointed him to the philosophy section with a wry smile. "Close enough," he said. The boy grinned and disappeared into the shelves. Jonah moved like someone remembering how to be steady.

Mr. Beverly came in just before closing.

He greeted Jonah with a nod and lingered near the counter, waiting—not out of politeness, but habit. Jonah filled two mugs and nodded toward the front table.

They sat without ceremony. The clock ticked. The steam rose.

They didn't talk much.

When Jonah finally asked if the shop was worth saving, Mr. Beverly didn't blink.

"I suppose you have to ask yourself what you mean by it being saved," he said. "I think anything worth saving starts with someone deciding it matters. What about it matters to you?"

Jonah didn't answer right away. Mr. Beverly didn't push.

After a minute, the older man stood. Reached for his coat.

At the door, he turned back.

"Ask Ms. Wallace if she still likes lemon bars."

Jonah didn't reply, but his hand paused on the counter. It wasn't really about lemon bars. It was Mr. Beverly's way of saying something else entirely, and Jonah heard it.

He stood a while after Mr. Beverly left, hands resting on the wood, heart somewhere between tired and steadied.

Then he reached for his coat. Flipped the sign. Locked the door.

The day wasn't done—but the shop had given all it could.

That night, Jonah stood in the kitchen with a bag of lemons and the vague memory of his mother's recipe. The peel gave under the rasp with a soft resistance, oils catching the air— bright, sharp, familiar. He zested too hard in places, carving bitter white beneath the yellow. The crust came out uneven where the butter had softened too quickly. But the sugar crackled gold on top, and the smell filled the whole house— warm citrus and vanilla, edged with something just shy of burning.

The mixing bowl sat in the sink, streaked with batter and tipped slightly on its side. A spoon clinked once as it settled. Flour dusted the edge of the stove and the heel of his hand. A lemon rind curled near the cutting board, forgotten.

The silence wasn't empty—it was full of doing. Of effort. Of care.

He set the tray down to cool, then leaned against the counter, palms flat to the surface, and let himself breathe.

Tomorrow wasn't solved. The shop wasn't saved.

But something small had begun again.

And sometimes, that was enough.

9

SHIFTS AND STEADINESS

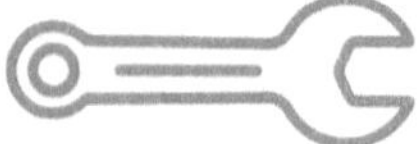

The shop had already emptied for the day. The tables were wiped, the pastry case gleamed, and the windows wore the dull reflection of early evening—that blueish-gray tint that made everything inside feel warmer than it really was. A few books had been left askew on one of the side tables, and Jonah made a mental note to reshelve them. A crumpled napkin sat nearby, abandoned next to an empty teacup with a lipstick stain, both catching the glow of the pendant lights like artifacts from a quieter century. Outside, the wind jostled a loose strand of tinsel someone had wrapped around the bike rack in December. It danced limply in the cold air.

He stood behind the counter, half-leaning against the espresso bar, thumb absently running along a chip in the laminate. The world was quiet except for the soft hum of the fridge and the tick of the wall clock above the door. He closed his eyes briefly and let the sounds settle into him, the way some people let music settle in their chest.

He didn't usually work closing. Patty had traded shifts with him that morning—something about a dentist appointment and an overdue nap. He didn't mind. The change had felt fitting somehow. A recalibration. Like the shop needed to breathe with a different rhythm tonight, and he'd been the one to match it.

The chair at the far end of the counter wobbled slightly as he passed. He crouched down, tugged a coaster from beneath the register, and shimmed the leg without fanfare. Small things. Quiet repairs. His version of prayer.

Ms. Wallace emerged from the back office with her glasses down and a box of invoices tucked under one arm. She paused when she saw him scrubbing beneath the tea rack. He didn't realize she was there until she spoke.

"You missed a spot."

Jonah turned. She stood just inside the kitchen archway, holding a dish towel and wearing the kind of weary expression that didn't come from sleep deprivation, but from thinking too much in too short a time.

He offered a tired smile. "Only one?"

She walked slowly across the room and handed him the towel. "Don't let it go to your head."

He took it, wiping at a phantom smudge on the edge of the counter. Then, as she turned toward the shelf by the pastry case, he quickly reached up and adjusted the crooked track light above them. It flickered once and steadied. Another minor fix. The light's faint buzz receded into the low thrum of the refrigeration unit, a sound so constant it had become invisible.

They stood in silence for a long moment. Not uncomfortable, but expectant—like something had to happen, and neither of them wanted to be the first to admit it.

Finally, Jonah broke it. He twisted the towel in his hands, allowing the physicality of it to absorb some of his tension. "I'm sorry."

Ms. Wallace didn't move. Her eyes, still and calm, stayed on him like a patient teacher waiting for the real answer.

"I was out of line," he continued. "The other day. I made it sound like this place didn't mean anything to you. That was unfair."

She nodded. Not acceptance, not dismissal. Just acknowledgment.

Jonah looked down at the towel. "The truth is, I've been coming here so long, I stopped noticing how much I rely on it. On you."

Ms. Wallace stepped closer, resting her hands on the counter between them. "When something feels safe for too long," she said, "we forget it can also disappear. That's not your fault. It's just... being human."

He nodded slowly.

She glanced around the shop. "This place—Grind & Bind—it's never been about the margins. Never even really been about the books or the beans."

Jonah looked up, curious.

"It's about the pause," she said. "That's all. People come here to stop. For a few minutes or a few hours. To be seen without having to perform. I built it for those moments of quiet."

There was something different in her voice. Not fragile, but more open than usual.

Jonah looked around the room too—the soft leather of the corner armchair, the faintly slanted bookshelf near the window, the table with the paint stain nobody bothered to scrub away. A teenager had spilled art supplies during an open mic night three years ago. No one had the heart to sand it out. Even now, if the light hit it just right, you could still see a smudge of cerulean caught in the grain of the wood, like a permanent echo of joy.

"I don't want to lose that," he said.

"Neither do I," she replied. "But we might."

That truth hung in the air. Cold, quiet, real.

"But I'm not giving it up without seeing what's left in the tank," she added. "And if you're still willing... I'd like your help."

He nodded, almost before she finished.

"Good," she said. "Because I was going through old lease paperwork," she said, lowering the box onto the counter. "Back when we first opened. Rent was... manageable. The coffee was worse. The shelves wobbled if you breathed too close."

She gave a faint smile at that, half-remembered fondness curling at the edge of her mouth. Jonah watched her hands brush a layer of dust from the lid of the box before she slid it aside.

Jonah straightened, leaning his rag on the counter edge. "Are you thinking about letting it go?"

She didn't answer at first. Then: "Every winter I think about it. And every time I choose to stay, I wonder if that's strength or stubbornness."

He looked at her, uncertain. "And now?"

She glanced over at him, eyes unreadable behind her lenses.

"Now I'm thinking about who else might keep the lights on when I can't."

Jonah stilled. His throat tightened, but he said nothing.

"You don't have to answer," she said, turning away. "Just... think about it."

Later, as he stepped out onto the sidewalk, the night had cooled just enough to fog the window behind him. His breath curled upward in soft plumes, fading into the stillness. He turned back and saw Ms. Wallace still inside, flipping pages on a notepad, glasses perched low on her nose. She looked like she belonged more than anyone ever had in that space.

The shop looked different tonight. Not lighter. Not safer. Just shifted, as if holding itself a little straighter. A couple of candles still flickered at the center tables, their light catching on the spines of nearby books. In the far corner, a regular had left behind a scarf, now draped over the back of a chair like a forgotten echo.

As Jonah made his slow way home, he passed Mr. Beverly's porch. The older man was seated in his usual spot, coat zipped to the collar, a chipped mug steaming in his hands. The porch light cast a faint amber cone over his lap, and a moth traced lazy circles through it, undeterred by the cold.

Jonah stopped. "You out here to philosophize again?" he asked.

Mr. Beverly smiled into his mug. "I came out for the silence. But I'll make room."

Jonah leaned against the porch rail. "Got time for a visitor?"

"I always have time. The question is whether you've got anything worth saying."

Jonah smirked. "Not sure. Maybe I was hoping you did."

The old man chuckled. "Now that's a clever deflection."

They sat like that for a moment—neither needing to fill the air. A dog barked somewhere down the block, distant and bored. A screen door creaked open and shut again, too far away to be seen.

Then Jonah asked, almost carefully, "Ever wonder if the things we build were ever really ours?"

Mr. Beverly didn't answer right away. He looked out toward the street, where the lamplight made soft halos in the mist.

"Ownership's a slippery idea," he said eventually. "We borrow things; places, people, even time." He took a sip from his mug. "But if you care for something properly while it's in your keeping... that tends to be enough."

Jonah didn't argue. He just looked down, the truth of it threading too close to where he didn't have answers yet. That quiet, restless part of him that wanted to hold on to what couldn't stay. He nodded, watching the faint clouds of his own breath. He shifted a loose nail out from the porch rail beside him, pressing it back into place with the heel of his boot. Another fix, small and unnoticed.

"Is there anything you'd like to talk about?" he asked, suddenly.

Mr. Beverly glanced over. There was a beat—a small hitch in the space between his inhale and answer.

"Not tonight," he said, gently. "But I appreciate the offer."

They sat a little longer.

And in that shared silence, something settled in Jonah—not an answer, but the shape of a question he needed to ask himself.

10

FLYERS AND FOOTSTEPS

The cold had settled in overnight, sharp and insistent. It made metal sting when touched, and turned every exhale into a brief ghost. The sky was a brittle blue, the sun more suggestion than presence. Jonah stood outside the Grind & Bind, his gloved fingers fumbling with the keys. The lock clicked open with a reluctant sigh. Three doors down, a wind chime rattled uncertainly in the breeze—off-beat, almost cautious, like it wasn't sure the day had earned its song yet.

Inside, the shop was still and dim, the early morning light filtering through the frosted windows, thin and amber, like watered-down honey. The air was stale from the night—coffee grounds, wood polish, and something faintly lemony that clung to the floorboards like memory. Jonah flicked the first bank of lights, and the shop slowly came to life. The mismatched pendant lamps above the bar flickered once before glowing steadily, casting warm pools of yellow over the espresso machines and countertop.

He moved through the space by habit, shrugging out of his jacket and draping it over the hook behind the counter. The grinder gave a low, grumbling whir as he switched it on, followed by the sharp hiss of the steam wand purging air. He prepped the register, straightened the tip jar, and restocked the sleeves and stir sticks in neat rows. The quiet was soothing, even purposeful, broken only by the soft ticking of the wall clock and the occasional creak from the rafters overhead.

Outside, the sky had paled to a dull gray-blue, and a slow drift of frost traced the edges of the front windows, feathered like delicate ferns. Jonah rubbed at a small patch of glass with the edge of his sleeve, clearing a circle just large enough to see the world waking up in layers—porch lights clicking off one by one, a jogger in neon gear exhaling clouds like a locomotive.

He crouched to inspect the footrail running along the espresso bar—he'd noticed the rightmost bracket had loosened again. He grabbed the flathead screwdriver from the drawer under the sink and tightened the screws until the metal bracket sat flush. The work was quick but grounding. He stood slowly afterward, resting a hand against the underside of the counter. It creaked faintly in reply, like two old friends acknowledging each other with a nod.

In the center of the counter sat a fresh stack of flyers—half-letter sheets, printed the night before. He picked one up, smoothing it against the counter.

The words felt too loud in the stillness of the shop, too formal. But it was a start. Something tangible.

SAVE THE GRIND & BIND
Community Night – This Friday
Readings. Live music. Local art.
Coffee and connection.
Donations welcome.

At 7:03, the bell above the front door jangled, and Brian barreled in like a man arriving from a different weather system entirely. He wore an unzipped hoodie layered over a "Spaced Out" t-shirt, one glove on, one glove stuffed into his back pocket. His cheeks were red, his hair flattened into some accidental geometry by his too-tight beanie.

"Man," Brian said, huffing warmth back into his fingers. "It's freezing outside. Like, actually painfully cold."

Jonah kept wiping the espresso bar. "Like frostbite level?"

Brian set his bag by the counter. "Well, I think I can keep my fingers and toes, but my face might actually be frozen to my skull. Is that a thing that can happen?"

Jonah slid a cup across to him. "No, I don't think so. But just in case."

Brian took a sip, shoulders easing. "Better already. Thanks."

Jonah gave him the faintest smile before turning back to the counter. "So, what'd you do with your day off? Something reckless, I assume."

Brian hesitated, then grinned. "Tried building that brew setup I was talking about. Glass chamber, heat coil, pressure valves, the whole thing."

Jonah raised an eyebrow. "And?"

Brian rubbed the back of his neck. "I may have underestimated how much steam it would throw off. It looked like a sauna exploded in my kitchen. I had to open every window before the smoke detector joined in."

That earned him a low chuckle from Jonah. "Sounds like progress."

"Yeah," Brian said, grinning wider. "Messy progress. But I think I'm onto something."

Jonah chuckled and handed him an apron. "We open in five. Go clean the pastry case."

By midmorning, the warmth of the shop had thickened into its familiar ecosystem—steam rising in slow curls from ceramic mugs, soft indie music humming from overhead speakers, and the faint rustle of book pages turning beneath the windows. A low sun filtered in through the eastern windows, angling across the wooden floorboards and catching the dusty glint of flour along the countertop.

The door chimed steadily through the morning—each arrival a minor shift in the rhythm, each departure leaving behind a trace of presence. Scarves were unwrapped, gloves tucked into pockets, laughter muffled but real.

The boards beneath Jonah's feet were wide-planked oak, old enough that their grain had darkened and softened with time. He'd always liked the feel of them underfoot. Something about the texture grounded him, made the place feel less like a job and more like a place he could breathe.

The flyers sat beside the register in a small, hand-cut block of walnut—courtesy of Herb's random woodworking habit. A few regulars had taken one with their order. One woman asked if her granddaughter could perform a song. Jonah said yes without hesitation.

Brian came back from his break holding a piece of printer paper with a rough sketch of a Grind & Bind logo shaped like a phoenix.

"Check it. Event rebrand: The Rebinding. Tagline: From grounds to glory."

Jonah glanced at it. "You're out of your mind."

"I know," Brian said cheerfully. "But it's part of my charm."

Jonah tucked the sketch under the register drawer once Brian wandered off again, amused and vaguely touched. Even absurdity had its place here.

The door swung open just before noon, and Patty stepped in, blowing into her cupped hands and stomping the snow from her boots. Her hair was pulled into a bun so tight it looked like it could deflect bullets, and she wore her usual oversized cardigan like armor. She walked behind the counter and poured herself a cup of the house blend.

"You know Mandy's got that monologue from Macbeth she's obsessed with. If this community night needs drama, you've got it."

"Shakespeare?"

"She's a high school sophomore. Everything is Shakespeare."

Jonah grinned. "I'll make sure she gets a spotlight."

Patty raised her mug. "Bless you. May your espresso shots be even and your tip jar full."

After she moved to the back office with her mug, the shop returned to a quieter hum. Jonah wiped down the espresso bar with the practiced grace of someone who knew when to linger over a task—not out of necessity, but as a way to settle the air. The rag passed over the counter in long, slow arcs. He adjusted a napkin holder, then unadjusted it.

A little after 2 p.m., Jonah stepped out with a half-full satchel of flyers and his scarf drawn tight across his neck. The cold had mellowed from the bite of morning into something quieter—a soft kind of chill that dulled the edges of the air but let him breathe a little easier. The sun was hanging low now, washing the streets in long angles of amber and brass.

The town unfolded like it always did, one familiar corner at a time. His boots echoed through the cold, each step amplified by the hush that settled on streets too empty for the hour. It wasn't silence—it was expectancy, like the town was listening.

He posted a flyer at the library first, tacking it to the community board just below an old announcement for a missing cat and above a penciled flyer for drum lessons. The woman at the desk nodded at him and smiled. He nodded back.

From there, he stopped by the antique shop with the hand-lettered sign and the ticking wall of clocks. The owner took two flyers and promised to put one in the front window. Jonah left with the quiet sound of grandfather clock chimes following him out the door.

At the laundromat, the warmth hit him in a wave of bleach and humidity. A young woman with purple headphones bobbed her head to a beat he couldn't hear while she folded towels with mechanical precision. Jonah added his flyer to the corkboard where notices for babysitters, old bikes, and handyperson services gathered like sediment.

He passed the bakery, still warm from the ovens, and paused long enough to watch the baker slip two loaves into a paper bag for an elderly couple. The bell above the door jingled as he entered. He didn't buy anything, but the baker gave him a powdered donut anyway—"for the cause," she said.

By the time he reached the hardware store, the sky was beginning to gray at the edges. Thin snow clouds gathered like rumors over the rooftops. The flyer joined a dozen others near the checkout: lost pets, upcoming church suppers, local 5Ks.

He slowed on the walk back.

The wind was still and the streets quiet, save for the crunch of grit beneath his boots. Christmas lights still clung to a few porches, unlit but stubborn. The town was aging—like an old flannel shirt stretched thin at the seams—but it was holding together. Somehow, in the ways that mattered.

He paused at a street corner on the way back, watching as a gust of wind dislodged a cluster of leaves from beneath a parked car. They skittered across the asphalt like they had somewhere to be.

He reached the shop again and stood outside for a moment, letting the warmth of the window glow spill across his boots. Inside, it looked soft and amber—the kind of light that made things feel gentler than they were.

He stepped in, the bell chiming low behind him.

Gen was seated near the front, at the corner window where the last of the golden light pooled like liquid glass. Her coat was draped neatly over the stool beside her. A sketchpad was open on the bar, her hand moving in deliberate strokes with a fine-point pen. A mostly-finished mug of coffee rested nearby, its steam long since faded. She sat facing the window, posture relaxed but upright, sketchpad angled just so under the slope of her wrist. Her pen moved lightly, almost reverently, across the page. She hadn't noticed him return—or maybe she had and decided not to acknowledge it yet. Either way, Jonah lingered by the espresso bar, watching the steady rhythm of her strokes before speaking.

"You always sketch in public places?"

She didn't flinch, but a faint smile pulled at the corner of her mouth.

"Sometimes," she replied, her voice quiet, almost meditative. "Light hits differently here."

Jonah moved closer, leaning slightly on the edge of the counter, arms crossed. "What are you drawing?"

She turned the sketchpad slightly toward him. It was the bar—not as it looked at that moment, but with a strange sense of timelessness. The woodgrain was exaggerated, the espresso machine rendered with sharp, mechanical precision. But the light—the way it pooled across the floor, caught the curve of a coffee cup, framed the glass in the front door—was unmistakably now.

"That's... really good," Jonah said, after a long pause. "You even got the crack in the third tile."

She shrugged, but there was a flicker of appreciation behind her eyes. "Flaws make it honest."

He nodded, still watching the sketch.

"There's something..." he started, then paused. "We're putting together a community night here. Kind of a last-ditch effort to remind people this place matters. Coffee, music, maybe some readings. It's this Friday."

She looked up from the page, brows slightly raised.

"Sounds... hopeful."

"More like desperate," Jonah said, dryly. "But I guess those don't need to be mutually exclusive."

"No," she agreed, closing the sketchpad gently. "They're not."

He hesitated. "Would you come?"

"To drink coffee? Or to participate?"

"Either. Both. Just be there, I guess."

Gen tilted her head slightly, studying him in that way she did —like she was peeling back layers, not to be invasive, just curious enough to make you notice what you were hiding.

"Why me?"

Jonah blinked. "What do you mean?"

She leaned forward a little, resting her forearms on the counter. "You don't ask easily. I can tell. So why ask me?"

Jonah glanced down at his hands. "I guess because you already notice the things most people don't. The cracks. The light. The small things."

She didn't smile, but the warmth in her eyes deepened.

"I'll be there," she said simply. "I'm curious to see how it turns out. But don't count on anything performative from me. I'm not hiding some secret talent with a guitar or anything like that."

"Fair."

She stood, slipping her sketchbook into her messenger bag and reaching for her coat. At the door, she paused, one hand on the frame.

"You might be more hopeful than you think, Jonah."

He looked at her, brow furrowed.

She tapped her bag. "That's what you're trying for here, isn't it? Bring some hope?"

He didn't reply.

"See you Friday," she said, then disappeared into the cold with barely a jingle from the doorbell.

"Friday," he muttered too late.

The door swung shut behind her, slow and silent, barely stirring the air. Outside, the street had settled into that late-afternoon stillness particular to small towns—where the world pauses between errands and dinners, where the snow begins to fall not with urgency but with permission.

Jonah stood there for a long moment, staring at the empty stool where she'd been. Her cup still sat near the edge of the bar, a faint ring left behind like a watermark on the day. He reached for it without thinking, holding it for a second before carrying it to the back sink.

The warmth of the dishwater pulled him out of his thoughts. He moved automatically, washing her mug, then his own. He rinsed the last mug, set it carefully on the drying rack, then reached for a towel and wiped the counter in slow, even strokes. When that was done, he circled the room once, nudging in chairs that weren't crooked, aligning things that didn't really need fixing. It wasn't about order—it was about motion. About doing something that stayed done. The kitchen clock ticked audibly from the back hallway—slow, steady, reminding him that time was always passing, even when it felt like nothing was moving.

He returned to the main room and let his hand rest briefly on the counter. The wood was smooth, worn, comforting in its texture. His fingers traced the natural whorls in the grain, following the knots and lines like rivers on a map. It wasn't new wood, wasn't perfect. But it held stories. Coffee spills. Quiet mornings. Arguments. Laughter. Lemon bars.

He let his hand rest there on the countertop—not for the sake of cleaning or adjusting or moving on, but just to feel it. To remember that permanence didn't always announce itself. Sometimes it just was, layered into the grain of things used daily and cared for quietly. He tried to imagine the shop without it—the counter, the light, the grain of the floor—but the thought wouldn't settle.

He turned and looked across the shop, now empty but not lonely. The light above the reading nook flickered faintly— something in the bulb or wiring, never enough to bother fixing, but always enough to notice. The scent of cinnamon and espresso still lingered, like the memory of warmth.

He picked up the dishrag from where he'd left it, now slightly damp and crumpled.

There was always something to wipe down. Always something to mend.

Outside, the snow had begun again—thin, slow, like ash drifting from an unseen chimney. It caught the last of the light in fits and starts, each flake briefly illuminated before settling into silence.

The flyers were out now, scattered like breadcrumbs. And maybe, beneath the steam and grain and ghosts of footsteps, the quiet work of hope was underway. He picked up the dishrag. There was always something to tend to. Always another reason to show up.

SIGNATURES AND SIDELINES

The bell above the door let out a tired clang as Jonah stepped inside, the kind that sounded more like a complaint than a welcome. He adjusted the strap of his satchel and let the door fall shut behind him. The air inside was warm and slightly sticky with steam and syrup, and someone had already brewed a pot of something dark and stubborn.

Patty stood behind the counter, one hand on her hip, the other tapping impatiently at the sign-up clipboard perched beside the register. She was wearing the red apron today—the one with the fraying corner seam she refused to retire.

"Morning," she said without looking up. "You're early."

Jonah dropped his bag behind the counter. "Couldn't sleep."

"Still?"

He didn't answer, but Patty grunted like she'd expected that. She flipped the clipboard around and held it out to him.

"You've been volunteered. Spoken word slot. Opening act. Friday night."

He blinked. "By whom?"

"Brian," she said with a shrug. "Said you'd 'set the tone.' I told him you don't like being watched, but he thinks brooding makes good theater."

Jonah stared at the clipboard. A few familiar names had scrawled their way onto the lines already—Amanda, obviously, in her dramatically loopy cursive. Mr. Beverly had signed up under the name W. H. Beverly, with a note beside it: Original piece to be read aloud. Claire, the violinist who sometimes busked outside the library, had claimed two ten-minute slots and underlined her name twice.

He passed the clipboard back. "I'm not doing spoken word."

"Tell Brian."

He moved behind the counter to grab a cup, but paused as he noticed the tiny wobble in the sugar caddy again. The wood underneath had warped just slightly from a past spill—he could feel the uneven rise through his palm. He lifted the caddy, reached below the counter, and grabbed one of the thin rubber feet they kept for uneven furniture. He pressed it into place under the affected corner, then tested the base. Solid now.

"You're allowed to leave things imperfect, you know," Patty said, eyeing him.

He tested it again, pressed down with the heel of his hand.

"Not this one." It wasn't much. But it held.

She snorted, then nodded toward the bookstore. "Local women's club is coming in for their monthly meeting. You know, the ones who treat you like a prize goat at the county fair. Do yourself a favor and disappear into the stacks before they get settled."

He raised an eyebrow.

"One of them called you a 'fine specimen' last time," she said, deadpan. "Don't make me defend your virtue."

Jonah took the hint.

In the back half of the store, the air smelled like cedar and old ink. The overhead lights buzzed softly above the metal staircase, and the upstairs floorboards creaked with each step, steady and familiar. Jonah made his way up, fingers trailing along the worn railing. There was a cart waiting at the landing —half-sorted, with paperbacks slouched like drunkards and a stack of hardcover donations still bearing library tags.

He pulled one at random—*The Book Thief*—and turned it in his hands. The spine was intact. Someone had underlined whole paragraphs in green ink. He shelved it silently, then moved on.

A burst of laughter echoed from below—sharp and unfiltered. Then came the murmur of voices rising and falling with animation. One voice called out, "Where's that handsome young lad?" Another replied, "Think I saw him go upstairs."

"Oh, I can't do stairs anymore," said a third, followed by a round of sympathetic clucks and a comment about someone's recent hip surgery.

Jonah pressed his lips together and turned down a quieter aisle.

A few customers wandered through the upstairs shelves—an older couple in matching quilted jackets, speaking in low tones about whether their granddaughter would "read something without dragons for once." A college student hovered near the armchair by the poetry alcove, headphones in, fingers twitching in the rhythm of a silent beat.

He kept moving, reshelving, straightening covers, pausing when his eye caught a crooked display. There was a comfort in it—this quiet fixing of things nobody noticed but him.

By noon, the clipboard had three new names. One woman had signed up to do 'interpretive movement' to a poem she'd written about compost. A teenager with a camera around his neck offered to 'project a montage of curated stills,' then asked Jonah twice whether his Canon would be "aesthetic enough for a post-capitalist café vibe." Jonah told him to ask Brian.

Patty rolled her eyes so hard they nearly made noise.

"Everyone's an artist," she muttered. Jonah was halfway through cleaning out the grinder chute when she added, "By the way, you're off tomorrow."

He paused. "What?"

"You heard me. Take the day. Don't come in."

"I didn't request—"

"Not a request," she said firmly. "You've been running on fumes and spite for a week, and this night actually matters. We need you sharp, focused."

She tossed a dish towel at his shoulder. "So take the day. Rest, recharge, whatever you need. No fixing lights, no alphabetizing the mystery section, no haunted stares into middle distance."

He didn't argue. Not out loud, anyway. But he felt the resistance bloom behind his ribs—part habit, part loyalty, part not knowing what to do when he wasn't here.

Still, he nodded. "Okay."

"Good. Maybe go on a walk. Talk to a human. Or whatever it is you pretend not to like doing."

Later that afternoon, while restocking the milk fridge, Jonah spotted Amanda perched at a window seat with her notebook open, humming something tuneless as she watched the snow begin to fall. She wasn't drawing—just tapping her pencil against the edge of the paper like she was waiting for a thought to arrive. The radiator ticked faintly behind her, its warmth fogging the bottom edge of the window.

He let her be.

Outside, the sky had gone that soft, weightless gray that made the world feel suspended in place. The kind of sky that held its breath.

Jonah stood behind the register, thumb idly brushing the corner of a flyer tacked just below eye level. The heading read:

Grind & Bind
Community Night: Come As You Are.

Below it, in Brian's handwriting:

BACK AGAIN. MUSIC, STORIES, POEMS, PROJECTIONS. ALL HEARTS WELCOME. MOST JUDGMENT RESERVED.

He looked at the names on the clipboard, then at the flyer. He didn't know if he had a poem in him. But he knew he'd be there. The shop would need everyone it could get.

When the counter cleared, Jonah drifted toward a nearby display—half poetry, half philosophy, spines leaning against one another like tired shoulders. He pulled a volume with a cracked leather binding, its gilt lettering nearly worn away. The first page he opened offered a declaration about liberty, sharp and ringing like a gavel. Too stiff. He set it aside.

A slimmer book smelled of dust and cloves. A sonnet on winter solitude stared up at him, knotted with rhyme that felt too neat, too fragile. He closed it carefully and reached for another.

An anthology yielded a fragment about love surviving across oceans, words swelling with certainty he didn't feel. Too grand. Back to the shelf.

Another: a dog-eared collection of folk ballads. He skimmed a verse about rivers carving stone, about strength in yielding. Too much like a sermon. Back it went.

A battered hardback of modern speeches offered him lines on progress, resilience, collective will. Each phrase rang polished, heavy with someone else's certainty. None of it felt like him.

He let the covers fall shut one by one, the quiet of the shop closing in around him. All voices that weren't his.

Outside, snow feathered against the glass in restless diagonals. Jonah returned the last book to its place, fingers trailing along its spine before letting go. The words would have to come from somewhere else. If they came at all.

12

MOVEMENT AND MEANING

The house had that particular kind of quiet Jonah only ever noticed on his days off—dense, ambient, almost structured. Not absence-of-noise quiet, but lived-in silence. A steady drip in the kitchen sink. The faint click of the thermostat. The wind pushing against the outer wall like it was checking for weakness.

He stood at the counter in socked feet, sipping from the heavy ceramic mug he generally used when he wasn't in a rush. Coffee brewed by hand this morning—French press, dark roast, a little over-extracted, but satisfying in its own way. He hadn't bothered turning on the overhead lights; the window above the sink let in just enough colorless morning light to find what he needed.

The linoleum in the kitchen had started to curl a little at the edge near the pantry—he'd need to patch that eventually. He made a mental note and immediately forgot it.

The living room was neat enough. A folded blanket over the arm of the couch. A stack of mail on the hall table, sorted but not yet dealt with. He'd vacuumed two days ago and planned to again before the weekend. Everything in its place. But even so, the house still carried the feeling of something waiting to be rearranged—not physically, but atmospherically.

He tried reading. *Calder Hale's Ledger*, still open to the dog-eared page he'd left untouched for a week. He read the same paragraph twice and absorbed none of it. The stillness pulled at him, not in a restless way, but like gravity—the soft kind that suggested motion without insisting on it. The book slipped from his lap, and he let it. A draft from the hallway stirred his legs into motion. He gave up on the book and wandered into the kitchen, more out of habit than hunger.

The kitchen smelled like nothing. Not coffee, not cinnamon, not even heat. Just air and memory. He stood there longer than he meant to, hands resting on the counter, as if waiting for something to rise. But there was no dough proofing, no oven ticking warm behind him. His hands felt too clean. He missed the mess—missed the small resistance of dough beneath his palms, the sense that something was rising, becoming. That there was still warmth to tend to. It wasn't a baking morning, but he still missed the quiet purpose of it. The weight of flour in his palms, the soft rhythm of shaping something that would become part of someone else's day.

By mid-morning, he'd decided a walk would help. Maybe fresh air. Maybe a little sun. Maybe nothing at all. Still, he tugged on his coat and gloves, laced up his boots, and stepped out into the day.

The town unfolded slowly around him. Familiar corners rendered unfamiliar by the angle of light or the scent of someone's chimney. The air held a mild sharpness, not biting but clean. Crisp enough to tint his breath white, soft enough to make walking pleasant.

He passed the library, its brick façade warmed slightly by the sun, and paused at the corner where the old hardware store used to be. The windows there were still covered with kraft paper, but someone had drawn little vines along the edges in green marker, like the building was trying to grow itself back into something.

A bus sighed to a halt a block away. Across the street, a teenager shoved earbuds deeper into place while navigating a skateboard through a thin slush trail that hadn't fully melted. He let his feet carry him toward the park without thinking much about it.

The paths were mostly clear but patched with stubborn ice and snow—fractured in the same places, patterned by footsteps. It reminded him of Kintsugi pottery, how the cracks became part of the design. Fixed, not hidden. The snow bore that same gold-thread logic: beautiful because it had been broken.

A jogger passed, bundled in bright fleece. A kid threw snow at a tree. Jonah noticed the shape of the old gazebo at the center of the park, boarded for repair. The duck pond was still half-frozen, its surface dimpled and opaque. Someone had tossed crumbs across the edge; a pair of mallards pecked lazily, unconcerned by the cold. The willow by the pond swayed gently despite the bare limbs.

And there was Genesis.

She sat alone on a low bench, one foot pulled up beneath her, the other steady on the ground. Her sketchpad lay across her lap, her pencil moving with an ease that didn't look rushed or performative. She was bundled into her coat, hood down, hair pulled back loosely. A thermos rested by her side, unopened.

Jonah slowed as he approached, hands in his pockets. Not wanting to startle her, he stepped onto the path with more weight than usual, the snow crunching deliberately beneath his boots.

Gen looked up and blinked once. "I've seen a few people walking the park today," she said. "Didn't expect you to be one of them."

"Didn't expect myself either," Jonah admitted. "Just felt like moving."

She tilted her head slightly, as if that answer made perfect sense. "Yeah, and has anything moved you?"

Jonah smiled as he responded, "The stillness, ironically. Feels like nothing wants to move, like it's all just waiting."

"And are you?" She asked.

"Am I what?"

"Waiting."

He glanced out at the water, then at the trees, giving himself a moment to think. "Maybe just being."

That earned a quiet exhale—almost a laugh, almost something else. She looked down at her sketchpad, the pencil stilled in her hand.

"This bench accepts all forms of being," she said, tapping the empty space beside her. "Introspective, extrospective, broody, moody, —I'd bet even quietly ponderous or existentially vague."

He sat—not too close, just enough to share the view and let the silence gather between them. A squirrel darted across the frozen grass behind them. The breeze picked up, tugging faintly at the corners of her sketchpad.

She didn't say anything else for a while, just returned to her drawing with a few gentle strokes.

Jonah tilted his head slightly, catching the page out of the corner of his eye. It wasn't a scene exactly. More a memory sketched in outlines—a bent tree limb, a suggestion of water, the trace of footprints curling away into empty space.

After a moment, he asked quietly, "When you draw—do you sketch what you see, or what you feel?"

She didn't look up. "Usually what I feel. But it helps to start with something visible."

Her pencil paused for a moment, then continued. "The world makes more sense when I turn it into shape and shadow. Not that it changes anything. Just makes it more understandable."

Jonah nodded, absorbing that. His breath clouded slightly in front of him, but he didn't move. The ducks near the edge of the pond shifted, rustling faintly in the reeds.

They sat like that for a while. Nothing pressing. Just the kind of quiet that didn't need filling.

Eventually, Gen closed her sketchpad and rose, brushing a smudge from her coat sleeve. A scrap of paper fluttered loose from between the pages—long and narrow, like a torn bookmark. It landed near Jonah's boot.

He picked it up.

The paper was heavy and soft at the edges. Charcoal smudged along one side. A single word written in small, neat script across the corner:

linger.

She glanced back and saw it in his hand. "Oh. That's yours now."

"You dropped it."

"I know," she said, slinging her bag over her shoulder. "But it didn't belong to anything. Might as well belong to something now."

Jonah looked down at the word again.

"Linger," he read softly.

She slung her bag over her shoulder, eyes on him now, not guarded. "Seems like something you're adept at."

He almost smiled at that—not because she was wrong, but because it sounded less like a flaw when she named it that way.

She stepped back onto the path, then turned with a small nod —half farewell, half something else.

"See you tomorrow?"

"Yeah," he said. "We're closing early to set up for the

community night. First cup's free if you show up before seven."

Her smile this time was real, unhidden. "No bribery necessary. I'll be there."

She turned and walked off, boots marking an unhurried line through the fractured snow.

Jonah watched until she disappeared behind the bend of willow branches, then glanced once more at the paper in his hand before tucking it carefully into his coat pocket.

'Linger,' it said. And for now, he did.

He stayed on the bench a while longer, letting the silence settle again. His breath came in soft clouds, fading as quickly as they formed. A child called out in the distance, the voice bright and echoing across the park, then vanished again. The breeze had picked up slightly, rustling the dry reeds at the edge of the pond and making the trees creak like old men settling in their chairs. The ducks had moved off, paddling slow arcs across the thawed edges of water. The stillness returned, not empty but whole—like a room just after someone leaves, still full of their presence.

Eventually, Jonah stood and stretched his legs. The cold had started to edge past his coat, but it didn't bother him much.

He walked slowly along the outer path, boots scuffing across patches of packed snow and half-thawed ground, beyond the loop of trail and the sagging gazebo, until he reached the far side of the park—where the trees gave way to an open field. He walked toward it without thinking, drawn more by direction than purpose.

The grass there was brittle and gold, wind-flattened and winter-worn. A low fence traced its perimeter—three boards wide, bleached and warped with age. Jonah stopped at the midpoint and rested his hands on the top rail, the grain rough beneath his gloves.

There wasn't much to see. No grand view. No hidden landmark. Just space.

But space had its own gravity.

He let his gaze drift across the field, the subtle dips and mounds in the land, the way the light bent slightly along the far ridge. A few birds cut across the sky in a loose V, so high up they barely seemed connected to anything.

He didn't know why the fence held his attention.

Maybe because it didn't try to be anything. It wasn't imposing or symbolic or meant to divide. It was just there. Weathered and leaning. A line someone had drawn long ago, not to keep things out, but to mark the shape of what they had.

There was something comforting in that.

In the idea that not everything had to move forward. Some things just stayed. Not stuck—steadied.

The wind pressed softly against his back, not pushing, just reminding him he had more day ahead.

The small market on Maple wasn't crowded. Jonah stepped in quietly, nodding to the older woman at the counter who always gave exact change, even when no one asked for it. The air inside was warm and a little dry, the heater ticking faintly from the ceiling vent. A few regulars gathered near the register, chatting softly about the weather like it was a shared neighbor they didn't fully trust. Jonah nodded politely and made a quiet loop through the aisles.

He didn't need much—just a few things to put lunch together. A small loaf of bread with a cracked top, a wedge of sharp white cheddar wrapped in waxed paper, and a handful of apples from a wooden bin near the door. He paused at the jam shelf on a whim and picked the fig preserves without overthinking it.

The walk home felt shorter. Or maybe just less linear. His thoughts looped and stretched as he went, touching things he couldn't quite name and didn't need to.

Back in the kitchen, the house felt the way it always did—cool and familiar, not impersonal but pared back. Jonah moved quietly as he prepared lunch: sliced the bread, layered the cheese, toasted it in the pan until it crisped. The fig jam turned out to be a good call—sweet and strange in a way he liked.

He washed the plate and pan afterward, not because he needed to, but because it felt like the kind of thing that helped a day make sense.

Then he made his way to the living room, still wrapped in the slow, deliberate rhythm of the afternoon. The couch blanket was cool to the touch, and the light coming through the front window had started to slide toward golden—just enough to make the corners of the room feel softer.

Jonah crossed to the coat rack near the door and slipped a hand into the inside pocket of his hanging jacket. He pulled out the narrow strip of paper, turned it over once, then carried it with him to the couch.

He picked up *Calder Hale's Ledger* from the side table and settled in. He opened to the same dog-eared page but didn't start reading right away. His thumb found the edge of the paper now tucked gently between the pages—the one Gen had dropped.

When he finally turned the page, the words met him gently, like someone speaking in a low voice in a quiet room:

> *"There are days when all we do is carry the weight of our own presence. Not for lack of motion, but because we feel the echo of what we've chosen not to chase. Stillness isn't failure. It's the hour before the idea. The space where the heart takes inventory."*

Jonah let the line roll around in his mind, slow and deliberate, like tasting something unfamiliar just long enough to recognize it. He remembered what Mr. Beverly had said—that some books notice you back. At the time, it had sounded like something older people said to sound wise. But now... now it struck a chord that continued to resonate through him.

He read the passage again, slower this time. He glanced at the strip of paper peeking above the pages of the book. He let the book rest lightly in his hands, the paper soft beneath his fingers. He closed his eyes for a breath.

Linger.

Not a command. Not a question. Just a possibility.

When he opened them again, the room was the same, but steadier somehow. He turned the page and continued reading.

13

ACTS AND ARTICULATION

The bell above the door jingled as Jonah walked a regular to the exit, holding it open against the rising hush of early evening. Outside, the street had begun to dim beneath a wash of slate-blue sky, and the streetlamps flickered to life with a sort of reluctant dignity.

"We'll be open again in a couple of hours," Jonah said, offering a practiced but genuine smile. "Community night— performances, readings, music. First cup's on the house if you show up before seven."

The woman hesitated at the threshold, clutching a book half-wrapped in a scarf. "I'm not much for crowds."

Jonah shrugged. "Neither are most of the people performing."

She chuckled softly and stepped out. "I'll think about it."

He let the door close behind her and flipped the sign from Open to Preparing Something Worth the Wait, the hand-lettered script curving around a coffee ring. He locked it with a solid click and leaned against the glass, watching the street outside.

They had a few hours.

The sidewalk beyond the window had quieted. A thin dusting of snow caught in the crevices of brick and curb, glowing faintly in the half-light. The town was beginning to tuck itself in—or perhaps, readying for something worth staying up for.

Inside, the shop felt like a theatre just before the overture— lights dimmed to a low golden glow, shadows long but soft. Jonah moved deliberately, rearranging tables, pulling the mismatched chairs into loose semi-circles around the small platform stage they'd set up near the poetry shelves. He swapped the music to something instrumental and let it fill the room.

He tested a few bulbs above the register, gently tapping one that buzzed faintly. It steadied under his fingers. The espresso machine hissed once in approval, and Jonah gave the counter a final wipe with a cloth and an application of lemon cleaner and elbow grease.

The air smelled of cinnamon and citrus—a strange combination, but honest.

Amanda arrived first, bundled in her winter coat and already brushing snowflakes from her hair with theatrical flair.

"You're early," Jonah said.

"I like to pretend I'm punctual," she replied, unwrapping her scarf with a spin. "Makes up for all the other areas in which I'm allegedly lacking."

Jonah handed her a roll of painter's tape. "Stars on the front window?"

She took it with mock solemnity. "The people demand atmosphere!"

Together they crouched by the window, taping gold-foil stars onto the glass in uneven constellations. Outside, the reflection of their movement shimmered in the pane—Amanda's grin, Jonah's focused scowl, the shared warmth of preparation.

The bell jingled again, and Brian burst in like a walking tech rehearsal—arms full of tangled cords, a fold-up projector screen, and what suspiciously resembled a fog machine he definitely hadn't asked permission to bring.

"Stand aside! I'm about to elevate this ambiance from charming to cosmic."

Amanda narrowed her eyes. "Tell me that thing doesn't flash."

"How truthful are you wanting me to be in this moment?"

"Brian! I would have thought you had learned your lesson."

Brian raised his eyebrows in mock offense, shifting the screen higher on his hip. "No one had a seizure last time. There was just that one guy who got spiritually overtaken by the rhythm of the poetry, but that's totally different."

Jonah nodded toward the poetry shelves. "Stage is there. Try not to melt anything."

Brian grinned. "I make no promises."

Amanda smirked. "We want atmosphere, sure, I just hope he keeps it in the stratosphere and not the exosphere."

Jonah arched an eyebrow. "Have you been studying that in school?"

She grinned. "Aced the quiz last week."

Jonah glanced back at Brian, who had now stepped into the projector's glow and was throwing dramatic shadow shapes onto the wall. There was no stopping him, Jonah knew. And honestly, he didn't really want to.

By six o'clock, the shop had transformed. Tables arranged in welcoming clusters, warm light tucked into corners, chairs pulled into soft arcs around the impromptu stage. Mismatched throw pillows had somehow multiplied—a contribution from Ms. Wallace, who emerged from the back with a basket of extras like she'd been hoarding them just for tonight.

"These aren't just for show," she said quietly, nudging a cushion into position. "People tend to stay longer when their back isn't arguing with a chair."

Jonah gave her a rare smile. "Noted."

The scent of ground beans and baked sugar had begun to layer the air. Someone lit a cinnamon candle near the returns shelf —unofficial, unsanctioned, but effective. The air shimmered with the hush of anticipation.

Herb arrived soon after, muttering about traffic and the inferior quality of recent biscotti deliveries, though he still managed to compliment the seating layout.

"This place is almost too cozy," he said, setting down his battered thermos and grumbling at the folding chairs. "I might fall asleep in the middle of someone's sonnet."

Patty swept in from the back, clipboard in hand, already halfway through the mental checklist she'd made days earlier.

"I need one of you caffeinated idiots to make sure the hot water tap isn't leaking again," she barked as she passed the counter. "And somebody get those lemon bars out where people can see them—they're not going to advertise themselves."

Brian pointed to the tray on the front counter. "Already staged, Captain Patty."

She narrowed her eyes at him but said nothing—which, for Patty, was high praise.

The display case gleamed with the afternoon's work—three dozen of Jonah's cardamom cookies, shaped like crescents and dusted with pearl sugar; mini quiches with spinach and Gruyère, their crusts golden and flaky; and his signature item for the evening: honey cakes shaped like books, each one iced with edible gold leaf along the spine.

"You've outdone yourself," Amanda said, peering through the glass. "These look too pretty to eat."

"That's the point," Patty called from behind the espresso machine. "We want people to remember this night."

The first guests arrived just after six. Amanda greeted them with unearned authority and the charisma of a community theater lead.

"Welcome to the Grind & Bind! Please silence your pagers, your cellular phones, your self-doubt, and any overly critical inner monologues."

Herb manned the coffee urn with the solemnity of a priest offering sacraments, grumbling at anyone who tried to add flavored creamer.

By six-thirty, the room buzzed in a low, hopeful murmur—mugs clinked, scarves were shrugged off, laughter burst from a table and dissolved as quickly as it came. Someone spilled tea and apologized twice. Someone else brought a thermos from home and received Herb's glare like a benediction. Children pointed at the stars on the windows, tracing imaginary lines with mittened fingers. It smelled like nutmeg and old pages. The walls held it all.

The show began with a high schooler reading three original poems—shaking hands, cracking voice—but the room stayed with her the whole way through. The silence between lines was its own kind of reverence, the kind that made even the coffee machines pause. Someone at the back set down their cup with exaggerated care. An older man with a harmonica and a long, braided ponytail played a haunting blues melody, bending notes that settled into the wooden beams like dust, at which point Brian's projector kicked into gear, casting soft visuals behind the performers: gently falling pages, abstract watercolors, looping typewriter animations.

The lights shifted and ebbed—slow dissolves between hues, more feeling than spectacle. In the audience, faces flickered with reflection: some uplifted, some inward. One woman wiped her eyes, though whether from the music or memory, Jonah couldn't tell.

The crowd's reactions varied—some leaned forward, drawn in;

others sat back, slightly unsettled by the sensory layering. Jonah caught snippets of whispered commentary:

"Reminds me of grief… or maybe Monday morning."

"Feels like my dreams look."

Amanda passed by again, this time whispering behind her hand: "Brian's either a genius or a menace."

"Both," Jonah replied. "In stereo."

Somewhere during the third act—a woman reading from a collection of letters she'd never sent—Jonah noticed a subtle shifting in the crowd near the door. She'd stepped in quietly, already sketchbook in hand. She wore a charcoal-gray coat with the collar flipped up, snow still melting along the sleeves. Her eyes took in the room, then narrowed slightly—not in disapproval, but in focus, like she was framing the composition in her head.

She didn't speak to anyone. Just found her usual stool by the side window and sat down, flipping open her sketchpad without looking up.

Jonah brewed a fresh mug, added a splash of milk the way she'd ordered it once before, and crossed the room silently. He placed the mug beside her and walked away without a word.

She didn't notice at first.

Her pencil moved in slow arcs, then faster strokes, her brow furrowed in concentration. When she reached for a piece of charcoal and accidentally nudged the mug with her elbow, she paused, glanced down—and then up.

Her eyes met Jonah's across the room.

She offered a quiet nod.

Jonah returned it, his chest tightening—not with clarity, but something like presence. Not hope. Not yet. Just the quiet, steady ache of being seen. He felt the warmth of the moment more than the coffee steam. It wasn't big, or bold, but unmistakable. Something understood.

Another performance began—a young man reciting slam poetry with a voice too big for his frame. Complete with a staccato verse about train stations and loneliness. He paced the stage, tapping rhythm into his thigh, every syllable like a footfall on old pavement. More acts followed—a cello solo that vibrated through the floorboards, a dramatic reading of a children's book that had everyone laughing, and a quietly mesmerizing duet between a man and woman whose voices wrapped around each other like threads.

Between acts, there were moments—soft refills, murmured compliments, brief glances shared between strangers who had never before sat so close. The shop had become something else, something whole. Alive.

The night unfolded in waves—each performer a new ripple, each projection from Brian a tonal shift: warm sepia, deep blue, sudden bursts of gold.

Amanda flitted around like a caffeinated stage manager, passing Jonah now and then with whispered reviews. Jonah smiled more than he expected to. The noise of it all—chairs scraping, cups clinking, applause rising and falling like tides—didn't feel chaotic tonight.

The applause from the previous act—a pair of middle schoolers performed an enthusiastic, if slightly chaotic, tap dance number—softened like rain tapering off a rooftop. Patty leaned over the clipboard near the register, tapping the next name with her pen.

"Well now," she said. "He's actually going through with it."

Heads turned as Mr. Beverly stepped slowly toward the small wooden platform. He carried a single slip of folded paper, held delicately between two fingers like something fragile.

He didn't climb onto the stage so much as arrive at it, nodding once to the front row before settling his stance with quiet dignity.

"I don't write poetry," he said plainly, "but sometimes... I carry it."

A pause.

"And sometimes, it carries me."

He unfolded the paper, eyes soft as parchment, and read:

> *I have lived long enough to know*
> *that nothing stays exactly where you put it.*
> *The world shifts —*
> *a gate sags,*
> *the stars move,*
> *a promise fades in the weather.*
>
> *But a fencepost,*
> *sunken deep into earth,*
> *will hold a field in place*
> *long after the house is gone.*
>
> *You don't notice it when it's doing its job.*
> *You only notice when it's gone.*
>
> *I've stopped chasing the birds I can't name.*
> *I watch the wind through dry grass*
> *and count it as prayer.*
>
> *If I am remembered at all,*

let it be as the fencepost —
upright,
weathered,
quietly keeping the shape of things.

He folded the paper with reverence, a kind of ritual silence in his movements.

"Title's "The Fencepost,"" he said, eyes distant but kind. "Author unknown."

But Jonah caught the subtle curl of a smile—a secret kept, not for vanity, but for peace.

The applause was gentle, deliberate. A thank-you rather than a celebration. Jonah saw Amanda discreetly dab her eyes with her sleeve.

Mr. Beverly stepped down to the gentle applause, returning to his seat without fanfare.

A man performed a comedic retelling of his failed attempt at sourdough starter. One couple sang a Simon and Garfunkel cover that made half the room sway without realizing it. And then, the shop stilled.

A small girl—maybe ten years old—took the stage with a violin nearly as long as her arm. She played slowly and carefully, notes wobbling like baby birds, but steady. Brian's projection softened to a gentle snowfall drifting across the back wall.

Nobody moved. Even the air seemed suspended, like it was holding its breath with her.

When she finished, the applause came like a wave held too long—restrained, then bursting.

Jonah stood behind the counter, a rag in his hand he hadn't used in twenty minutes. The warmth in his chest felt untethered from caffeine or heat. It was something else entirely.

The applause dwindled and a quiet settled, heavy and expectant, before Amanda stepped onto the small wooden platform. She didn't carry a script. She didn't take a dramatic breath. She just stood there, arms loose at her sides, and let the quiet stretch a second longer. She looked hesitant, like she was on the verge of a decision. Not nerves—resolve. The room responded to her stillness the way fireflies respond to darkness —with quiet attention.

"When I signed up for tonight," she began, "most people, including me, assumed I'd pick something dramatic.

Something with Shakespeare or a corset or at least one fake death."

A soft laugh rippled through the crowd.

"But I decided not to be someone else for a change. I decided to be... here."

She paused. Her eyes scanned the room, not as a performer, but as someone trying to memorize it.

"This place—the Grind & Bind—it's not just where I sneak pastries or dodge my mom's side-eye or harass the staff with questionable music requests. It's where I figured out that I could belong somewhere without pretending."

A few heads nodded. Someone near the counter murmured an appreciative "mm."

"When I was younger—younger than I am now, I mean—I thought love would look like fireworks. Big, bold, obvious. But it turns out sometimes it looks like remembering how someone takes their coffee. Or being handed a rag before you realize you've spilled something."

She glanced, briefly, toward the counter.

"Sometimes love isn't loud. It's quiet. It listens. It shows up. It sees you... even when you're trying not to be seen."

Jonah's hand tightened slightly on the edge of the register. He didn't move.

"I've learned a lot here," she continued. "About books. And espresso ratios. And how much grief a broken mug can cause."

Scattered laughter now.

"But mostly, I've learned that it's okay to grow in unexpected directions. Even dandelions bloom in winter... if the light's warm enough."

The words lingered like shimmers in the stage light, visible only when you looked at just the right angle.

She smiled—small, not performative—then stepped down.

The applause that followed was slow to start, like the crowd wasn't sure whether to clap or hold onto the moment a little longer. It was the kind of ending that didn't call for celebration, but for stillness. Like everyone in the room understood they'd been part of something rare, and to move too quickly might scare it away.

Jonah stood still, watching her return to her seat, cheeks slightly flushed, shoulders squared.

He didn't say anything. But he felt the truth of her words settle around him like steam rising from the bar.

Ms. Wallace rose from her chair near the back, smoothing the crease of her skirt as she stepped forward. She didn't climb onto the stage, only lifted her voice just enough to carry.

"Thank you," she said simply, eyes moving across the faces gathered. "This place has always been about more than coffee or books. Tonight proved it again. Music, stories, poems... even a few experiments with projectors." A ripple of laughter softened the edges of her words. "It isn't always perfect. It doesn't have to be. What matters is that we gather, and that we make space for one another." A small smile tugged at the corner of her mouth. "Get home safe. And keep making things worth sharing."

The crowd answered with warm applause, chairs scraping as people stood and bundled themselves back into coats. Jonah busied himself with stacking mugs on a tray, listening as the conversations drifted toward the door.

Amanda came up beside him and nudged his shoulder with hers. "We pulled it off."

"We?" he teased.

She rolled her eyes. "You looked less broody than usual, so I'm calling that a team victory."

Brian slid in from the other side, a little breathless. "That last projector cue was timed perfectly. Emotional crescendo. Light swell. I've peaked artistically."

"No," Jonah said dryly, but thankful for the interruption. "That was three transitions ago."

Brian grinned and bowed anyway.

The shop began to thin out. Conversations softened into farewells. The bell over the door jingled steadily, like a heartbeat winding down.

Jonah moved slowly through the motions of cleanup. He collected mugs, wiped tables, tucked wayward napkins into a bin under the counter. He glanced toward the window.

Gen was still there.

She hadn't performed. Hadn't even spoken. But her sketchpad was full—he could see the edges of inked figures and the suggestion of movement across the pages. She closed it gently and rose to leave. This time, she gave him a look as she passed —not a nod, not a smile. Just a look, like she saw something he hadn't yet. It stayed with him even after she was gone.

Patty yawned and stretched. "I'll finish the count tomorrow. Go home, Jonah. You earned it."

He looked around at the shop, the scuffed floor and folded chairs, the low murmur of departing voices still caught in the rafters. He ran a hand across the wood grain of the front counter—a surface worn smooth by years of elbows, books, and conversation. Beneath his palm, the knots and imperfections felt familiar. Steady. A silent architecture of meaning built one touch at a time.

Amanda lingered near the poetry shelf, pretending to reorganize chapbooks that hadn't been touched all night. Jonah caught her out of the corner of his eye. He walked over, not with heavy footsteps but with the easy weight of familiarity.

"That was a beautiful monologue, brave," he said softly.

Amanda shrugged, not looking at him. "It was just words."

"You say that like words don't matter."

She shrugged.

"They do," he added. "Especially when they come from you. You'd be surprised how many things get diminished by the word *just*. That was more than *just* words. They were yours. That matters."

She finally turned. Her smile was tight around the corners, like it had been rehearsed but not for this kind of scene. "You don't have to say anything, you know."

"I know."

A beat passed. Long enough for everything unsaid to stretch out between them like a clothesline full of delicate things that might tear if tugged too hard.

"I just wanted you to hear it," she said. "Even if you..." She paused, then gave a quiet, ironic laugh. "Just—" She shook her head. "Even if."

"I did hear it," he said, voice low and kind. "And I'm really glad you said it."

Amanda blinked fast but nodded, swallowing whatever else was in her throat. She stepped back, still wearing that careful smile.

Jonah spoke softly, just for her to hear. "Goodnight, Mandelion."

"You know," she said, voice lifting just a touch, "it's not so bad. Dandelions aren't meant to be picked, anyway. They're meant to spread."

Jonah smiled, warm and real, but tinged with something quieter.

She nodded again, turning toward the door. She paused in the doorway. Gave him a small, proud little bow, as if exiting the stage of her own story.

Then she was gone.

The shop was dark except for the lamp above the register and the low flicker of candlelight from the poetry shelf. Jonah had stayed behind to count tips and reset chairs.

He hadn't expected her to knock.

Gen stood outside, one hand on the doorframe, sketchpad under her arm, eyes cautious.

"Didn't mean to interrupt," she said when he opened it.
    "You're not."

She stepped inside and sat quietly, not at the counter but near the back, by the window she always chose. Jonah poured her a cup, no questions.

When he brought it over, she looked up. "You ever draw a line and not know why until later?"
    Jonah sat opposite her. "I don't draw."

"Figures," she said softly. "But you build things. You fix things."

He didn't deny it.

Gen opened her sketchpad, flipped to a half-finished page.

"It's my sister," she said. "I used to draw her when we fought. I kept sketching until I could remember what it was like to love her again."

Jonah looked at the lines—sharp, unfinished, beautiful.

"She's gone?" he asked gently.
　"No," she said. "But I am."

The candlelight shifted as if leaning in, softening the hard corners of the night.

The silence between them deepened.

Then Jonah said, "You can always start again."

She looked at him—not with challenge, but with something raw.

"Maybe," she said. "But not always in the same place."

He nodded slowly, eyes tracing the candle's flicker. Maybe not. But maybe that was okay. Not every story had to have a clean ending to be worth telling.

14

NOTES AND NOTICING

The shop was still dim when Jonah arrived.

He unlocked the front door with practiced movements, boots brushing faintly against last night's salt dust. The bell overhead rang out as usual, but its echo felt softer somehow, as if the air had thickened overnight—still saturated with applause and murmured laughter. He stepped inside and paused, letting the door shut behind him.

The chairs weren't in their usual places. One of the wingbacks still faced the makeshift stage, and a few stools were clustered like they hadn't quite decided to leave. Jonah left them be. He moved through the shop slowly, as though anything louder than a whisper might shatter what lingered. He passed the side table near the window and gently righted a candle holder that had tipped during cleanup, the wick curled in on itself like a closing eye. A folded program from the night before was wedged behind the lamp cord—he straightened it, but didn't move it. It felt earned.

Lights. Machines. Register. Everything moved in sequence, but the rhythm felt different—off-tempo, like a song missing its chorus. The espresso machine hissed as it warmed, steam curling upward and fading like breath in cold air.

Jonah poured himself a cup and set it on the counter. The mug, warm in his hands, grounded him—but didn't anchor him. He stared at it for a while, sipping in silence, eyes drifting toward the front window.

He took his time restocking the pastry case. The cinnamon rolls were imperfect today—slightly uneven in their spiral, one tilted off-center like it had dozed off mid-rise. Herb would call that "character." Jonah left it right where it was. He had just finished organizing the case when the door clicked open and Brian stumbled in, hat askew and coat unzipped halfway.

"Why is it," Brian grumbled, "that every time I do something mildly meaningful, my immune system thinks it's earned the weekend off?"

Jonah raised a brow. "You look like you lost a fight with a laundry basket."

Brian held up a crumpled granola bar. "Breakfast of the unrested."

Jonah slid a mug across the counter. "Here. Caffeinate."

Brian accepted it like communion, sipping with

exaggerated reverence. "Bless you and the donkey you rode in on."

They sat in the easy silence of people who were too tired to force conversation. Brian flopped into the reading nook chair with his mug. "You know, the whole night felt like the town cracked open a little. In a good way."

Jonah gave a half-nod.

"I mean, I wasn't expecting Amanda to go full-sincerity mode," Brian continued. "I was bracing for, like, dramatic soliloquy vibes. But she... surprised me."

Jonah formed a subtle smile as he remembered her performance. "She does that."

Just then, the door blew open with a gust of wind and a flourish of scarf—it was Amanda, unmistakably Amanda, with a grin already forming.

"And I have arrived, just in time to save the morning from being too quiet."

Her boots squeaked faintly on the floor as she made her way in, cheeks flushed from the cold, and her hair slightly windswept under a knit beanie dotted with pins.

"Did I miss anything good? Philosophical angst? Existential brooding?" She leaned her elbows dramatically on the counter. "Should I just assume the usual?"

Jonah smirked, but Brian answered. "We were just talking about how you broke character last night and made people feel things."

Amanda pretended to be scandalized. "You mean they weren't expecting a heartfelt soliloquy about soft places and first love and how bookstores smell like safety?"

"Not from you," Brian said. "I was betting on a dramatic Shakespeare excerpt or a moody reinterpretation of 'Wicked.'"

Amanda grinned. "I contain multitudes."

"Hey!" Brian exclaimed. "That's my line."

She pulled a lemon bar from her coat pocket—wrapped in foil, half-crushed—and held it up like a prize. "Breakfast."

Jonah chuckled. "Is that one of the leftover ones from last night?"

Amanda took a bite. "This one's mine. I claimed it. I said, 'this bar is for feelings,' and then I saved it in honor of my emotional maturity."

Brian looked at Jonah. "We should start charging her rent."

Amanda ignored him and turned her attention back to Jonah. Her voice softened.

"Did you know it was about you?"

Jonah looked up from where he was wiping the counter, towel paused mid-circle. He didn't respond right away.

"I figured," he said finally.

She waited.

"I don't know if I deserve all that," he added.

"It wasn't about deserving," she replied. "It was about being."

He looked at her, really looked, and saw in her eyes not the girl from yesterday, but the young woman who had stood under those lanterns with her voice steady and her hands shaking just a little.

"Thank you," Jonah said quietly. "Really. For trusting me with that."

Amanda gave a half-smile, bittersweet and proud.

"It's out in the universe now, spoken into being."

She straightened, brushed a few crumbs off her coat, and started for the door.

Brian called after her, "Where are you going?"

"To be mysterious!" she said.

"You're quite adept at bringing genuine smiles." Jonah raised his mug slightly. "Goodbye, Mandelion."

"Blooming in winter, remember?" she called over her

shoulder, arms spread in mock grandeur. "It's kind of my thing."

Her head tilted down just a little too low, a little too long, before she turned back to give a wave and a smile that didn't reach her eyes.

The door shut behind her, leaving stillness in her wake.

Jonah stared at the closed door a moment longer. Not because he thought she'd turn back—just because part of him wished she would. Not for him, but for herself.

"To everything there is a season." He whispered quietly, to himself.

He returned to the counter and placed his mug beside the register. The window reflected his outline in the glass— blurred, layered with the street beyond. He watched himself for a moment, uncertain whether he felt seen or obscured.

The day drifted forward. Customers came and went in their usual patterns, the weight of the previous night slowly absorbed by the return of routine. Jonah cleared tables and cleaned counters, slipping into the rhythm. A small knot of families gathered in the children's corner mid-morning, coats piled on chairs as Brian took up a book with mock-serious flourish. His voice rose and dipped with cartoonish dramatics, earning giggles that rippled through the aisles. Jonah caught sight of him holding the book sideways so the pictures faced the kids, eyes bright despite his complaints of exhaustion earlier. The sound carried gently through the shop, not breaking the quiet so much as rounding it out.

By late afternoon, Jonah noticed a napkin tucked under the dispenser by the corner stool—not crumpled, but folded neatly. He didn't remember seeing it earlier. He opened it gently, expecting notes or doodles. What he found instead was a sketch. Rough. Rushed. But unmistakable. It was him. His profile, tilted in concentration, a towel in one hand, a coffee mug in the other. The lines were soft, incomplete, and yet it held something true—an outline of presence. Not performance. Just being. There was no exaggeration, no embellishment—just him, mid-motion. He hadn't realized he looked that steady.

He stared at it for a long time. He didn't need a name to know who had left it.

Behind the register, as he reached to file the napkin beneath the drawer, a yellow Post-it caught his eye. It hadn't been there this morning. Ms. Wallace's tight handwriting filled the square:

"The room felt fuller than it should've. Good work, Jonah.
— W"

Just that.

He read it twice before pressing it flat beside the sketch and closing the drawer.

The bell over the door gave a sharp jingle, and Patty blew in with the cold, the scent of peppermint lip balm and wind-chapped wool trailing behind her.

"Afternoon, sunshine," she called, tugging off her gloves with quick snaps. "Please tell me the machines are behaving. I don't have the emotional bandwidth for another espresso tantrum."

Jonah turned, smiling faintly. "Crankily cranking away, as always."

"That's the dream." She moved behind the counter, dropping her tote bag with a thud and peering into the pastry case. "Did Brian eat half a cinnamon roll and leave the other half?"

Jonah glanced over. "He called it a 'strategic pause.'"

Patty snorted, flipping on the backroom light. "Of course he did."

She paused then, scanning Jonah's face like she was checking for signs of overwork or existential spirals.

"You holding up?"

He shrugged, then nodded. "Yeah. Actually... yeah."

She narrowed her eyes but didn't press. Instead, she reached into the drawer beneath the counter and pulled out a clean towel, flicking it open like a magician about to perform a trick.

"You did good last night," she said offhandedly, rearranging cups that didn't need rearranging. "The place felt alive."

Jonah didn't answer right away. He didn't need to. Patty nodded once and moved on, muttering something about inventory counts and misbehaving scones as she disappeared into the stockroom.

Jonah turned back to the front window just in time to see Mr. Beverly crossing the street, bundled in his long coat, with the slow determination of a man who meant to be somewhere even if time wasn't in a hurry.

The bell jingled again, softer this time.

Mr. Beverly stepped inside with the grace of someone who'd once been quick and still remembered how it felt. His coat held the cold like a memory, and he paused just beyond the threshold, letting the warmth of the shop catch up to him.

"You open for wanderers and the weary?" he asked, removing his hat with a slight bow.

Jonah smiled. "Only if they pay in exact change or riddles."

Mr. Beverly chuckled as he crossed to the counter. "I've got no riddles today, Mr. Ashford. Just the need to borrow a few moments of your time. If you've got any to spare."

Jonah poured him a cup without asking, steam curling into the air like punctuation.

Patty peeked out from the stockroom. "Hey, Mr. Beverly," she called. "You here to stir up wisdom or just hog the cinnamon muffins again?"

He raised his cup in a toast. "Depends on who's asking."

"Smart answer," she said, disappearing back into the shelves.

Mr. Beverly took a sip and let out a low, contented sigh. "There's something holy in a cup like this."

Jonah leaned on the counter. "You said you needed a few moments?"

Mr. Beverly glanced around the shop, as if weighing whether the walls would listen in. Then he gestured toward the door with a tilt of his chin. "Walk with me?"

Jonah hesitated, eyes flicking toward the back where Patty was humming under her breath.

"I'll cover," she called. "I'm not deaf, you know."

"Never said you were," Jonah replied, already grabbing his coat.

Mr. Beverly waited just outside, sipping from his mug as he studied the clouds above, as if they'd written something worth reading. Jonah joined him on the sidewalk. The cold had mellowed into something tolerable—brisk but no longer biting. The streets were still wet from the melt, and the sky hung low, a pale canvas waiting for brushstrokes.

They started walking without comment, shoes finding their rhythm against the concrete. Jonah waited. Mr. Beverly always began things like this—with silence first, as if tuning the instrument of conversation before playing a single note.

"I didn't sleep much," Mr. Beverly said eventually. "Happens more often these days. I find myself thinking about things I thought I'd made peace with."

Jonah glanced over, but the older man's gaze was fixed ahead. Measured, unreadable.

"Last night..." Mr. Beverly continued, "something in it stirred old dust. Not in a bad way. Just—memories, I guess. The kind you wrap up and store neatly, only to find them shifted slightly on the shelf."

They turned down a quieter street. One of those in-between places, where the houses still wore Christmas lights half-unplugged and the mailboxes leaned slightly from the freeze.

"You ever think about how rarely we let people surprise us?" Mr. Beverly asked. "We think we know their shape, their tone. But then something happens. A girl stands under warm light and speaks the truth with trembling hands. A shop fills with voices that never thought they'd be heard. And suddenly the world feels... rewritable."

Jonah nodded slowly. "Yeah. I think about that more than I let on."

Mr. Beverly gave him a small smile. "You always struck me as someone who sees more than he speaks."

"Sometimes I think I see too much and say too little."

"Same affliction as every man who's tried to keep his heart from spilling."

They walked a bit farther. The wind picked up for a moment, tugging at the edges of their coats.

"I appreciated what you said earlier," Jonah offered. "About needing a few moments. Not everyone asks like that."

"There's not enough asking these days," Mr. Beverly replied. "Just telling. Or shouting. I've come to value the kind of silence that comes with consent."

They rounded a corner near the old library, its bricks dark with moisture, windows steamed from within. Mr. Beverly slowed slightly, as if calibrating how to say something.

"You asked me the other day if there was anything I wanted to talk about," he said. "And I meant it when I said not yet."

Jonah kept pace, quiet.

"But I will tell you this, Mr. Ashford," Mr. Beverly continued. "When I lost my wife, the world didn't stop. Didn't flinch. Just kept turning. The mail kept arriving. The sun kept rising and setting. The lights didn't even flicker. But there were moments—small, almost dismissible—when someone made space. No grand gesture. Just a chair pulled out. A hand on the shoulder. A cup of coffee without asking how I take it."

Jonah looked over at him. The edges of Mr. Beverly's eyes crinkled, not from grief now, but from something quieter. Resignation, maybe. Or calm.

"I see the way people lean toward this place," he said, nodding back in the direction of the shop. "And I see the way you hold it open, even if you don't realize that's what you're doing."

"I'm just showing up," Jonah said.

"And some days," Mr. Beverly replied, "that's the holiest thing a person can do. You're steady—like sunrise or tide. I don't think you see that in yourself. But it's there."

They stopped near a lamppost that hummed faintly even in daylight. Mr. Beverly reached for his cup, now nearly cold, and drank it anyway.

"I don't have much wisdom left," he said. "But if I've got a little, it's this: keep noticing. Keep letting the world happen in front of you. Most people close their eyes halfway through."

Jonah nodded. He tucked his hands into his coat pockets, thumb grazing the edge of a receipt he'd forgotten to throw away. He left it there.

They stood there a moment longer before turning back, walking in silence again, their breath fading behind them. Proof that they'd been there, however fleeting.

15

CRACKS AND CLARITY

The bell gave a reluctant chime as Jonah unlocked the front door and stepped into the quiet.

It was colder inside than out—something about how the shop held on to night air longer than it should. He left the lights off for a moment, letting the filtered gray of morning seep through the front windows. Dust motes hung like lazy snowfall in the sunbeam strip across the register. The place felt paused, not asleep. Like a held breath. The rent letter sat on the counter. Next to it, the leaves of the fiddle-leaf fig were drooping, a subtle echo of the day's weight.

The supply delivery box by the counter was smaller than usual, just enough ingredients for a single batch of muffins. Jonah stared at the meager supplies, calculating. They could make it through the day, maybe tomorrow if customers didn't expect much variety. He glanced at the case, hesitated, then arranged what he had as if it were enough.

Patty had left her usual post-it on the counter, but even that felt abridged.

> *Inventory low—don't bother restocking the hibiscus. No one drinks it but me.*
> *— Patty*

Patty always signed her notes the same way—dry humor, a squiggle, sometimes a doodle if she was feeling generous. This one felt stripped bare. Jonah didn't need context to know something was off.

He set his satchel down behind the bar, checked the drip brewer even though he knew it was clean, and let the sounds of the shop settle around him—the low mechanical hum of the fridge, the occasional creak from the beams overhead, the distant, indecisive flutter of something loose against the front door.

He walked over and found it: a hairline crack just below the brass handle, maybe four inches long, almost invisible unless the light hit it wrong. He ran a finger over it. Cold. Smooth, but wrong. A single vein threading its way across otherwise perfect glass.

Not urgent, he told himself. But it will be.

He retrieved a roll of clear tape and a Sharpie from the drawer, sealed the crack in a makeshift X, and scribbled a note on a folded receipt:

CHECK THIS LATER

He pressed it to the door with a flat palm and stepped back.

It helped, but only a little.

The morning passed without rush. A few regulars came and went—quiet hellos, a few light jokes, a to-go order misspelled on the cup that made the customer smile instead of correct him. Jonah appreciated the grace.

Just past eleven, the door opened with a creak and a gust of cold that carried the street in with it. Amanda stepped in, not with flair or commentary, but simply, quietly—hood half-down, binder hugged to her chest.

"Hey," she said, smiling without tilt or tease.

Jonah raised a hand from behind the bar. "Hey."

She slid onto a stool at the counter. "Don't worry, no performance today. Just needed a break from pretending to understand quadratic equations and irrational numbers."

"Sounds pretty radical." Jonah quipped as he poured her a hot chocolate without asking.

"Hardly," she muttered, then accepted the mug. "This helps."

She took a sip, winced a little—still too hot—and set it down carefully.

There was a moment of quiet between them that didn't feel loaded. Just shared space.

"I applied for something," she said finally, brushing a bit of lint off her sleeve. "Summer program. Theater intensive. Based in Denver. Regional rep troupe, travels a little. Kind of a big deal, if I get it."

Jonah blinked, pleasantly surprised. "That's awesome."

"I think so. It feels... big. But also, like, overdue?"

"Yeah," Jonah said, nodding. "Sometimes things show up only when you're ready to notice them."

She gave him a look—half curiosity, half appreciation. "That's either really profound or something you read on a coffee sleeve."

He smirked. "Must those be mutually exclusive?"

Amanda twirled her spoon in the mug absently. "It's not forever. Just a few months. But... I need to know what else I can be, you know? Not just the girl who reads things aloud and cries at the right moments."

"You're a lot more than that already."

She smiled. "You'd say that even if I wasn't."

He paused, then shrugged. "That doesn't really sound like me."

A longer silence settled in. Amanda broke it gently.

"I used to think this place was magic because you were in it."

Jonah looked up from the espresso machine, mentally preparing a subtle deflection.

"But now I think it's magic because you made it feel that way. That's a better kind, I think."

He didn't know what to say. So he nodded, once, slowly.

Amanda reached across and squeezed his hand just once before pulling back. No lingering. No flutter. Just gratitude.

She finished her drink in three careful sips, packed up, and left with a backward glance that didn't ask for anything in return.

The shop was quiet again until late afternoon, when Gen walked in with her sketchpad tucked under one arm and her scarf only half-tied. Her eyes were restless.

Jonah was shaping tomorrow's croissants—a laborious process of rolling and folding butter into dough, creating hundreds of delicate layers. He watched her hover near the counter, then drift toward the fiction wall before returning. She eventually settled on her stool by the window and opened her sketchpad, glancing at him as he rolled the croissant dough on the floured countertop. His sleeves were pushed back, forearms dusted with flour, each movement precise—fold, rotate, press. She didn't speak, just angled her sketchbook slightly toward the light. Her pencil moved slowly at first, then faster. She was drawing his hands. Again.

She watched in silence as he worked, her sketchpad now resting idle in her lap. "How long does that take?" she asked finally.

"Three days, start to finish. Has to rest between folds." He dusted flour from his hands. "Can't rush it."

"Three days," she repeated, like the concept was foreign. "I don't think I've planned three days ahead in... maybe ever."

Jonah looked up. "That's not necessarily a bad thing."

"Isn't it?" She traced patterns on the counter with her finger. "Sometimes I think about what it would be like. To know where I'll be next Thursday. To make promises I could keep."

"Is that what you want?"

She was quiet for a long moment. "I think I want to want it. I don't know. Do you ever get the feeling," she said, tapping her pencil against the counter edge, "that you've outstayed a season?"

Jonah tilted his head. "Like a calendar season, or something less... weather-based?"

Gen smiled, barely. "The kind that doesn't change on its own. You just wake up and realize you're late to leave it."

She didn't sit. She just leaned her hip against the counter, scanning the space like she might redraw it all if she looked long enough.

"I think I'm restless," she said, but it didn't feel like a confession. More like a breadcrumb she left behind. She pressed her thumb along the edge of the table, tracing the grain like it might give her direction. Beneath it, her knee bounced just enough to make her spoon tremble against the rim of her mug.

Jonah didn't answer right away. He wondered if she meant the town, the moment, or him. Maybe all three. He set down the cloth he'd been using to wipe the counter and leaned his hands against the edge, not too close—just enough to face her without asking for more than she wanted to give.

Gen tapped her pencil twice against the edge. Then again. A syncopated rhythm like her thoughts couldn't find a steady beat.

Jonah tilted his head slightly. "Restless isn't always a sign you need to leave," he said. "Sometimes it just means something's changing. Could be inside the room. Or it could be something inside of you."

She didn't look at him. She just kept her gaze on the books

along the far wall, her thumb still tracing the grain of the table, slower now. Like she was listening with more than her ears.

"And how do you tell the difference?" she asked softly.

"You don't," Jonah said. "Not until whatever it is finishes changing, or it disappears."

That made her pause. The pencil went still.

Then she said, "And what if I'm what disappears?"

Jonah studied her for a second, then turned and reached under the bar. When he straightened, he had a book in his hand—softbound, the cover worn along the spine. *Calder Hale's Ledger*.

"I've been reading this," he said, flipping through it carefully. "There's a part—hang on—"

Gen's eyes tracked the book more than his words. Not the title, not the dog-eared page—but the sliver of cardstock tucked near the middle. A makeshift bookmark, thin and cream-colored, with a faint pen mark near the top. Her pencil stilled against her sketchpad. She didn't say anything. Just looked at it for a beat longer than necessary, her expression not curious, but recognized.

Jonah didn't notice. He was frowning at the page numbers, muttering under his breath until he found the line he wanted.

"Here," he said, holding it up between them. "Gray says—well, it's not dialogue, it's just him thinking, but—'Maybe we don't outgrow places so much as shed the parts of ourselves that needed them. And then we look around and everything feels smaller, but it's not. We've simply grown past the corners we used to fit inside.'"

Gen didn't say anything.

Jonah lowered the book a little. "It hit me," he said. "Not the most elegant phrasing, but... it felt real."

He read the line again. The words didn't just hit him; they named a hollow space he'd been feeling for months. The shop, the town, his father's silent house—they hadn't shrunk. He had simply outgrown the person he was when he first walked in. The thought was less a comfort and more a verdict.She smiled faintly, more with her eyes than her mouth.

"Do you think it's possible to stay somewhere without staying the same?"

Jonah looked up, brow creasing—not in confusion, but thought.

"I think it depends on whether the place changes with you," he said. "Or if it only remembers who you were when you arrived."

Her fingers traced the edge of her sketchpad absently. She looked like she wanted to say more, but didn't quite find the shape of it. He had the sense she was working her way toward something.

She looked at him then—really looked—and for a moment, neither said anything.

"I've got errands," she murmured, already stepping back. "I'll see you soon."

She left a folded paper on the counter as she turned to go.

Jonah waited until the bell stilled before picking it up.

The sketch showed the front window of the Grind & Bind, drawn from outside. His figure was barely visible—blurred, like seen through rain or old glass. The shop behind him glowed softly. A space of warmth viewed from somewhere colder.

He stared at it, wondering if he was part of the glow or just standing where the light happened to fall.

———

Evening came with a kind of hush.

Jonah was wiping down the counters when the front door opened, and Ms. Wallace stepped in, buttoned coat, scarf perfectly wrapped, folder tucked under her arm. She looked like she always did—put-together, composed—but her steps were slower.

"Evening," she said.

"Didn't expect you," Jonah replied, setting the cloth aside.

"Didn't expect to come," she said, glancing around. "I was nearby. Thought I'd check in."

She set the folder down and rested her hand on it—fingers still, as if deciding whether it needed to be opened.

"How've things been since Friday?" she asked.

"Quiet. Good kind of quiet, mostly."

She nodded. "That's something."

Jonah waited, but she didn't elaborate.

When she turned to go, hand on the folder but still not opening it, she paused.

"I'll need to make a final decision by next week," she said softly.

He hesitated. "Do you already know what you're going to do?"

Ms. Wallace turned back. Her eyes were tired but clear.

"I know what I can afford," she said. "Not sure yet what I can carry."

And then she left.

Later, after he'd locked up and turned the lights low, Jonah returned to the front door.

He peeled off the tape, cleaned the edge of the crack with care, and fitted a proper sealing strip. It wasn't perfect—it never would be—but it held. It mattered that he'd done it.

He stood back to inspect the fix.

In the darkened glass, his reflection layered over the shop interior—coffee bar, bookshelves, the glow of one dim bulb overhead. All of it now bisected by the repair. And something about the shape of it reminded him of Gen's sketch. Like he was both inside and out. Held and half-gone.

He reached out once, fingers touching the glass.

And then he turned off the last light.

REPAIRS AND REPETITION

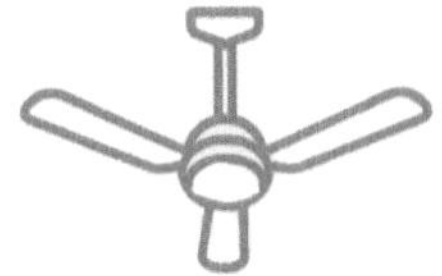

The house made its usual complaints as the day warmed—groaning faintly in the walls, wood flexing in its joints, the slow stretch of a structure remembering how to hold itself together. Somewhere down the hall, the thermostat clicked, the ductwork rattled, and the house seemed as if it were breathing a sigh. A floorboard eased beneath no one's weight.

Jonah padded into the kitchen barefoot, the cold linoleum pressing up through his heels. He'd slept later than usual, not by much, but enough for the light outside to be full and slanted, spilling across the counter like poured milk. The French press was already out. He measured the grounds by feel, filled the kettle, and waited in silence as it came to a boil.

Outside the window, the neighborhood was already in motion. A jogger passed in rhythmic strides, breath fogging with each exhale. A man adjusted the straps on a child's backpack at the curb. The faint rumble of a school bus echoed somewhere distant, though Jonah couldn't remember if it was Monday or Tuesday. The days were beginning to blur. A dog barked from two houses down—sharp, territorial—then loped back to the spot it had been guarding from, unmoved and unbothered.

Jonah poured the water in slow spirals, pressed the plunger with his palm, and poured the first cup without ceremony.

At the kitchen table, his father sat with an open binder planner and a radio murmuring softly in the background—something dry about road resurfacing and budget reallocations. His pen scratched once against the page, paused, then moved again in small, neat loops. He didn't look up as Jonah crossed the room, just nodded slightly and reached for his own mug, turning a page with his thumb.

"Morning," Jonah said, voice still rough from sleep.
  "Mm," his father replied, more hum than word.

Jonah pulled out the chair opposite, settled into it, and wrapped his hands around his mug. The table was tidy, as always. A small stack of paid bills marked with the transaction date. A pen aligned parallel to the edge. His father's coffee had gone lukewarm, but he drank it anyway.

They sat like that for a while—two men bound by silence more than conversation. Outside, a breeze scraped dry leaves along the sidewalk. Inside, the only real sound was the slow turning of planner pages and the soft droning of voices from the radio. They drank in silence for a few minutes. The planner pages were already well-marked—ink bleeding slightly at the edges where time had collected. A few clipped receipts rested beside it, corners aligned. The pen rested near his father's fingers, uncapped, precise.

"Garage could use reorganizing," Jonah offered.

His father nodded without looking up. "Been needing it."

Jonah let the quiet settle again before speaking. "Things at the shop've been shifting. Might be more changes coming."

"That so," his father said, drawing a line beneath something.

"Yeah."

His father paused. Set the pen down carefully. "Most things aren't meant to last forever," he said. "Doesn't mean they didn't matter while they did."

He didn't say it like comfort. Just fact. A line added to the day's ledger.

Jonah didn't speak, not right away. He traced the rim of his mug with his thumb. He watched his father's hand move— steady, familiar, careful. He remembered those same hands smoothing Ovaltine powder into coffee, flipping pages of a paperback by the porch light, tightening the bolts on Jonah's old bike without comment.

"You ever leave something you didn't want to?" he asked finally.

His father leaned back a little, one arm resting across the back of the chair. "Had a buddy at the hardware store. We ran tools together, stocked the shelves—him longer than me. One day, he decided he was done. Smart guy. Loved the job. But he got it in his head he was meant for something else—went back to school at thirty-nine. Quit with nothing lined up but a tuition payment."

"What happened?"

"Didn't pan out, not like he thought. But he said it felt better failing at the thing he chose than staying in something safe just 'cause it was there." He took a sip of his coffee.

"What about you?" Jonah asked.

"I stayed longer than I should've," his father admitted. "Comfort gets heavy if you carry it too long. Staying put ain't always the brave choice. But neither's running. Depends on the reason."

Jonah nodded, though he didn't quite know what part he was agreeing with.

His father turned and met Jonah's gaze—not intense, not pressing, just steady.

"Whatever you pick—make sure you're the one doing the picking."

The radio kept on, low and unimportant. Jonah nodded. His father returned to reviewing his planner. The moment passed. Jonah stood and walked to the sink, rinsed his mug, let the water run over his fingers for a moment, and stood watching the steam rise from under the tap.

By late morning, the sun was high but diffuse, like it hadn't quite committed to the day. Jonah zipped his coat and slung his bag over one shoulder, stepping outside with a little more weight behind his stride than usual.

As he walked, the conversation with his father replayed itself— not as a clear narrative, but as fragments and echoes. Whatever you pick... Comfort gets heavy... Better to fail at something you chose...

There wasn't an answer in any of it. Just angles to hold up to the light. He wasn't even sure what he wanted to choose— whether it was about the shop, or Genesis, or the version of himself that sometimes looked back in the mirror and seemed to be waiting for permission to move.

The air had a bite to it still, but it was softening. One of those slow thaws that happened almost unnoticed. The sidewalks were dry now, though the gutters still held grit from the last storm. He stepped over a discarded fast food cup, nudged it to the side with the toe of his boot, and kept walking. Some things weren't his to pick up.

At the Grind & Bind, he hung his coat in the back and bypassed the café entirely. Patty and Brian had the front covered—he gave them a wave but didn't stop to chat.

Instead, he turned his attention to the quiet corners of the shop—the ones that had been waiting for someone to notice.

He tightened the hinge on the cabinet beneath the window display, the one that always groaned when opened too far. He replaced the missing bracket under the philosophy section, where the shelf had started to lean. He sanded the lip of the checkout counter drawer so it slid without catching. He even took apart the wobbly coat rack in the back hallway, realigned the base, and reassembled it screw by screw.

The tasks didn't need thanks. They just needed doing.

Late in the afternoon, while he was sorting hardware into a drawer under the register, Mr. Beverly arrived.

"Good afternoon, fine proprietors," he said warmly, greeting Patty and Brian with a smile.

"Hey, Mr. Beverly," Brian said, pulling the milk pitcher off the wand. "We still owe you applause from community night. You crushed it."

Mr. Beverly chuckled. "I appreciate your appreciation, but no applause is necessary. I'll take your light roast, and one of those cinnamon buns with the nuts."

He chatted easily with them while Jonah continued his work, crouched near the floor, reorganizing a shallow drawer full of mismatched screws and orphaned Allen keys.

From the book side, Herb appeared without warning, a clipboard in one hand and his usual scowl in place.

"Well, if it isn't Mr. Fix-It," he muttered, tilting his head toward Jonah. "The cart by the local history section's got a wheel that's gone rogue—nearly tipped the whole thing when I moved it."

Jonah glanced up. "Front left?"

"Of course, front left. It's always the front left."

"I'll take a look."

"And while you're back there," Herb added, pivoting to go, "there's a drip in the men's room sink again. Like a metronome off beat. Slowly driving me insane."

Patty, passing by with a tray of clean mugs, grinned. "Might explain a few things."

Jonah stood, dusting off his knees. "Got it."

He wheeled the cart into the back hallway first, flipped it onto its side, and tightened the bolt holding the caster in place—then locked the wheel's pin with a sliver of scrap plastic trimmed to size. It rolled smoothly after that. He returned it quietly to its place near the worn spines and creaking floorboards.

In the men's washroom, the faucet handle had loosened at the stem. Jonah tightened it with a hex key and added a rubber washer. The drip stopped. Just a slight shift in pressure and angle. Sometimes that's all it took.

By the time he stepped back into the café, hands damp from rinsing off grease, Mr. Beverly was settled at a corner table near the window, coffee in one hand and a half-eaten cinnamon bun on a napkin. He was listening to Brian, who was speaking animatedly, waving a spoon like a conductor's baton.

"—and if wormholes are real, it wouldn't be about speed, right? It'd be folding space entirely, like punching a hole through two corners of a map."

Mr. Beverly nodded thoughtfully, chewing with care. "I'm not sure I follow the mechanics," he said, "but I like the image. I admire how your brain insists on finding ways through things."

Brian beamed, clearly encouraged.

Jonah lingered for a moment near the hallway, unnoticed, watching the exchange. There was something grounding about it—the rhythm of small routines, the way each person in the space seemed to fit a groove worn just for them. He checked his watch. His shift was nearly done.

Mr. Beverly met his eye across the room and gave a small nod, like they'd already agreed to something.

Jonah set the rag down and made his way over.

Mr. Beverly gathered his empty mug, brushing a crumb from his coat sleeve. "Mr. Ashford," he said with a slight bow of his head, "you've got the air of a man who's kept the world spinning one quiet repair at a time."

Jonah huffed a small breath of amusement. "Or at least kept it from rattling off its hinges."

Mr. Beverly gestured loosely toward the counter, where Brian was still explaining something to Patty using salt packets and dramatic hand motions. "And I believe young Brian has me entangled in a theory involving dark matter and espresso shots. I'm not sure if I've learned anything, but I do feel cosmically implicated."

Jonah smiled. "That happens sometimes."

Mr. Beverly set down his mug and reached for his coat. "You headed home?"

"Yeah," Jonah said. "Just about."

"Mind if I walk with you?"

"Not at all," Jonah said easily. "I'd like the company."

Outside, the air had cooled again, the light going long and gold across the storefronts. It caught in the windows of parked cars, in the sheen of power lines overhead. Their footsteps echoed lightly on the pavement. The breeze tugged at the corners of signs and curled dry leaves across the sidewalk. They passed an intersection where the traffic signal blinked a steady, unhurried yellow, cautioning no one in particular. The sky held that signature late-afternoon stillness—blue fading at the edges, waiting for night.

"We could take the direct way," Mr. Beverly offered, adjusting his scarf. "Or something a bit more roundabout."

Jonah looked down the quieter street, then toward the row of older houses off to the left. "Meandering might fit my thoughts better."

Mr. Beverly gave a quiet chuckle. "I had a feeling."

They turned down the side street together, steps unhurried, shadows stretching out ahead of them. Their footsteps echoed lightly on the pavement. They walked side by side, not in a straight line, meandering through side streets that felt familiar but slightly off in the changing light. The neighborhood was quieter than usual, weekday rhythms beginning to wind down.

"Cold's hanging on," Mr. Beverly said. "Thought I'd be out in the garden by now."

"Spring's always stubborn," Jonah replied.

"Mmm." A pause. "Community night was something,"

Mr. Beverly said, hands tucked into his coat pockets. "I noticed you didn't take the mic."

Jonah shook his head. "Didn't really have anything to say."

"Nothing? Hm, I suppose most of your contributions occur behind the scenes. Unnoticed, but no less necessary."

Jonah didn't argue with that. Just kept walking, gaze on the sidewalk.

"Amanda's piece stayed with me," Mr. Beverly continued after a beat. "She had a clarity to her. Like someone finally speaking in her own voice."

Jonah nodded. "She usually tells other people's stories. Scripts, monologues, lines written by someone she's never met. That night... I think it was the first time she didn't feel like she had to translate."

Mr. Beverly gave a quiet hum of agreement. "Well, it landed. Sometimes, the unscripted things ring truer than the ones we rehearse."

Jonah kicked a stray rock into the gutter. "She didn't tell me she was going to do it."

"She didn't need to," Mr. Beverly said gently. "Some truths don't wait for permission."

They passed a yard with broken fencing, a child's scooter tipped on its side near the porch. The wind moved through the trees in soft sheets.

"I think someone I care about is going to leave," Jonah said finally.

Mr. Beverly nodded slowly, like the thought didn't need context to be understood. He was quiet for a long time, watching a sparrow hop along the gutter. "My wife," he said finally, "she'd leave the back gate unlatched for the neighbor's cat. Never fed it, never called it. Just left a space it could come through if it wanted." He opened his empty hand, palm to the sky. "Some things you can't hold. You can only leave a gate open."

Jonah swallowed. "How do you know if you're supposed to follow?"

"You don't," Mr. Beverly said. "But if standing still starts to feel like being left behind, it might be time."

They turned the corner toward their street. The shadows were longer here, stretched thin across sidewalks and brick walls. Jonah felt the tension of the day loosen slightly.

Mr. Beverly tucked his hands into his coat pockets. "I met my wife in a post office," he said.

Jonah blinked. "Really?"

"Mmhm. She'd come in every Thursday to mail a letter. Same time, every week. Never the same address. I asked her once who she was writing to, and she said, 'All the places I might've lived if I'd made different choices.'" He chuckled. "That's how I knew."

"Knew what?"

"That she didn't need fixing. Just someone to walk beside her. To be there with her."

They slowed near Jonah's driveway. The house was washed in the last light of afternoon, golden and warm against the cool exterior. It looked slightly unfamiliar in that light—like a memory he hadn't visited in a while. Familiar lines cast differently.

"Well," Mr. Beverly said. "I'll see you tomorrow, I expect. Good evening, Mr. Ashford."

Jonah nodded. "Yeah. Goodnight, Mr. Beverly. Thanks for the walk."

They parted with a small wave, and Jonah stood outside the door for a moment before going in.

He dropped his bag by the door, peeled off his coat, and let it hang lopsided from the hallway hook. His shoes landed with a soft thud beside the bench. He didn't bother with dinner.

Upstairs, he lay down on the bed without pulling back the covers, limbs splayed awkwardly like he'd fallen, not chosen. The ceiling fan turned slowly overhead—its blades catching and releasing the last threads of sunlight as they slipped behind the horizon. The blades kept turning. His thoughts with them. Slow arcs. Quiet repetition. His father's voice: Make sure you're the one doing the picking. Mr. Beverly's reply: If standing still starts to feel like being left behind...

He closed his eyes. Opened them again.

The fan kept turning.

And Jonah kept counting—each rotation, each quiet hinge in his memory—wondering how many times he'd let something pass before he was ready to follow.

17

THRESHOLDS AND THREADS

The morning delivery came in a brown paper bag instead of the usual crates. Three pounds of coffee beans, enough flour for a single batch of muffins, and a handwritten note from the supplier:

Final delivery until account settled.

The phrase echoed. Ms. Wallace hadn't said much after Community Night, but Jonah remembered her expression when she'd looked at the ledger—like someone watching a foundation crack.

Jonah set the bag on the counter with the careful precision of someone handling something fragile. The weight of it—or lack thereof—seemed to echo in the empty shop. He'd arrived earlier than usual, not by design but because sleep had become a suggestion his body no longer took seriously.

The silence felt different today. Not expectant, like most mornings, but resigned. Like the shop had exhaled and forgotten to breathe back in.

He measured what he had with the deliberate attention of someone stretching a meal. One batch of blueberry muffins, their batter thin but workable. A handful of yesterday's scones, arranged to look abundant in the nearly empty case. The coffee would last through the morning rush, maybe into lunch if people ordered smaller cups.

The ovens warmed with their usual blue flame dancers, but even they seemed dimmer. He slid the muffin tins inside and set the timer, the tick joining the shop's diminished symphony —fewer instruments now, playing softer.

Brian arrived on time, which meant something was wrong.

"Morning," he said, voice uncharacteristically subdued. No theatrical entrance, no commentary about the weather or his dreams or the cosmic implications of caffeine. Just a quiet greeting and careful eyes that took in the sparse counter, the single tray of muffins, the way Jonah moved like he was walking through water.

"Light inventory today?" Brian asked, tying his apron with uncharacteristic precision.

"Something like that."

They worked in companionable quiet, rationing their usual abundance. Brian didn't suggest any experimental drinks. Jonah didn't mention the supply situation. They both knew. They both pretended not to.

The batter came together thinner than usual, not quite right. Jonah folded in the blueberries with the care of someone repairing something already too far broken. They'd rise, probably, but not with the same heart.

At one point, Brian took a long inventory-style glance at the back shelves, then quietly refilled the sugar jars like it might help stretch the supplies. He wiped down the counter without being asked, slower than usual, careful not to dislodge the illusion of normalcy they were both trying to maintain.

The morning regulars came and went, most too polite or too preoccupied to comment on the reduced selection. Ms. Curlee took her usual black coffee and asked for a blueberry muffin with the casual assumption that there would be one. Jonah handed it over, still warm, and watched her bite into it with the contentment of routine unchanged.

"Perfect, as always," she said, leaving exact change and a smile.

Jonah watched her go, wondering if she'd taste the difference —the slight desperation in the batter, the careful conservation in each measured ingredient. Probably not. People tasted what they expected to taste, especially in places that had never disappointed them before.

Around ten, the bell chimed and Gen stepped in, but something was different. She carried herself with the fluid certainty of someone who'd made a decision, though she hadn't announced it yet. Her sketchpad was tucked under her arm, but she also carried a manila envelope, thick and official-looking.

"Coffee?" Jonah asked, already reaching for a cup.

"Actually," she said, settling at the counter, "just tea today. Something light."

He paused, cup halfway to the machine. In all the weeks she'd been coming here, she'd never ordered tea. Never ordered anything but coffee, black, sometimes with a splash of milk when she was feeling indulgent.

"Everything okay?"

She smiled, but it carried weight. "Everything's... changing. But maybe that's the same thing."

He brewed her chamomile, watching steam curl from the cup like incense. She wrapped her hands around it but didn't drink, just let the warmth seep through her palms. The light slanted differently this morning—cooler, sharper, falling across the counter in pale stripes. Outside, someone pushed a stroller past the window, wheels creaking against the uneven sidewalk. Jonah leaned on the counter, resting one hand on the warm surface beside her cup. The scent of chamomile filled the space between them, gentle and strangely dissonant in a room that usually smelled like espresso and cinnamon.

Gen didn't speak right away. She stared at the rising steam, her thumb grazing the handle of the cup in slow circles, like she was trying to ground herself in the heat without letting it scald.

"I got news yesterday," she said finally. "About a residency program. Three months in Oregon, then maybe California after that. Art cooperative, shared studio space, the whole thing."

Jonah felt something shift in his chest, like furniture being rearranged in a dark room. "That's... that's incredible. You applied for it?"

"Months ago, before I even came here. I'd forgotten I was waiting." She turned the envelope over in her hands. "Funny how that works. You throw seeds everywhere and forget where you planted them until something starts growing."

"When would you go?"

"Next month, most likely." She looked up then, met his eyes directly. "Spring seems like the right time for new beginnings, don't you think?"

The timer chimed from the kitchen—the last tray of muffins, there wouldn't be a next one to follow. Jonah excused himself and pulled them from the oven, their tops golden and perfect, releasing clouds of sweet steam that seemed almost mocking in their abundance.

When he returned, Gen was sketching absently on a napkin—not the shop this time, but something abstract. Lines that curved and intersected without forming anything concrete, like roads on a map to somewhere that didn't have a name yet.

"The thing is," she said, not looking up from her drawing, "it's not just about me going. The program has space for... collaborative residents. People who bring different skills. Artisans, writers, ...bakers. People who understand that art isn't just what hangs on walls."

She set down her pencil and looked at him directly.

"I keep thinking about what you said once, that day the oven burned everything. You said baking doesn't lie. How it shows everything—your attention, your care, whether you're distracted or present." She paused. "That's art, Jonah. What you do here, it's art."

He started to shake his head, to deflect, but she continued.

"I've been watching you. The way you fix things before they break. How you remember exactly how everyone takes their coffee. The way you make this place feel like home for people who might not have one anywhere else." She leaned forward slightly. "You think that's not creative? You think that's not making something beautiful out of raw materials?"

"Gen..."

"I know it's crazy," she said quickly. "I know you have a life here, responsibilities. The shop, your father, Amanda..." She trailed off at the last name, something flickering across her face. "But sometimes you have to step outside the script, sometimes we say crazy when what we really mean is brave."

She slid the envelope across the counter toward him. The manila paper whispered against the polished wood, a sound that seemed to swallow all the others in the shop—the hum of the fridge, the distant traffic, the soft tinkling of mugs settling on dishes. "The application deadline isn't for another week. If you wanted to... if you thought you might want to..."

She hesitated then, fingers resting on the edge of the envelope. "I wasn't going to bring it up, honestly. I told myself you wouldn't be interested. That it wasn't fair to ask." She gave a quiet laugh, almost a breath. "But then I kept picturing you baking. Fixing the hinges on the door. Bringing me that mug without saying a word. I started thinking maybe you belonged somewhere that saw that kind of thing as valuable. Not just... expected."

She met his eyes again, softer now. "You're more than the glue holding this place together, Jonah. I think you've just gotten used to being useful."

Jonah stared at the envelope like it might burst into flames. Inside, he could see the edges of forms, official letterhead, the bureaucratic framework of possibility.

"I don't know the first thing about art residencies," he said finally.

"Neither did I, six months ago." She smiled, and this time it was lighter, less weighted. "But I know about starting over. I know about taking the leap and trusting that something will be there to catch you. Or at least that the fall will teach you how to fly."

The bell chimed again—brighter this time—and Patty stepped inside, clutching a brown paper bag in one hand, something from the deli down the street judging by the grease stains near the bottom, and a folded envelope in the other. She paused just past the threshold, eyes moving from Genesis to Jonah, then down to the envelope resting on the counter.

"Didn't mean to walk in on anything," she said, voice low but unapologetic.

Gen rose smoothly, tucking away her sketchpad and slinging her bag over her shoulder with deliberate calm. "You didn't. Just... finishing a thought."

Patty gave a small nod, not pushing. "One worth finishing, by the look of it."

She paused near the counter, giving Jonah a look that was part curiosity, part concern, and all Patty.

"Think about it, Jonah," Gen said softly. "Not forever. Just... think."

The door clicked closed behind her a moment later, leaving traces of chamomile and charcoal in the air.

Patty set her lunch on the counter, removed her coat with practiced movements, and pulled up a stool beside Jonah. She didn't speak right away, just followed his gaze to the envelope.

"Well," she said finally, as she unwrapped her sandwich and nodded towards the envelope in Jonah's hands. "That doesn't look like a utility bill."

Jonah turned the envelope over in his hands, not quite ready to open it but unable to set it down. "Job opportunity. Out west."

"For you?"

"Apparently."

Patty studied his face with the careful attention of someone reading weather patterns. "And you're considering it?"

"I don't know." He looked up at her. "Should I be?"

She was quiet for a long moment, watching Brian rearrange the sparse pastry case to make it look fuller than it was. He kept shifting the same three muffins around like he was playing pastry chess. Occasionally he stepped back, tilted his head, then moved one an inch to the left. It was a performance of abundance, as if the illusion could hold if he just got the angles right.

"You know," she said finally, "I've been working here for six years. Watched this place through good times and lean ones. Watched Ms. Wallace worry herself sick over rent and supplies and whether we'd make it through another winter."

She leaned against the counter, her voice dropping lower.

"But I've never seen her look at this place the way she's been looking at it lately. Like she's already saying goodbye."

Jonah felt something cold settle in his stomach. "What do you mean?"

"I mean, she's been in twice this week, going through old papers, taking pictures of the bookshelves. Yesterday, I caught her writing down the paint colors on the walls." Patty's voice was gentle but unflinching. "People don't do that unless they're trying to remember something they're about to lose."

The envelope felt heavier in his hands now, less like possibility and more like a life preserver thrown from a distant shore.

"Community night bought us some time," Patty continued. "Donations, goodwill, people remembering why they love this place. But time isn't the same thing as money, and money isn't the same thing as hope."

She straightened, adjusting her apron with brisk efficiency.

"I'm not saying you should go or stay. That's not my choice to make. But if someone's offering you a chance to take your talents somewhere they'll be appreciated, somewhere you can grow..." She shrugged. "Maybe that's not a coincidence. Maybe that's the universe being surprisingly efficient for once."

She moved toward the back office, then paused.

"Besides," she added, her voice carefully casual, "if this place does close, at least one of us should land somewhere soft."

The rest of the day passed in a kind of suspended animation. Customers came and went, but there was an undercurrent of farewell in everything—the way the afternoon light slanted through the windows, the sound of pages turning in the corner reading nook, even the hiss of the espresso machine seemed more poignant than usual.

Jonah found himself paying attention to details he'd always taken for granted: the exact shade of brown in the wooden shelves, the way dust motes danced in the window light, the soft thud of books being set down on tables. As if he were trying to memorize everything at once, storing up sensory details against some approaching winter.

Amanda didn't come by after school. Neither did Mr. Beverly. The shop felt smaller without them, more fragile somehow, like a house with half its foundation gone.

Brian lingered a little longer than usual, cleaning the steam wand twice and pretending not to watch Jonah. He muttered something about needing to email a professor and slipped out with a subdued "See you," the chime of the door somehow quieter behind him.

At closing time, Jonah locked the door and flipped the sign, but instead of leaving, he sat in one of the reading chairs and opened the envelope Gen had left behind.

The forms were straightforward but comprehensive—work samples, personal statement, letters of recommendation. A description of the program that made it sound both terrifying and extraordinary: communal living, shared meals, collaborative projects, the chance to explore what art meant when it wasn't confined to traditional galleries or stages.

There was a section for "artisan applications"—people who worked with their hands, who understood that creation didn't always happen with paint or words. Bakers, woodworkers, potters, weavers. People who made beautiful, functional things that nourished the body as well as the spirit.

At the bottom of the packet, Gen had tucked a small note card, her handwriting neat and careful:

> *The best art happens when someone takes what they know and shows it to people who've never seen it before. You know how to make a place feel like home. That's rarer than you think. —G*

Jonah read it twice, then folded it carefully and slipped it back into the envelope. Outside, the street lamps were flickering to life, casting long pools of yellow light on the empty sidewalks. The town looked peaceful, settled, content with its rhythms and routines.

But inside the shop, surrounded by books and empty coffee cups and the lingering scent of baked goods, Jonah felt the first stirrings of something he hadn't experienced in years: the possibility that maybe, just maybe, there might be another way to live.

He sat there for a long time, listening to the shop breathe around him—the settling creak of a beam, the soft sigh of the cooling oven. The envelope in his lap was no longer just a packet of forms; it was a lens, and through it, everything in the shop looked different. Not less beloved, but suddenly, achingly finite. The questions it contained didn't feel like burdens anymore. They felt like keys.

Somewhere down the street, a dog barked once and fell silent. The town was settling into evening, unaware. Jonah sat still, one hand resting on the envelope, not reaching for a pen, not yet. But for the first time, imagining its weight in his hand.

18

INK AND INCLINATION

The light through Jonah's bedroom window was gray and directionless, the kind that made it hard to tell whether morning had really begun or just never ended. He sat on the edge of his bed in socked feet, the envelope from Genesis resting on the nightstand beside his alarm clock and a half-drunk glass of water. He hadn't opened it again. He didn't need to—he knew the shape of it now, the questions folded inside.

Downstairs, his father's coffee mug clinked softly against the counter. A rhythm he knew without looking. He rose, dressed in practiced silence, and left the envelope where it was.

The shop was still dark when he arrived, the key slipping into the lock with a tactile familiarity he didn't have the heart to resent. He clicked on the overheads, started the ovens even though there wouldn't be much to bake, and filled the kettle for tea—not because he wanted any, but because the act felt gentler than coffee. Less bitter. More like growing things.

The air inside still carried yesterday's scent: sugar, cinnamon, and something faintly floral.

At the center table, he began arranging the items Ms. Wallace had left in a box the week before—blank stationery, black and sepia pens, small tent cards with prompts like "Write a letter to someone you miss." He positioned everything with the careful precision of someone dodging a decision, each pen straightened like it might anchor something.

A card fell from the box and fluttered to the floor. Jonah bent to retrieve it and paused when he read the prompt:

WRITE SOMETHING YOU WISH YOU'D SAID, EVEN IF IT'S TOO LATE.

He slipped it quietly into the stack.

Brian arrived mid-morning, windblown and under-caffeinated but carrying a bundle of misplaced energy like he was trying to compensate for yesterday's quiet.

"Oof," he said, dropping his backpack with a thud. "This

morning's got the vibe of a black-and-white documentary about loneliness."

Jonah handed him a cup without a word.

Brian eyed the stationery display while sipping. "So... this is the handwriting thing, huh?"

Jonah nodded. "Ms. Wallace wants people to write letters. Pen pals, postcards, whatever moves them."

Brian leaned in, reading the prompts aloud. "Dear Future Me, Things I Can't Say Out Loud, One Last Goodbye... jeez, man, this is like emotional karaoke."

Jonah almost smiled. "You think it's too much?"

Brian shrugged. "Nah. I think people are weirder and more sentimental than they let on."

He grabbed a blank index card from behind the bar and scribbled something, then taped it to the side of the display. The heading read:

THE SUGGESTION BOX (NO PROMISES, BUT WE MIGHT READ THEM)

Below that, he wrote in smaller letters:

TELL US SOMETHING YOU'D NEVER POST ON A USENET GROUP.

Jonah raised an eyebrow. "Really?"
Brian grinned. "Trust the chaos, my dude."

By late morning, the shop was filling more than expected. A few customers sat longer than usual, sipping slowly, some scribbling quietly at the letter station. Jonah refilled the pen jar and cleared a half-finished muffin plate. The case was sparse again, but no one complained. Maybe they noticed. Maybe they didn't. People were good at rewriting what they loved to match what they remembered.

Around noon, a folded sheet of paper appeared in the letter station, left behind under a mug. No name. Just careful handwriting on heavyweight cream paper:

I used to come here with someone. We always sat by the window. They'd read aloud if it was raining. I didn't think it mattered until it stopped happening.

Thanks for not changing the chairs.
—M.

Jonah stood with the letter in his hands longer than he had intended, the heavy paper suddenly feeling like a weight. He read it again. *I didn't think it mattered until it stopped happening.* The words echoed in the sparseness of the shop, a quiet testament to all the things that became precious only in their absence. He was unsure whether to save it or pretend he'd never seen it. Eventually, he folded it again, the crease sharp and final, and slipped it into the pocket of his apron.

Amanda burst through the front door mid-afternoon like she'd been launched from a slingshot. Her hair was half-pulled back with a pencil, and her bag was threatening to shed every binder it contained.

"I'm here, I'm caffeinated-adjacent, and I have opinions," she declared, marching toward the counter.

Jonah glanced at the clock. "You're early."

"I made a dramatic exit from Algebra II. Felt appropriate. This—" she gestured to the letter station "—is adorable, and I fully intend to overshare."

She dumped her bag on a nearby chair and pulled a stool up to the table like she was claiming territory. "Do we get to read the letters or are they sacred?"

Jonah smiled faintly. "Mostly sacred. Though there's a suggestion box now."

"Dangerous," she said, delighted. "I'm going to pretend it's for performance reviews. My first one: Brian needs to stop pretending soy milk is a personality."

From the bar, Brian called back, "Soy milk is a personality, and mine is complex."

Amanda laughed and began flipping through the pens with theatrical intensity. "Alright. I'm writing to my future self. Or my multiverse variant. Whichever one owns a dog and doesn't forget to water her plants."

She wrote a few lines, paused, then looked up at Jonah. "You look like you're thinking about something. Like, really thinking."

He kept polishing the already-clean counter. "Do I?"

"Yeah. You've got that look—the one you get when your brain is way ahead of your words. What's going on?"

He hesitated, then shrugged. "Just trying to figure out what's next."

Amanda leaned forward slightly. "You've been quiet since the community night. Not just quiet-quiet. Jonah-quiet."

He gave her a look.

"That's different," she insisted. "Normal quiet is, like, reading-a-book quiet. Jonah-quiet is existential." She tapped her pen twice. "Did something happen?"

"Maybe."

"Are you okay?"

"I think so."

Amanda studied him for a second, then softened. "You don't have to tell me if you're not ready. But I hope you do eventually."

She turned back to her paper, writing with more care now. "If I could write to my future self, I'd say... 'Be kinder to your weird impulses. They're probably trying to tell you something.'"

She glanced up. "What would you say to your past self?"

Jonah folded a towel along the counter's edge. "I think I'd say—"

'Don't let the fear of losing something good prevent you from pursuing something great.'

Amanda didn't answer right away. When she did, her voice was quiet. "That's beautiful."

She folded her letter carefully and slipped it into the basket. "You better write one too. Even if it's just to your oven."

Before she left, she pulled on her coat and added, "And Jonah?"

He looked up.

"Don't get stuck. Not even in a good place."

Genesis didn't stop by.

Jonah noticed in the quiet way people do when they've gotten used to someone appearing at a certain time and space. He didn't expect her, exactly, but the absence felt outlined. Like a seat left empty on purpose.

Maybe she was giving him space. Maybe she didn't want to seem like she was pushing. Or maybe it didn't mean anything at all. But he noticed.

He found himself glancing once at the door before closing, like she might slip in under the wire with a mug request and a half-smile.

But she didn't.

———

As they closed up, Brian lingered near the letter station, collecting a few of the notes left behind. He cleared his throat with mock gravity.

"Ready for the gold?"

Jonah nodded once, drying a tray.

"This place has the best lighting to cry in public."

"The barista with the metal band shirts makes me feel like I'm cool enough to order a cortado."

"This isn't a suggestion. I just wanted to say I had my first date here five years ago. It didn't last, but this place stayed."

"Y'all need to bring back the lavender shortbread, or I'm staging a coup."

Brian held that one up with mock outrage. "They spelled 'coup' like the chicken sound! But I feel the passion."

Jonah laughed softly, folding a towel. "We might have to bring it back."

Brian dropped the cards into a folder. "Even if this place is falling apart... it's someone's safe place. Probably more than one someone."

Jonah didn't respond right away, but something in him stilled, like the words had brushed against a bruise he'd forgotten was there.

That night, at home, Jonah made tea—something floral, gentler than coffee, with a quiet steam that curled upward like thought. He sat at the old desk in his bedroom—the one with a shallow drawer that still smelled like pencil shavings and notebook paper. He cleared a space and set the envelope from Genesis to the side. He didn't open it. Not yet.

Instead, he took out a yellow legal pad from the drawer and uncapped a pen.

The page stayed blank for a long time. He tapped the pen on the desk as the earlier prompt echoed in his memory. 'Something you wish you'd said.'

He wasn't sure what he was writing—an application, a confession, a letter to himself. The words came slowly.

I MAKE THINGS WITH MY HANDS.

NOT BECAUSE IT'S EASIER THAN SAYING THEM OUT LOUD, BUT BECAUSE IT LASTS LONGER.

THE THINGS I FIX STAY FIXED. THE THINGS I BAKE FEED SOMEONE OTHER THAN ME.

I'VE ALWAYS THOUGHT THAT MATTERED.

He stopped, pen hovering over the last word, which suddenly seemed insufficient.

Then he drew a single, clean line through the whole thing, the ink stark and decisive. He flipped to a new page, the paper crisp and full of potential, and started again.

19

FRAMES AND FORECASTS

The rain had started sometime before dawn, a steady hush against the windows that blurred the edges of morning. Jonah walked purposefully, with his hood pulled low and his collar turned up, but still, the rain found its way in. It slipped past seams and soaked into his sleeves, clung to his cuffs, and dripped from the hem of his coat. He opened the shop to the sound of water trickling down the gutters and the metallic patter of drops hitting the tin awning over the front door. The world felt muffled, like someone had turned the volume down just enough to let the silence speak.

Inside, he flipped on the lights and stood for a moment in the quiet glow—damp, half-rooted in the storm. The air smelled faintly of damp stone and old paper. He peeled off his jacket and hung it on the hook by the back door, where it hung heavily, darkened with rain. Then, circling back with a towel, he wiped up the drops he'd trailed across the wood floor, moving with quiet care.

There was no heat yet—the ovens hadn't been started. The air in the shop felt still and chilled, the kind of cold that sank in slowly and stayed awhile.

Ms. Wallace arrived not long after he'd unlocked the front. She stepped in without her usual quiet, her umbrella dripping and coat speckled with rain, a brown cardboard box balanced on a hip and tucked under her arm. She didn't shake off the weather like she usually did. She let it follow her in.

"Good morning," she said, setting down the box and tugging off her gloves.

Jonah nodded. "Morning."

"Supplies," she added, nodding to the box and indicating that Jonah should take it. "Let's get those shelves restocked, shall we?"

He picked up the box and peered inside. It contained coffee, flour, some dry goods, and several containers of fresh blueberries. He carried it behind the counter as Ms. Wallace followed. She didn't move toward the office. Instead, she stood at the counter, watching Jonah as he unpacked the box and carefully placed the items in all of their designated places.

"A place for everything, and everything in its place," she spoke softly. Then, in a more assertive tone, "The landlord reached out yesterday. He wants an answer by the end of the month."

Jonah didn't speak, just continued organizing shelves.

"If we renew, it's a long lease—three years minimum. And a hike." Her voice was calm, but her shoulders were tighter than usual. "If we don't... well. He has other offers."

She turned to face him fully. "It's not just about what we want anymore. It's about what we can do."

Jonah nodded slowly. "So, what are you thinking?"

She hesitated. "I'm thinking that I've poured a lot of years into this place. And I'd pour more, if it made sense. But I also think... there's a difference between letting go and giving up. I'm still working out which this would be."

Jonah watched her as she glanced toward the bookshelves, as if memorizing them again. She unzipped a side pocket of her coat and pulled out a folded notice. Without fanfare, she walked to the bulletin board and pinned it to the cork—lower right corner, beneath an old poster for a banned books display. She smoothed it once with her hand, her thumb lingering for a fraction of a second on the corner, as if pressing a seal onto a fate. She checked its alignment, and stood there a moment in quiet reverence before giving him a soft, tired smile and disappearing into the office. Jonah started to speak, but the words caught somewhere behind his teeth. Some questions needed silence more than answers.

He brewed tea instead of coffee—something gentler. The herbal steam rose like quiet encouragement. It felt right.

As he leaned against the counter, letting the warmth rise into his chest, the bell above the door jingled softly. Brian stepped in, brushing water from his hoodie, but stopped short when he saw Jonah glaring at the puddle forming at his feet.

"Whoops—almost made an entrance," Brian said.

Jonah nodded, then tossed a towel over to him. "Make sure it's not slippery near the door."

Brian tread carefully across the mat, wiping water as he moved. "Rain's theatrical today. Like someone broke the sky and just let it spill."

They continued through their usual opening rhythm. Jonah started the ovens and double-checked the dry stock. Brian lined up the mugs without comment. It was a quiet companionship, steady. The shop gradually warmed as the ovens kicked in, and the air took on the gentle aroma of batter and baking spice.

By midmorning, the storm softened into a steady drizzle, but people still came. A few peeled off wet coats and stood near the heaters. Others took their usual spots, grateful for dry chairs and warm drinks.

One older man shook water from his umbrella and said with a grin, "Days like this, I'm glad you're open. Coffee just hits different when it's raining."

A college student near the windows curled her feet up on her chair and buried herself in a blanket and a book. A mother with a toddler asked for a muffin and then sat by the register reading aloud from a children's poetry collection.

"This place," one woman murmured near the door, pulling off her gloves, "is exactly where you want to be when the weather forgets how to behave."

Jonah didn't say much, but he noticed. The way people eased into the shop, the weight they let go of as soon as they crossed the threshold; like this small corner of the world held firm while everything outside blew sideways. He couldn't fix the storm, but here, inside, he could offer stillness.

Patty arrived around midday, umbrella under one arm and a deli bag in the other.

"You ever notice how rain makes you feel nostalgic?" she said, shaking off her coat. As she passed the bulletin board, she slowed—eyes lingering on the new notice. She read it fully, face unreadable, and then kept walking, saying nothing. She set down her umbrella and hung up her coat, then turned toward Jonah and Brian with the same sharp energy as always.

"What did I miss? Emotional letters? Existential cappuccinos? Brian's latest flirtation with soy milk foam?"

Brian grinned. "I'm saving the soy milk revelations for the weekend."

Patty dropped her bag on the counter. "Shame. I was hoping for enlightenment."

Jonah raised an eyebrow. "Rough morning?"

"Let's just say if I'd stayed home, I'd be arguing with my shower drain right now. This place smells better and judges less. Speaking of, is that fresh pastries I smell?"

"Ms. Wallace brought in some restock supplies this morning," Jonah replied.

They fell into rhythm, the three of them, comfortable in their familiar roles. Brian humming under his breath, Patty arguing with the toaster, Jonah making tea for a customer who asked if they had anything "calming and also vaguely magical." He handed out drinks with precise warmth. The storm rolled on, but inside felt intact.

The bell chimed softly, and Amanda stepped inside, hugging a folder under her arm, her curls damp and cheeks flushed.

She didn't announce anything this time—just gave a little wave and a sheepish smile.

Brian, already holding a towel, tossed it to her. "I think you might want this. You look sort of like a drenched poodle."

"Thanks," she said sardonically, toweling her hair quickly. "It's really coming down out there."

She paused just past the door, taking in the warmth of the shop, the scent of fresh muffins curling through the air.

"It's raining, I'm cold, and this place smells like comfort and—ooh—poor impulse control," she said, already reaching for a muffin from the tray near the counter. "Honestly, of all the corners of the universe to land in, this one might be the coziest. Pretty sure the universe sent this storm just to boost your foot traffic. I see a lot of occupied seats."

"Patty said my latte art looks like it's trying to apologize," Brian said.

"It should be. That foam had regrets. Honestly, I think the cow that gave that milk expected her contribution to be part of something more... inspired," Patty said, not looking up.

Amanda laughed and made her way toward the letter station. She sorted pens for a moment, then called over, "I've been working on a monologue. Want to hear it?"

Jonah nodded, and Patty gave a little wave of her hand like: Go on, let's hear the drama.

Amanda stood straight and began:

There's a girl sitting at a bus stop, right? Rain's coming down sideways, and she's wearing the wrong shoes—because she always wears the wrong shoes.

She's waiting. Not for the bus, not really. For a sign. A person. A reason. Something that'll tell her she isn't crazy for hoping.

She checks her watch, then the street, then the sky. Everything's wrong. The weather, the moment, the timing.

But here's the thing: she stays. She doesn't leave. And maybe that's the point. Maybe she misses the bus on purpose.

Because sometimes the thing you're waiting for isn't a ride—it's a reason to stay in the rain a little longer. Just in case.

She paused, then added with a grin, "Also, she probably has to pee, but that feels like a different metaphor."

Brian clapped. Patty gave a satisfied nod. Jonah smiled. He wasn't sure if Amanda was talking about herself, or trying to remind him of something he'd forgotten. Maybe both. But for the first time that day, the storm outside felt like it might be passing.

"That was... really good," he said.

"Yeah?" Amanda asked. Her grin faltered just slightly. "I've been trying to get it right for the acting troupe showcase. It's supposed to be personal, but not... too personal. Like, honest without oversharing."

"It's well-formed and intentional," Jonah said. "Hits that line just right."

Amanda looked relieved, then tucked the monologue back into her folder.

"I'll revise it a hundred more times anyway," she said. "But thanks. Hey, Mom—did you ever pull that book I needed?"

Patty didn't look up from the receipt drawer. "I think Herb grabbed it. Check upstairs—he's cataloging again."

Amanda gave a small groan but headed for the staircase anyway, muttering something about maze-like shelves and cryptic filing systems as she disappeared into the stacks.

Genesis arrived just after lunch, stepping in with her hood half-down and her sketchpad tucked tight beneath her coat. She didn't order anything. She just walked up to the counter and offered a small nod, a quieter version of her usual presence.

"I forgot this last time," Jonah said, holding up the mug she'd once claimed as her unofficial favorite. It had been washed, dried, and set aside. She took it with both hands.

"Thanks."

She lingered at the counter. No sketching this time, no preamble.

"I'm leaving," she said quietly. "Monday, probably. Going to try and get things settled in before the residency gets underway."

Jonah nodded. "You all packed?"

"Mostly. Still a few things left to figure out. But the big parts are in motion." She paused. "That includes letting go of the habit of hovering."

He raised an eyebrow.

"I've been thinking too much about whether you'd apply," she said. "And I realized that's not mine to carry."

He didn't respond right away.

"I'd still like you to come," she added, "but I won't ask again."

Jonah looked down at his hands on the counter. "I haven't decided yet."

"I know."

She reached into her coat and pulled out a folded piece of paper. "This is the address where I'll be staying, in case you do decide. Or in case you want to visit and pretend you didn't." Her smile was soft, a little wistful.

He took it without a word. It was just paper, but it carried more than he was ready to unfold.

Before leaving, she looked around the shop, eyes tracing the shelves, the worn counter, the letter station still neatly stocked.

"You made something here," she said. "Whatever happens, that matters."

She looked at him then, really looked, her gaze steady, searching, like she was trying to find the shape of something she didn't quite know how to name. It held for a long moment, a pause thick with things unspoken. Like if she looked hard enough, she could will a decision out of him.

But then her expression shifted, just slightly. The smallest sigh. The softest release. A quiet recognition that it wasn't her choice to make.

And then she left, as quietly as she'd come, the door chime sounding oddly delicate in her wake.

Later in the afternoon, Brian wandered back to the letter station, flipping through the stack of anonymous notes with a grin tugging at his mouth.

"Oh man. Okay, here we go," he said, clearing his throat like a town crier. "First up: 'More book recommendations, please. I trust you all more than Amazon.'"

Jonah looked up from wiping down the espresso machine. "We should put that on a T-shirt."

Brian continued. "'Replace all chairs with beanbags. Embrace chaos.'"

He paused, tilting the card. "I bet I know who wrote that one."

From across the counter, Patty didn't look up. "It wasn't you?"

Brian smirked. "You can't prove that."

He picked up another. "'Please never get rid of the mismatched mugs. They make me feel less alone.'"

That one they let hang a little longer. Jonah felt something small settle in his chest.

Brian broke the quiet with another. "'Can we get one of those library ladders that rolls? I won't use it. I just need to know it's there.'"

"Seconded," Amanda said from her seat without looking up. "I need something dramatic to lean against during monologues."

Brian read another. "'Do the books get rotated, or is that just the caffeine talking?'"

Jonah chuckled. "Depends on how much caffeine they've had."

Brian held up the next card. "'Please add a menu item called "The Usual" that's completely random every time.'"

"That's a customer service nightmare," Patty said.

"That's a branding opportunity," Brian countered.

He picked up the last one and read it a little slower. "'I proposed to my partner at the table by the window. She said yes before I finished my sentence.'"

Jonah blinked. He remembered—two winters ago, snow piling against the windows, the quiet tremble in the man's voice, the way she laughed through tears. He'd brought them two mugs and a slice of banana bread, on the house.

He hadn't thought of that day in a while. He said nothing now, but the memory sat beside him like a folded page in a well-loved book, warm, certain, like something worth believing in.

By the time Jonah was locking up, his jacket was still damp from the morning. As he reached for it, his eyes caught the corner of the bulletin board. The notice was still there—centered, smooth, deliberate. Just as she'd left it. He hadn't forgotten—it was just easier not to look straight at it.

He didn't bother trying to stay dry. The rain had become a fine mist again, soaking in quietly. The streets were quieter now. Puddles reflected streetlights in liquid gold, and the wind whispered through bare trees like someone telling secrets softly. He took his time walking, hood pulled up, steps deliberate. Streetlights buzzed softly, glowing amber in the gloom. Water beaded on mailbox tops, and the wind smelled like something shifting.

Mr. Beverly was on his porch, as always, cardigan draped over his shoulders, a mug steaming beside him.

Jonah paused at the gate. The porch light glowed soft against the rain.

"Evening," he called.

"Mr. Ashford!" came the reply. "You look like a man walking with something heavy that doesn't want to be named."

Jonah cracked a small smile and stepped up the walk. "Got a minute?"

"Hopefully, I've got more than that. Sit."

The porch creaked under Jonah's weight as he lowered himself into the extra chair. Rain tapped steadily against the gutters, a soft rhythm around them.

They sat in silence for a beat.

"I might apply to something," Jonah said finally.

"Something or someone?" Mr. Beverly asked, the corner of his mouth twitching.

Jonah huffed a laugh. "A residency. Out west. One of those artist things. But art can be anything, I guess. There's a community. A place where people go to figure out if they're brave."

Mr. Beverly nodded, unsurprised. "And what do you think you'll figure out?"

"I don't know." Jonah glanced toward the street. "It's not even an offer, really. It's just an application, but it feels like more than that."

"Sometimes the doorframe matters more than the key."

Jonah looked down at his hands. "I'm not sure if I'm afraid of going, or afraid of staying."

Mr. Beverly let that settle between them, then asked, "Is there someone else involved? Someone who might make either choice feel bigger than it is?"

Jonah didn't answer immediately. "Maybe. I mean, I think so, but I'm not really sure."

"Someone worth considering?"

Jonah nodded once.

"Well then," Mr. Beverly said, "consider them. And consider yourself, too. Both deserve a seat at the table."

Jonah leaned forward slightly. "If I go... I don't know what I'm walking into. But if I stay..." He trailed off.

Mr. Beverly waited, giving Jonah time to complete his thought.

"...I might already know how that story ends."

"People think courage is about action," Mr. Beverly said. "Sometimes it's about stillness. Knowing when something's finished, or when it still needs tending. To everything there is a season. What time is it for you now?"

Jonah gave a slow exhale, pondering. "The shop might not make it."

"I know."

"If I leave now, I abandon it."

"Should you stay for the sake of loyalty alone?" Mr. Beverly asked gently. "Make sure you aren't mistaking familiarity for good."

Jonah looked out at the streetlight haloing the mist. "It just feels like... if I make the wrong call, I lose something important."

Mr. Beverly shifted in his chair. "It sounds like if you make the right call, you lose something important as well. Try to ask yourself: is what you're holding on to still holding you back?"

Jonah didn't answer.

They sat together for a while, listening to the hush of the rain and the way the wind combed through the trees. Eventually, Jonah stood.

"Thank you."

"You don't owe me that."

"I know," Jonah said. "That's why it matters."

Mr. Beverly nodded once. "Whatever you choose, make it yours. Don't let it be chosen for you."

As Jonah reached the steps, Mr. Beverly added one final line, almost as an afterthought:

"You don't have to know yet. You just have to stay curious long enough to find out."

***

Jonah's house was quiet when he arrived. A single light glowed in the kitchen above the sink. On the stair banister, a clean towel hung neatly. On the sideboard table: a folded sweatshirt and a pair of dry socks.

He changed slowly, grateful. No words from his father, but the gesture had its own language.

In the kitchen, he made tea—chamomile, simple, warm. As he sipped, he thought of Gen—not the tea she ordered, but the way she held it. Palms curled around it like it offered something more than warmth. A reminder. A tether.

Upstairs, at his desk, Jonah turned on the small lamp and opened his legal pad.

He began to write.

> I WASN'T SURE I'D APPLY TO THIS. I'M STILL NOT SURE I'M THE KIND OF PERSON WHO BELONGS IN A RESIDENCY PROGRAM.
>
> I'VE NEVER CONSIDERED THE THINGS I DO TO BE ARTISTIC, BUT I'VE BEEN TOLD THAT WHAT I DO—BAKING, REPAIRING, MAKING COFFEE, REMEMBERING THE LITTLE THINGS—IS A FORM OF ART. I DON'T KNOW IF I BELIEVE THAT YET, BUT I'M WILLING TO FIND OUT.
>
> I DON'T HAVE GALLERY PIECES OR INSTALLATIONS. WHAT I HAVE IS A HISTORY OF PAYING ATTENTION—OF NOTICING WHAT NEEDS FIXING BEFORE IT BREAKS, AND SHOWING UP TO DO IT. I KNOW HOW TO BUILD COMFORT FROM SCRATCH. I KNOW HOW TO MAKE PEOPLE FEEL AT HOME, EVEN WHEN THEY DON'T KNOW THEY'RE LOOKING FOR ONE.
>
> I'VE LEARNED THAT CARE HAS A SHAPE, AND SOMETIMES THAT SHAPE IS A SPACE—A PLACE—WHERE PEOPLE FEEL SAFE ENOUGH TO STAY AWHILE.
>
> MAYBE THERE'S A PLACE FOR THAT KIND OF THING IN YOUR PROGRAM.

He underlined the last line, then paused. Beneath it, he wrote a single name:

Ms. Wallace

He circled it once—slow, deliberate. A quiet beginning. Not a declaration. Not yet. But something.

Tomorrow, maybe, he'd ask.

20

HINGES AND HORIZONS

The house was quiet except for the hum of the fridge and the occasional sigh of settling walls. Jonah stood in the kitchen in socked feet, watching the coffeemaker finish its cycle. His father was already at the table, reading a folded newspaper with half his toast gone and his mug waiting patiently between them.

Jonah first filled his father's mug, then poured one for himself and slid into the chair across from him. Neither of them spoke right away. Outside, the morning still carried the hush of yesterday's rain—clouds lingering, not threatening, just undecided.

Jonah, still nursing his first few sips, kept his eyes on the swirling steam before finally asking, "How do you know when it's time to change something?"

The question landed without rustling anything. His father didn't startle or shift. He just sat for a moment, thumb brushing the rim of his mug, before looking up and shifting the newspaper aside. He leaned back in his chair and took a long sip before answering.

"You mean like a job?"

Jonah shrugged. "Anything. Something that's been part of your life for so long, it feels like muscle memory. But then one day... it doesn't fit the same."

His father was quiet a beat longer, then said, "When staying started to feel like forgetting who I was supposed to become."

Jonah nodded slowly.

"You already know, Joe," his father added, voice softening. "You're just hoping someone will tell you otherwise."

Jonah sipped again, his thumb brushing the rim of his mug without thinking. Across from him, his father did the same. Unaware. Unspoken. On the table between them sat the small ceramic sugar bowl Jonah's mother had always used. It was chipped on one side, but neither of them had ever suggested replacing it. They drank the rest of their coffee without another word, but the silence between them felt understood.

The walk into town was damp around the edges, the sort of morning that hadn't made up its mind yet. Puddles clung to the uneven sidewalks, slowly pulling away from themselves and slipping into cracks. Water murmured through the culverts under the street as if a memory were being rinsed from the stone. The air held the faint scent of wet bark and thawing soil. The sunlight had shifted just enough to suggest it might stick around today.

Jonah passed by Fielding's Hardware store and made a mental note: hinges for the back room cabinet, lightbulbs for the hallway sconces, something to reseal the cracked tile grout in the restroom. The shop always had small wounds, and he preferred to patch them before they became infections.

The Grind & Bind appeared through thinning mist like something rooted, old, and patient. Jonah unlocked the front, let himself in, and turned on the lights one at a time. There was something ceremonial about it, something grounding. The lights came on with their usual reluctant flicker. He hung his coat and began the slow process of warming the place. He swept the entryway, wiped down the counter, and restocked the napkin holders. Familiar rituals. Measured ones. Steadying ones.

Brian arrived a little after seven, bouncing on the balls of his feet with his usual chaotic energy compressed into his limbs like a spring under tension, his hoodie half-zipped, and headphones still hanging around his neck.

"Morning," he said, already swaying to music only he could hear. "I had two waffles and got sucked into a documentary about prehistoric fungi."

"You're vibrating," Jonah observed, wiping down the espresso machine.

"Could be the caffeine. Could be the excitement of another weekend. Hard to say."

Jonah held out a handwritten note. "Then channel it into usefulness. Take this to Fielding's. Hinges, bulbs, grout sealant."

Brian blinked. "You think I should go now?"

"You're dancing like you're halfway there already. Might as well shimmy your way over before it gets too busy."

Brian saluted with two fingers and spun on his heel. "Aye aye, Cap'n. Be back in two shakes. Maybe a few more."

With Brian gone, the morning settled into its rhythm.

Jonah helped an older couple find a gift for their granddaughter, guiding them toward the illustrated hardcovers with foil-stamped covers and ribbon bookmarks. The grandfather made a dry joke about needing a degree in glittery packaging to pick a book these days. Jonah smiled and suggested one about a fox who held conversations with the moon. The grandmother tapped her chin and said, "She loves foxes. That's it, then."

Ms. Curlee arrived early for story hour, as she often did, her gray braid tucked beneath a rain hat and her canvas tote bumping softly against her hip. Jonah made her a latte—half decaf, extra foam, just how she liked it—and slid it across the counter before she asked.

"You always remember," she said, eyes crinkling at the corners.
"Some people are worth remembering," Jonah replied.

She gave him a nod of approval, then made her way to the rug circle, laying out cushions with methodical grace. Herb arrived not long after, looking like he'd been up for hours but had only just arrived. He made his way behind the counter without a word, filled a mug nearly to the brim with the strongest black coffee available, and gave Jonah a curt nod. He didn't speak, just grunted softly and made a beeline for the children's section, a box of puppets under one arm and a stack of picture books tucked against his side like precious cargo.

Jonah watched him settle in across from Ms. Curlee, the two of them murmuring briefly about the reading list. Herb examined the cover of a book featuring a raccoon in a bowtie and raised an eyebrow. Ms. Curlee simply patted his knee and said, "Trust the process." Herb muttered something about bowties being historically suspicious, but stayed put.

A teenager hovered near the poetry shelf and asked without looking up, "Do you have anything that's not, like, super lame?"
Jonah pointed toward the rotating display stacked with

Nikita Gill, Ada Limón, and a few copies of the Milkweed Editions anthology. "That Nikita Gill might surprise you," he said. "Honest, hits you where you don't expect."

She nodded once and tucked a copy of Wild Embers under her arm before drifting back toward the couches.

Patty and Ms. Wallace arrived together, sunglasses pushed up into their hair and voices mid-conversation. Their steps fell in tandem as they hung their jackets on adjacent hooks, moving with the practiced synchronicity of people who'd worked together too long to fumble the choreography.

"We need to post the revised schedule today," Patty was saying. "Or we'll end up double-booking Brian again, and then we'll have to make it up by letting him invent some unholy concoction involving latte art and interpretive dance."

"And that would be terrible," Ms. Wallace replied dryly, though the corner of her mouth twitched.

They disappeared into the back, murmuring about invoices and shifts, their voices folding into the shop's steady hum.

The place began to breathe. Quiet voices, pages turning, the soft thud of books being reshelved. Somewhere near the letter station, a mechanical pencil scratched across thick paper. A child giggled from the story rug as Herb adjusted the puppet on his hand and gave it a dignified British accent. Ms. Curlee played along without missing a beat.

It was a Saturday morning again.

The bell jingled and Brian returned, carrying a small paper sack and grinning like someone who'd just discovered something worth telling.

"Look who I ran into at Fielding's!" he called.

Amanda trailed behind him, reviewing a folded list with most of the lines crossed off.

"Had to place an order for the spring production," she said. "We're apparently out of everything except duct tape and desperation. And speaking of desperation, someone" she added, hitching a thumb toward Brian, "started flirting with a mannequin wearing a toolbelt."

"Guilty," Brian said, unapologetic. He handed Jonah the supply bag. "Hinges, bulbs, grout sealant. Also, Mr. Fielding threw in some extra wall anchors—said we looked like the kind of place that patches things often."

"Thanks, could you just set them in the back," Jonah asked.

Brian nodded, stepping away. As he returned and began tying on his apron, he added, "Oh, and he said if I'm ever looking for a change of scenery, he might have something opening up this summer."

Patty, her interest clearly piqued, looked up from the register drawer a little too conspicuously. "Rusty Gus said that?"

Brian paused. "I mean, I don't know about any Rusty Gus, but Mr. Fielding made that offer, yeah."

Amanda picked up on the subtle pink rising into Patty's cheeks. "He's sort of handsome in that *'Come with me if you want to live'* sort of way. Don't you think, Mom?"

Patty blinked. "Excuse me?"

"Come on," Amanda said, grinning. "All that quiet competence. Tools. Flannel. You may act like a gargoyle sometimes, but you're not made of stone."

Patty rolled her eyes, her cheeks now fully pink. "He smells like sawdust and linseed oil."

"Could be worse." Amanda added, smirking.

"I'm going to pretend I didn't hear that," Patty said. But she was smiling.

A little before noon, Jonah stepped into Ms. Wallace's office. She looked up from her desk and smiled. The office always smelled faintly of old paper and citrus oil. The light from the desk lamp made the room feel smaller, like it had pulled the walls in to help her focus. Ledgers and file folders were stacked with her usual brand of meticulous clutter. She sat at her desk, papers in loose stacks around her, a cup of coffee going cold beside her keyboard.

He didn't sit. Just stood in the doorway, nervously fingering the paperwork in his hand.

"It feels like you're about to ask for more than just a day off," she said, setting aside a ledger.

"I am," Jonah said. "I need a letter. Of recommendation. For something I'm... thinking about doing."

He set a folded printout of the program details on the edge of her desk—the dates underlined, the submission link circled. She didn't look at it right away, but removed her glasses, folding them slowly.

"Just thinking? Or is it something more?"

He hesitated. "It's for a residency program. On the West Coast. It's for artists, kind of—but also for makers. People who build things, who tend places, who create something that matters, even if it doesn't hang in a gallery."

Her expression didn't change, but her eyes softened.

"I'd be honored," she said. "I mean it. You've built something steady here. You've made this place better."

She tapped the printout once on her desk. "Whatever you do next, I hope it gives back as much as you've given. You've been good for this place, Jonah. Steady. Thoughtful. Quietly exacting."

He smiled faintly. "That's one way to put it."

She tapped the printout gently against her palm. "And if this next thing is something that lets you be all those things in a bigger way, you should go for it."

Jonah nodded, murmured a quiet thanks, and turned to leave.

Amanda was waiting near the reading nook, sipping something herbal. The mug looked oversized in her hands, but she held it with both palms wrapped around it like she was trying to gather something fragile and warm. She didn't look up right away, instead watching the steam curl toward the ceiling, the way people do when they're letting thoughts settle before they speak. Sunlight spilled through the front windows in soft sheets, catching the edges of her curls and casting faint patterns across the floorboards.

"You okay?" she asked finally, her eyes meeting his.
    "Yeah," he said, after a breath. "Just... took a step."
    She raised an eyebrow. "For all mankind?"
    He huffed a quiet laugh. "Not quite that dramatic. There's a residency I'm applying for. An artistic thing. I asked Ms. Wallace to write a recommendation."

Amanda gave a slow nod, absorbing that. She traced the rim of her mug with one finger, then asked, more quietly:

"Is it just you?"

The question floated there for a second—gentle, but not weightless. Jonah didn't answer right away. He shifted his stance, and looked past her toward the rows of books that didn't ask anything of him.

"I'd be going on my own," he said eventually. "But the idea didn't start with me."

Amanda studied him, her brow creased just faintly. "Even milkweed seeds need a little push to drift," she said.

Jonah let out a quiet breath. "You always did know how to say things without saying them."

"Occupational hazard," she replied. "Growing up in a bookstore with a mom who labels emotions like inventory."

He smiled. "You're still my Mandelion."

Her face softened, and she ducked her head just a little. "Feels like you've been calling me that since forever."

"Maybe it started as a playful nickname, but now it's hard to think of you as anyone else."

She looked back up, something steadier behind her eyes now. "Some names still fit, even after they've been worn in."

She smiled into her mug, like the warmth might reach the part of her that still answered to it. A silence settled, shared. Then Amanda leaned back slightly, her voice lighter again:

"Well... if you go, you have to write. A letter, a postcard, anything! Though letters would be preferred. Let us know how the great wide somewhere is treating you."

She hesitated, then added with a playful half-smile: "I'll miss the muffins, obviously. And the way you just instinctively take care of things. That too, but mostly the muffins."

***

Ms. Wallace met him near the register, envelope in hand, her expression as unreadable as ever, but her eyes held something quieter. She offered it to him without ceremony—a single sheet clipped neatly to the front.

"Hope I've done right by you," she said.

Jonah took the envelope carefully, the weight of it disproportionate to the paper inside. "I'm sure you have."

She gave a small nod. "You've done right by us. Whatever happens next, I hope you carry that with you."

He held her gaze. "Thank you, sincerely, for more than just the letter."

"You're welcome," she said simply. "Now go on. It looks like the sun's trying to find its way back out."

He tucked her sealed letter into his jacket pocket, where it lay flat against his chest, and stepped out into the afternoon light.

The day had worn a little thin at the edges, and he felt the pull of quiet. He walked indirectly, knowing he'd eventually make it home but not by way of the shortest path. He meandered through the town, past shopfronts that had traded owners or purpose more times than he could remember. The old tailor's was now a yoga studio with a chalkboard sign out front offering peppermint tea and candlelit classes. The hardware store still had the same creaky door, but the display window had been updated. There was sleek signage where there used to be handwritten sale tags in sun-bleached marker.

The next block over, he paused outside a squat brick building that had once been a video rental store. He'd spent summer afternoons there, tracing rows of faded cases and pretending to know what made a movie 'critically acclaimed.' Now it was an insurance office with drawn blinds and a CLOSED sign that never flipped.

He passed the corner where he and the Mikes used to play tag after school, their backpacks tossed in a heap near the curb while they chased each other around the utility poles. One had moved away after his dad got a job out of state. The other, a year later, when his mom remarried. Jonah had still walked that same route for a while afterward, slowing near the corner, out of habit more than hope. The silence felt heavier without the thud of sneakers and shouted dares. Across the street, a lamppost still leaned slightly from the time the older Mike tried to ride his bike with no hands. Jonah remembered the shout, the crash, the panicked laughter as both Mikes scattered and he stood rooted to the spot, unsure whether to laugh or run.

He hadn't spoken to either of them in years. The way kids lose touch without meaning to—no falling out, just life pulling at different threads. He wondered where they'd ended up. If they remembered that corner. If they ever thought of him the way he sometimes thought of them, suddenly and without warning, like a song he hadn't heard in a while.

Farther down, he paused outside a storefront with dusty windows and a faded For Lease sign curling in one corner. The paint was flaking, but the doorframe still carried the outline of old lettering, Coop's Scoops & Sodas, if he remembered right. It had been an ice cream parlor once. Red vinyl stools at the counter. Two pinball machines in the back that ate quarters and jammed half the time. He'd come here on Saturdays when his mom still packed his lunches in wax paper and made him promise not to ruin his dinner.

He remembered standing on tiptoe to point out a flavor, fingers smudging the glass, trying to decide between bubblegum swirl and mint chip like it was a decision that could change his life. Sometimes she'd let him get both. The place had closed the summer before high school, replaced by a boutique that lasted less than a year. Since then, the windows had gone dusty and the lights hadn't come back on.

It struck him, standing there, that the town had always been changing. He was only just noticing. It hadn't changed all at once. It had shifted in quiet increments—storefronts fading, sidewalks cracking, trees growing up and over the old paths.

He kept walking, swinging wide through the park. The bench was empty. The wood was still damp from where yesterday's rain had hidden in the shadows of the overhanging tree branches, the metal legs slightly sunken in soft soil. He stood there for a long moment, where words had passed in quiet doses, careful and close. Clear memories of a sketch scribbled, a drifting piece of paper. Linger, it had said. And so he did. He didn't sit, just let the silence move around him, soft and familiar.

Then he moved on.

At home, Jonah shed his work clothes and pulled on an old sweatshirt, soft enough to make him feel like the day could stop pressing in. He moved through the house in socked feet, the floor cool beneath him, the hum of the fridge filling the quiet like a low, steady breath.

He filled the kettle and set it on the stove, then opened the narrow tin of tea bags and paused, fingers brushing the paper tags as if waiting for a sign. He chose chamomile. Simple. Familiar. He thought of how Gen had once held her mug like a small tether—thumb grazing the rim, steam curling up like it carried something she couldn't quite name. It still meant something. Maybe more now than it had then.

When the water was ready, he poured it slowly and watched the color bloom, golden and soft. He cradled the mug in both hands for a moment before carrying it upstairs, past the creak in the fourth step, past the shelf where a bulb had gone dim and he hadn't yet replaced it.

The desk by the window still held his legal pad and the manila application envelope he'd left open with the flap slightly curled, as though waiting. Afternoon light spilled across the surface in a quiet slant, warming the wood and casting the faintest shadow of the pen where it rested beside the pad. Dust motes floated in the air like held breath.

He sat down, the chair giving a soft groan beneath him, and took a long sip. The tea was slightly too hot, and it settled in his chest like a small anchor. He looked down at the letter, still hesitant to touch it. Not out of doubt, but reverence.

The handwriting was steady, more so than when he'd first started. He read it again from the beginning, purposefully, line by line, his eyes tracking the loops and angles of each word, each sentence. There was no flourish, no exaggeration. Simply care, and truth.

The pen felt cool in his fingers when he picked it up. He turned it once, then set it to paper and signed his name. The action was deliberate, measured. No pause.

The scratch of ink was faint but final.

He folded the pages slowly, creasing the edges with the same care he used to fold butter into croissant dough. He slid them into the addressed envelope. The flap resisted for a second, then gave way. He pressed the seal firmly with his thumb, a final, quiet repair. Final, but not farewell. Not quite.

Outside, a breeze stirred the last of the leaves in the yard. Somewhere, a dog barked once, then stopped. The light through the window had softened further, golden and low, the kind of light that made even cracked things look whole.

Jonah exhaled. Not relief. Something quieter.

Tomorrow, he would send it.

And tonight, perhaps, he would finally sleep without waiting for the right moment to begin.

21

CADENCE AND CALM

The week passed by without hurry, as if the air itself had decided not to rush him. Streets still held a trace of rain in their seams, the blacktop darker where the sun hadn't reached. The Grind & Bind's windows caught the light differently each morning—sometimes bright with a clean, early shine, sometimes muted beneath slow-moving clouds. Inside, Jonah's motions were steady, unencumbered, as though a quiet weight had been set down somewhere behind him. He wiped a ring of water from the counter with the heel of his hand, straightened the small brass placard by the tip jar, and listened to the grinder's soft climb and fall like a heartbeat he could rely on.

A father and daughter came in just after one mid-morning lull, the door's chime followed by the sound of her boots scuffing across the mat. She was small enough that her knit hat kept slipping sideways over one eyebrow. They paused at the counter, the father leaning down to check with her before ordering.

"We'd like two hot chocolates," he told Jonah.

"Say please," the little girl whispered.

"Please," her father quickly amended.

The girl tilted her head upwards. "Can mine be magical?"

Jonah kept his expression serious. "I'll see what I can do."

She grinned like she'd just secured a secret pact, and followed her father to the corner table near the bottom of the spiral stairs. On the way, she began talking excitedly, loud enough for Jonah to overhear, that she was going to write a story about magical chocolate, "but not the kind that makes you fly. That's been done."

Her father pulled out a chair for her before taking the seat opposite and pulling out a notepad and pencils. Her boots didn't reach the floor; they swung, slow and deliberate, like she was keeping time for the shop. She picked up the pencil and immediately began writing on the notepad, verbalizing her intent with each new line.

Jonah brought their drinks over a few minutes later. He set the first mug—plain, dark, no frills—in front of the daughter, then the second, crowned with a careful mountain of whipped cream and a dusting of cinnamon he'd drawn into a tiny heart with the tip of a spoon, in front of the father. He paused. "Oh wait," he said, swapping them with a practiced flourish. "The magic went into this one."

Her eyes lit up, the kind of light that doesn't burn out quickly, and she pulled the mug close as if the heat might slip away. Jonah stepped back toward the counter. Behind him, her voice was smaller now, but still curious. "If a character is quiet, can they still be the main one?"

Her father paused, smiled. "Sometimes those are the only ones worth listening to."

Jonah didn't turn, but the answer settled somewhere beneath his ribs and stayed there.

By late morning, the light shifted—thinner, brighter. Two friends spread a map across a table, its folds refusing to lie flat. "Do we go through the state park or cut over at Millford?" the taller one asked. The other circled a town with a pencil from the mug on their table and said, "Let's earn the view." Jonah brought them a plate of lemon cookies and, because it felt right, two mismatched napkins. They thanked him like he had added a landmark to their route.

Patty swept in with the particular energy of someone who'd started her day at double speed and saw no reason to slow. "Good morning," she said, tapping a knuckle against the pastry case as she leaned over to inspect the bottom shelf. "How's it been?"

"Rather pleasant," Jonah said, sliding a tray into place.

"Had a few ideas for recipe tweaks so I started testing a couple of them this morning."

She shifted a plate of muffins a quarter inch to center it. She reviewed the case with a newly critical eye, "Hmm, on the streusels?"

"Yeah. Less butter," Jonah said, brushing a crumb from the counter, "and just a touch more salt."

A woman waiting at the counter turned toward him. "Did you say more salt? I love a little salt with my sweet. I'll take one."

Jonah gave a small nod, reached into the case, and slid a warm streusel into wax paper before handing it over. "Still fresh from the oven," he said. The woman tucked it into her bag with a thank-you that sounded more like anticipation.

Patty adjusted a display tag, then straightened and pointed toward the back. "You've been on your feet all morning. Grab something before the rush."

"I'm fine," Jonah said. "I'll eat later."

She tilted her head, still fussing with the tag until it sat just right. "Later's too far away. Go have something now." When he hesitated, she flicked a glance at him over the top of the case. "Not a request."

Jonah lifted his hands in mock surrender and stepped toward the back. The faint aroma of coffee and cinnamon followed him through the doorway, the low murmur of Patty's voice already drifting toward the bookstore side as she greeted someone new. By the time he returned with a sandwich from the cooler, she was halfway through ringing up a customer, one hand on the register keys and the other gesturing toward the pastry case like she was orchestrating the whole shop without breaking stride.

Around mid-afternoon one day, the door seemed to breathe open with the wind, and an older man stepped in, both hands held slightly away from his sides as if he'd misplaced something he couldn't quite name. "It's blue," he said to no one in particular. "The cover. Or maybe my copy was blue. A man walks into a... not a bar. A workshop? He carries a—good grief, what is it called?" His words drifted upward and scattered like dry leaves in a draft.

Jonah came around the counter. "Let's see if we can narrow it down. Was it a novel or nonfiction?"

The man squinted. "Novel."

"Contemporary? Historical? Mystery?"

"Not mystery. Quieter than that. A few decades old, I think." He pressed a hand to the side of his head, as if nudging the memory into place. "There were... details. He kept track of things. Like bookkeeping, but... different."

Jonah could feel the frustration tightening in the man's voice, the way a knot draws in on itself. He shifted tactics. "When you read it—what did it leave you with?"

The man blinked, then let his shoulders ease a fraction. "Lonely, I think. But not in a bad way. Like... like he noticed the world too closely. There was a ledger?"

The click came quietly in Jonah's mind, a puzzle piece finally finding its space. "I think I may know what you're looking for. Let's go take a look in our Used Books section."

He led him to the shelf, the book exactly where it should be. "*Calder Hale's Ledger*?"

"That's it!" The man brightened as if a light had been switched. "The library said it was out of print."

"Well, thankfully we have this copy in paperback. The pages are a bit softened at the edges, and the spine is cracked, but it's all there." Jonah said, smiling as he observed the tranquility washing over the man's face.

The man lifted it from its place on the shelf with both hands, running his thumb along the worn spine as if reacquainting himself with a long-lost friend. "On the quietest days," Jonah quoted, the words surfacing from memory, "the pages seem to notice you back."

The man looked up. "You've read it?"

Jonah gave a small nod. "It was recommended to me by one of the greatest men I know."

"I didn't think I'd ever see it again," the man said quietly, the words settling into the space between them.

Jonah waited a moment, watching the man's shoulders ease as he turned the book over in his hands. "Let me get you a coffee," he said, his voice low. "You can sit for a bit... take your time with it."

A few minutes later, Jonah set the mug on the table beside him and stepped back without a word. The man didn't look up, already lost to the first few pages.

Later, two college-aged customers hovered at the poetry shelf, their shoulders almost touching as they scanned the titles. One held up a glossy-covered collection. "This one looks important," she said, "but it also looks like it's trying too hard."

The other flipped open a slimmer volume with a worn spine. "And this one looks like it belongs in a coat pocket next to some bus tickets."

They spotted Jonah passing and grinned. "Okay, we need an expert's opinion. Which one?"

"Normally for expertise, you'd want Herb," Jonah said, pausing beside them. "But between the two..." He nodded at the smaller book. "That one'll follow you around easier."

They ended up buying both. On their way out, the student with the pocket-sized book glanced back. "You called it," she said, and it landed with a quiet, satisfying weight before the door closed behind them.

Almost immediately after they left, the door swung open with a short gust of cool air, and Brian stepped in with a battered handyman's manual under his arm. He set it on the counter and started tying his apron, missing the loop the first time.

"Hinges, light fixtures, espresso machine," he said, tapping the book. "Figured if I'm going to work part-time at Fielding's, I might as well learn how to fix the kind of stuff that breaks here too."

"Smart," Jonah said, moving a stack of mugs closer to the register. "He'll be glad to have you."

Brian flipped a page to a diagram of a gear assembly. "How'd you get good at this stuff, anyway? You're the one everyone calls when something's rattling or squeaking."

Jonah paused, resting his forearms on the counter. "My mom used to worry about how much time my dad spent fixing things—always taking something apart, putting it back together. She'd send me out to keep him company. Said it'd be good for both of us."

Brian leaned in a little, listening.

"I learned a lot just watching," Jonah went on. "Eventually, he'd hand me a wrench or ask me to hold something in place. Half the time I didn't know what I was doing, but... you pick things up." He shrugged lightly, as if it were nothing, though the warmth in his voice gave it away.

Brian tapped the page again. "Guess I'm starting late."

"You're starting," Jonah said. "That's the important part." He reached for a rag to wipe down the counter, then glanced back at Brian. "How's school? You're getting close, right?"

Brian ran a hand through his hair as he did a quick mental calculation. "A semester and a half. Feels like it's taken forever, but I'm getting there."

"That's something," Jonah said. "Not everyone does."

Brian gave a small, lopsided smile, more to himself than to Jonah. After a pause, he started straightening chairs like it was just another day. Only, every few steps, his eyes flicked back to the open manual on the counter. He mouthed the words on the page, trying to fit in quick reads between chairs, never quite breaking his stride.

The hours found their own shape, and the days all flowed together—not in monotony or solitude like it used to feel, but in the way patterns eventually reveal their quiet value. Jonah found himself noticing how sameness held subtle variations: how the light stretched farther across the floor some mornings, or how the reflection off the front window could pool in a new place before fading.

One morning, he carried bags to a customer's car during a sudden drizzle; the paper handles softened under his grip and left a damp line across his palm. Another, he tightened the upstairs railing with the stubby screwdriver he kept in his apron pocket. Later in the week, Ms. Wallace paused at the serving counter while he showed a curious teenager the difference between pour-over and French press. She didn't interrupt—just observed with a half-smile, taking quiet stock of the exchange. By the time he glanced up, she was already heading for her office.

"Jonah," she said later from the doorway, the word a soft summons. "The craft station for next Friday, I think we should keep the sign in your handwriting, yes?"

"Yes, ma'am."

"Your penmanship is kinder than mine," she said, then added appreciatively, "And...thank you for fixing the railing. It feels much more secure."

He offered a quiet nod, content to let her thanks drift between them, unclaimed.

The bell gave a modest chime, and Ms. Curlee stepped in with a neat stack of children's books pressed to her chest. She always brought in a selection from the library ahead of each Saturday's storytime. She set them on the counter, straightened the edges once, and gave Jonah a small smile. Her voice carried a faint rasp. "Good morning, Jonah. I'm afraid I'll need you to cover this week's reading, if that would be alright? My throat's not quite right, and I'd rather not make it worse."

"Not a problem," Jonah said. "You might try tea instead of coffee today. It's more soothing, gentler on the voice."

"That sounds lovely, and just what I need," she said, the corners of her mouth hinting at gratitude. "Surprise me."

Over in the half-stacks, Herb was crouched low, sliding a book into place with deliberate care. At her voice, his movement slowed just slightly before he reached for the next one. He didn't turn, didn't speak, just dusted the top edge of the shelf with his fingertips as if it were part of the shelving process.

Ms. Curlee's eyes drifted toward the aisle. "He keeps these shelves neater than anyone I've seen," she said, her voice softened with something almost private. "Looks after the books like they're his own children."

Jonah glanced over. "He could probably give you the synopsis of most of them," he said, keeping his tone light.

"Not sure how he's had time to read them all, but I wouldn't bet against it."

"No, I don't imagine I would, either," she said, her tone light but pointed enough that it might have been meant for him. Herb's hand stilled on the spine in front of him for half a beat before moving again.

She accepted the tea from Jonah, offering an appreciative nod and toast, and gave her usual two taps on the counter before heading for the door. Herb's gaze shifted to the reflection in the front glass as she stepped out, then he adjusted the last book in the row until it lined up perfectly with the one beside it. He cleared his throat, twice.

"Damn weather," he muttered, half to himself. "But I'm not about to start drinking leaf water. I'm not a woodland creature, though I do enjoy the occasional singing princess."

He walked behind the counter and poured himself another mug of black coffee. "This'll do," he grumbled to no one in particular.

That Thursday evening, Amanda swept in with her scarf the color of school buses and warning signs. She shook a fine mist of cool air from her coat as the bell stilled above her. "They came in," she said without preface, pointing her chin toward the back. "Scripts for the theatre department. An entire box. Herb emailed to let me know."

"Herb has email?" Brian quipped from behind the counter.

"And he knows how to use it!" Amanda replied. She leaned an elbow on the counter, grinning toward the bookstore as if Herb might appear to defend himself.

"I'll get them," Jonah said, sliding his towel onto the counter and stepping toward the storeroom where shipments waited to be shelved. The box was heavier than it looked; it seemed to thrum with a papery weight that suggested a hundred voices crammed inside waiting for their turn.

Jonah shifted the box against his hip as he came back through the café. "I can take it the rest of the way for you," he told Amanda as she moved to take the box from him.

She started to protest, then caught the slight tilt of the box in his arms and let the refusal die. "If you insist."

Jonah glanced toward Brian. "You good to finish closing?"

Brian waved a hand. "I've got it. Can't have Amanda here carrying a box as big as she is." He turned back to the espresso machine, already pulling out a cloth to clean the steam wand.

Jonah walked with Amanda along the sidewalk that still held thin ribbons of damp at the cracks. The weight of the box pressed steadily against his hip, the cardboard edges biting faintly into his forearm. A bead of sweat formed along his cheek despite the evening chill, catching the glow of the passing streetlights as they flickered into their nightly rhythm.

One or two late commuters passed by with heads down against the breeze, their footsteps scattering into the quiet.

She began flipping through one of the scripts, reading a snippet aloud before stopping to shake her head. "That came out wrong," she said, laughing. "I've got the tone all wrong." She tried it again, slower this time, then grinned. "Better... but still not right."

"Still, that's an impressive range," Jonah commented.

"Something's different this week," Amanda said after a stretch of silence.

"With the script?" Jonah asked, glancing over at her.

"No, not that. With all...this," she replied while waving her hands at everything and nothing in particular.

"Oh, you sensed that, too, huh?" He agreed.

She nodded, thumbing through the script in her hands. "Maybe it's the season changing. Not the obvious kind of change; no flowers yet, and no real warmth to speak of, but winter's starting to loosen its grip. Like the ground underneath is already awake."

Jonah nodded. "Just waiting for permission," he mused. "The light's been different the last few days. Mornings feel sharper, the evenings not as dark."

She glanced at him. "So—have you heard back from the residency yet?"

"It hasn't even been a week," Jonah said. "Not sure how long they take to decide... or if I'll even hear back at all. But sending it in... it did something. Helped me see things a little differently. Even if nothing comes of it, something came from the act of trying. Does that make sense?"

"I think so. Kind of like my branching out with the acting troupe. I know it seems that I like being the center of attention sometimes," she smiled shyly, catching Jonah with a big grin of agreement. "But signing up for that really feels as if I'm stepping out of my comfort zone. What if I try with a new group of people and I find out that I'm really not very good?"

"That's a valid concern," Jonah said, still smiling.

"Hey!" Amanda responded with incredulity, giving Jonah a slight push to throw him off balance.

"In all seriousness," he continued, "you are incredibly talented. You have a real gift, and I'm glad that you've chosen to share that with the people around you."

They rounded the last corner, passing houses with porch lights spilling in uneven pools across the sidewalks. "This street always smells like bread at night," she commented, changing topics. "Not the fresh kind of bread when it's direct out of the oven, more like the warm air from a bakery after it's closed."

"Ha, like those flavored water drinks that don't have much flavor?" He joked.

"Yes!" She exclaimed in agreement. "The flavor names should be more along the lines of 'We sliced a lime in the same room as this open water' or 'We bottled this while juggling a grapefruit and some mint.'"

Neither of them could contain their laughter. Amanda looked around, eyes catching on the glint of damp pavement. "Oh, and this block—" she gestured toward a row of houses, "the light always hits differently here. Same houses, same porches and yards, but somehow it feels more welcoming."

"I've never noticed that," Jonah said. "Probably has

something to do with the paint colors. There's more yellows than blues. Makes it feel warmer."

"Or maybe it's just one of those things you can't measure," she said, smiling to herself.

As they stepped onto her porch, she pushed the door open with her hip. "You can set the scripts just inside the hallway, here." He stepped in and lowered the box to the floor, its weight leaving his arms with a pleasant ache.

From the kitchen, Patty called out, "Amanda? Is that you?" She appeared a moment later, drying her hands on a dish towel. "Oh, Jonah!" She exclaimed, noticing the box of scripts on the floor and the few drips of sweat still glistening on his face. "You didn't have to do that, but thank you. Amanda, go wash up for dinner. Jonah, you're welcome to stay and eat—there's plenty."

"I appreciate it," Jonah said, "really, but I should get going." Patty gave a small, understanding nod and disappeared back into the kitchen.

Jonah stepped out onto the porch, his foot just finding the first step, when the door creaked open again. Amanda stepped through, moving like a decision finally made, and wrapped him in a sudden, solid hug.

"What was that for?" he asked, pulling back just enough to see her grin.

"Just felt appropriate. Thanks again!" She stepped back,

blowing a ridiculous, theatrical kiss in the air to cut the sincerity, then slipped inside, closing the door behind her.

As Jonah walked down the path, he could still feel the ghost of her arms wrapped around him, holding in the warmth. He glanced over his shoulder. Through the front window, mostly hidden by the curtain, Amanda was still watching him go.

On the walk back, the night had settled fully, carrying the layered sounds of the neighborhood: wind chimes in a polite breeze, a dog collar ringing with each step, distant tires rolling over damp pavement. Looking down the next row of houses, Jonah recognized a familiar silhouette. The old man from earlier in the week sat in the fading light of his porch, head bowed over the copy of *Calder Hale's Ledger*, turning each page with the slow care of someone who knew there was no need to rush. Jonah slowed for a step, the sight lodging in his mind like a bookmark, before continuing home.

Friday came and went without pretense, the steady turn of tasks carrying it toward closing. When the last customer stepped out into the evening and the bell stilled above the door, Jonah walked purposefully over to the bookshelves. The shop smelled faintly of paper and the day's last pot of coffee, the air carrying the hush that came after the music was switched off. He moved among the shelves with intention, a slow, deliberate rhythm, pulling titles with the care of someone choosing more than a gift.

For Herb: *The Daughter of Time* by Josephine Tey, a quiet, deliberate mystery solved entirely from a hospital bed, its detective relying on persistence and observation rather than running down dark alleys. Jonah imagined Herb appreciating the economy of it; no wasted words, no nonsense. Next to it, he placed *A View from a Broad* by Bette Midler, a wry, chatty memoir he suspected Herb would pick up "just to skim" and then read in full, claiming it was "educational" while clearly enjoying every bit of its theatrical bite.

For Patty: *No One Belongs Here More Than You* by Miranda July, short stories edged with odd, sharp humor. Just the kind of thing she might pick up during a lull and accidentally finish before her break ended. The corners of the bright yellow cover were already a little softened, the kind of wear that fit her better than a pristine copy.

For Brian: *The Left Hand of Darkness* by Ursula K. Le Guin, its political and cultural debates woven through a landscape of ice and survival. The copy Jonah chose had neat, slanted handwriting in the margins, presumably from the previous owner. There were comments, underlined passages, and the occasional question mark. He could picture Brian reading them like an argument left behind, grinning as he talked back to the page and adding his own counterpoints in the same cramped space.

For Amanda: *The Carrying* by Ada Limón, poems with an easy rhythm and deep-rooted honesty, the kind that settled differently when spoken aloud. Jonah had seen her pause after certain lines before, letting them hang in the air as if they might change something.

For Ms. Wallace: *The Sense of an Ending* by Julian Barnes, a novel as concise as it was intricate, each detail intentional, each silence purposeful. Jonah thought she'd appreciate the precision, the way every word carried weight. An ironic title, to be sure, all things considered. But fitting in the natural order of things.

For his dad: *The PreHistory of the Far Side* by Gary Larson, hefty enough to feel like a project, paired with *Strange Planet* by Nathan W. Pyle, whose dry, literal humor might earn one of his father's quiet smirks. He could already see him at the kitchen table in the early morning, coffee at his elbow, a book open to a panel that no one else had seen yet, the kind of amusement he'd keep to himself until asked.

For Mr. Beverly: he paused longer than he expected, fingers grazing spines, pulling one down only to set it back again. A memoir felt too personal, a novel too distant. Nothing quite matched the steady, patient wisdom in the man's voice. Not yet. He left the space in his stack open, trusting the right book would show itself when it was ready.

Each chosen book received a blank card tucked inside, like planting a seed he might never see grow. The words for each hovered in his mind, already beginning to take shape—not speeches, just lines meant to travel, to last. He closed the last cover and stood for a moment, the stack balanced in his arms. When he clicked off the lights, the silence felt less like an ending and more like the pause before a story begins.

22

MORNINGS AND MESSAGES

Jonah woke before the alarm, the kind of waking that felt unearned but welcome. The light was still soft through the blinds, holding the pale gold of early day. He sat up, eyes catching on the stack of books at the corner of his desk, each one with a notecard tucked just far enough to show. The sight made him smile—small, private—like greeting a row of old friends already mid-conversation.

Downstairs, the kitchen was warm in a way that didn't come from the heater. His father stood at the stove, turning bacon with the same measured patience he gave to almost everything. The smell drifted toward Jonah before he'd even cleared the last step.

"Morning," his father said, without looking away from the pan.

"Morning." Jonah crossed to the counter, found two mugs clean and waiting, and poured coffee.

"Eggs?" his father asked.

"Sure." Jonah set the mugs down and reached for plates.

They moved around each other easily, no wasted steps. Jonah cracked eggs into a small skillet, watching the edges go from glassy to opaque, the yolks holding their centers like tiny suns. His father plated the bacon, then added toast to one side.

As they sat, his father tapped the table once, like he was marking a beat. "Need to stop by the post office later. Out of stamps."

Jonah nodded, chewing. "Might be busier this morning—story time at the shop."

His father gave a faint smile. "Better you than me."

The early morning passed without commentary beyond that, but none was needed. Father and son moving in a choreography that was never practiced, but perfected over years, each aware of the other's presence without demand. It wasn't indifference, rather it was mutual understanding, the kind of harmony that needed no explanation.

The Grind & Bind smelled faintly of paper and cinnamon by the time Jonah had the children's section arranged. Chairs in a semicircle, the bright rug smoothed flat, a stack of picture books waiting on a low table. The light coming through the front windows angled across the spiral staircase, catching in the polished spines of the half-shelves.

Somewhere behind him, Herb was reshelving with his usual slow deliberation.

By the time the small crowd settled in, Jonah recognized a familiar knit hat slipping sideways over one eyebrow. The girl from earlier in the week—hot chocolate, magical request—slid into a seat between her father and another child. She spotted Jonah and grinned. "Do you have more magic today?"

Jonah leaned down a little. "Only if you promise not to tell the others. They'll all want some."

She nodded solemnly, as if sworn to secrecy.

The tables were pushed back, the rug rolled out, and the stack of books waiting at Jonah's elbow carried the color of well-worn spines. He glanced over the titles before starting, his thumb brushing the top one in the pile. It struck him that Ms. Curlee might've chosen them deliberately, not just for their bright covers or popularity, but for what they carried with them—quiet lessons tucked between pages, small, essential kinds of courage disguised as children's tales. He smiled as the realization came full bloom. He wasn't sure if she meant for him to notice, but the thought lingered as he opened the first book.

He turned the first page, fingers smoothing the paper, the sound barely louder than a breath.

At the back of the room, Amanda slid into a seat near the wall, arms wrapped around her knees. She didn't wave, just caught Jonah's eye with a small smile mixed with both mischief and encouragement. He nodded once before returning to the page.

He started with *The Snowy Day* by Ezra Jack Keats, the pages full of bright red snowsuits and crisp footprints. His voice carried a warmth that had children leaning forward as if closer would mean they could feel the snow under their own boots.

Next came *Corduroy*, the bear with the missing button. Jonah read the lines with a kind of gentle patience, and the children gasped in unison when Corduroy set out at night to search the grand store. Amanda, watching from a few seats back, smiled at their delight, her chin propped in her hand. Jonah tilted the book so the children could see the illustrations, each carrying the story forward beyond words: the escalator, the beds, the button hunt. He let them laugh at the bear's tumble. "He's okay," Jonah reassured softly to the younger children before turning the page.

A little girl in a purple puffer coat raised her hand, then spoke without waiting. "Why didn't anyone fix his button before?" she asked, curiously.

Jonah looked up, scanning the half-circle of faces. "Sometimes," he said, "grownups don't notice what needs fixing, or they think it too small to bother."

That seemed to settle something. She leaned back on her elbows, satisfied, as he reached for the next book in the stack.

He lifted *The Story of Ferdinand*, and his tone shifted, softer still. He described the bull who only wanted to sit beneath the cork tree and smell flowers, his words unhurried, almost reverent. The room seemed to grow quieter as the story went on, the children easing into the calm. Even Amanda sat straighter, eyes lingering on Jonah as he spoke. When he reached the part where Ferdinand sat peacefully in the bullring, unmoved by the crowd's cheers, Jonah paused just long enough for the silence to carry its own weight before finishing. A little hand shot up then, waiting patiently for acknowledgment. "He's brave," the child said. Jonah nodded, agreeing without needing more words.

From there, Jonah opened *Make Way for Ducklings* by Robert McCloskey. As he turned a page, one child yawned audibly; another adjusted her grip on the stuffed raccoon in her lap. His voice carried a lilt of humor as he read about Mr. and Mrs. Mallard waddling through Boston, searching for the right place to raise their family. The children giggled when policemen stopped traffic for the ducklings, their little heads bobbing proudly along. Jonah smiled at the laughter, but he let the ending soften—the simple bravery of finding a safe place in a busy world, and the kindness of those who helped them get there.

Then he opened *Star in the Jar* by Sam Hay. The children's eyes widened at the thought of a star small enough to keep, tucked in a jar. Jonah read the boy's excitement with a playful lilt, then slowed as the story turned toward giving the star back to the sky. His voice gentled at the farewell, each word brushed with care. The children leaned in, holding their breaths until the boy finally let the star go. A murmur of relief passed around the circle as the star found its place again, shining brighter because it had been loved.

Finally, he opened *Extra Yarn* by Mac Barnett and Jon Klassen. The tale of Annabelle and her endless box of yarn filled the room with a different kind of wonder. Jonah's voice carried the rhythm of stitches being pulled through loops, steady and sure. The children sat awe-stricken, watching as he tilted the book to show the growing sweaters, the bright colors spreading across the gray town. Amanda's expression softened as he read the line about the whole world being changed, not by force, but by something given freely. When he closed the book, the children sat hushed for a moment, as if the air itself was wrapped in the threads Annabelle had left behind.

As he set down the last book, Jonah looked at the stack again, feeling the weight of what tied them together. "You know," he said to the group, though it seemed that the entire café had gone silent at some point, "bravery isn't always loud. It doesn't shout or wave banners. Most of the time it's quiet, like choosing kindness, and staying true to yourself, even when no one else is watching." He rested his hand on the top book. "These stories express all kinds of bravery. Peter stepping out into the unknown just to see what the world felt like under his boots; Corduroy searching for what's missing; Ferdinand refusing to fight and holding on to what brings him joy; a mother duck who wasn't willing to settle for the wrong place just because it was easier, and the kindness of those who helped her reach the right one; a boy selflessly letting go of a star, his dear friend, because it's better for them; and Annabelle choosing not to sell her gift but keep sharing it." His eyes softened. "Different ways of being brave."

A boy near the front, with hair mussed from a hoodie tugged off too fast, spoke up without raising his hand. "But the box didn't really have yarn forever, right? That's not real."

Jonah smiled, not at the question, but at the earnestness in it.

"It exists in the story, yes," he said. "But sometimes a story isn't just about what happens. It's about how things feel. And that box that never emptied represented kindness. The more you share, the more it seems to grow."

As story time wrapped up, the applause was small but sincere. A few children began tugging on coats and boots, filling the room with the soft commotion of zippers and swishing fabric. Others clutched their parents' sleeves, already asking about snacks and sweets.

The little girl stepped toward Jonah as the room slowly emptied.

"That was magic," she declared.

He smiled, warmth catching at the corners of his mouth. "Glad it worked."

She skipped away, joyful and unhurried, straight into her father's arms. The man mouthed a quiet thank you to Jonah before lifting his daughter into a hug and turning toward the door.

Amanda lingered near the back of the room, pretending to straighten chairs. "That was a solid setlist," she said softly as Jonah passed. "Some of us grownups needed those reminders too."

Jonah smiled, half-turning. "I noticed. Grownups forget what bravery looks like sometimes."

She shrugged, eyes glinting. "Books are stealthy like that. Say one thing out loud, sneak something else between the lines."

"A book's a book," Jonah said. "They all have something to say."

The rest of the morning folded into the usual rhythm—wiping tables, refilling mugs, answering a question about used book pricing, replacing a light bulb over the counter. Afternoon slipped past in conversations half-heard from the bookstore side, the low hum of the espresso machine, and the occasional door chime breaking the quiet.

Toward evening, the bell rang again and Mr. Beverly stepped in, shoulders a touch stooped but eyes still clear beneath his cap. Jonah felt the familiar warmth of recognition, along with the realization that he hadn't seen him in several days.

"Good to see you," Jonah said, setting down the rag he'd been using. "I was starting to wonder. If I hadn't spotted you by tomorrow, I was going to come by your house."

Mr. Beverly smiled at that, amused but touched. "I appreciate the concern, Mr. Ashford. But I'm an old man, and sometimes old men just need a little extra time to take care of things."

Jonah nodded, understanding. "Well, I'm glad you came in today."

"As am I," Mr. Beverly said. His gaze swept the shop with quiet fondness before he headed toward the shelves.

The walk home was familiar, yet his mind kept replaying images from the morning: a bright yarn unfurling, a cork tree in quiet shade, ducklings trailing in a perfect line. Children's stories had a way of reducing things to their simplest truths, and in their simplicity, revealing what mattered most.

At home, an envelope sat at the edge of the kitchen table where his father had left it, addressed to Jonah, return address stark against the cream paper, printed in an even serif. Jonah didn't open the envelope, not yet. He wanted to hold on to the day a bit longer. He rested a hand on it for just a moment, then moved to the counter to begin preparing dinner. He sliced shallots thin enough to curl, their sweetness softening in the pan before garlic joined, whispering into warm olive oil. Mushrooms followed, earthy and familiar, with a pinch of red pepper flakes that made the air prickle. Rice ticked in a pot with the lid barely ajar. He added chicken to the skillet, turning it until it seared golden, then scraped up the browned bits, watching them dissolve back into the sauce. He squeezed half a lemon over the top, and turned the heat low to let the amalgamation simmer. Steam rose like a cloud, the smells grounding him, opening memories, a sense of belonging. To the house, to the moment, to the meal.

Cooking steadied him; it was a ritual of trust, of knowing that if he gave each step care, the end would hold together.

He ate without a rush, sleeves pushed to his forearms, tasting each bite as if the flavors themselves were a lesson. The envelope remained untouched, waiting with a patience that almost mocked him. He cleared the dishes, washed the counter until the sponge ran clean, then washed his hands, wiped them dry, and sat back down at the table.

He sat for several minutes with the letter before him, becoming part of the stillness, the silence. Momentarily unready, or unwilling, to allow any change to happen. He saw himself younger, perched on a low stool in the garage, holding a flashlight for his father as a wrench clinked against rusted metal. He remembered the ache of wanting to be useful and the surprise of realizing he was. He saw the mornings his mother handed him flour-dusted bowls, teaching him how to measure by feel, not numbers, the rhythm of kneading as ordinary and sacred all at once. He heard Brian's first shift, nervous chatter spilling out faster than coffee into a cup, and the way the shop slowly taught them both to steady their hands. He thought of Patty's voice cutting through chaos like a compass, of Amanda's laughter breaking silence into warmth, of Gen's sketchbook catching things he hadn't known he was showing.

The memories moved like lanterns on water—each one distinct, each part of the same current. Together they told him something he hadn't been ready to say aloud: he had not stood still all this time. He had been moving, growing, even here, even now. And the envelope on the table was not pulling him out of his life, but carrying him forward with it.

He tucked a thumb inside the corner of the flap, easing inside and underneath. The edge tore open cleanly, and he unfolded the pages inside. His eyes moved quickly, then slowed, retracing lines to be certain.

Dear Mr. Ashford,

On behalf of the admissions committee, it is my great pleasure to inform you that you have been selected for acceptance into the Spring/Summer cohort of the Redwood Arts Residency Program. Your submission demonstrated a rare clarity of vision and a quiet strength of voice that we believe will contribute meaningfully to the work of this year's group.

The residency will begin on April 1 and conclude on August 30, with fellows expected to reside on-site for the duration. Accommodations and studio space are provided, along with a monthly stipend of $1,000 to assist with living expenses. A detailed orientation schedule and logistical information are enclosed, including travel arrangements, materials lists, and guidelines for participation.

This year's program will bring together artists, writers, and performers from across the country, each invited for the unique perspective they carry. We are confident that your contributions will enrich the dialogue of the cohort, and that your time here will be one of growth, exploration, and renewal.

Please confirm your acceptance by returning the enclosed form no later than March 10. Should you have any questions, do not hesitate to contact our coordinator at the address provided.

We look forward to welcoming you into our community, and to seeing where your work will lead.

Sincerely,
Eleanor Briggs
Program Director, Redwood Arts Residency

He had been accepted. He skimmed the rest, the parts written in the practical cadence of logistics: arrival the first Sunday of the month, shared lodging in restored cottages, meals provided in the communal hall, a weekly seminar on artistic practice, quiet hours in the studios, mailing address for correspondence, optional evening lectures. The words flickered past him in neat rows, half-absorbed and half-ignored, as though his mind only wanted the shape of them, not the weight. What stayed was the certainty: there was a place waiting, one that expected him.

Jonah let the words rest in front of him, both hands on the table as if anchoring them there. He breathed once, twice, a long exhale that left his chest a little lighter. Whatever came next would not erase this proof, in ink and paper, that trying had led somewhere.

Upstairs, his desk light spread a quiet pool across the books he'd set aside the night before. He uncapped his pen, feeling the weight of it in his fingers. Ink, unlike thought, couldn't be undone with silence. To write was to make something stay. The pen felt heavier than usual in his hand, not burdened but deliberate, every movement a mark of intent.

For Herb, he whispered "For the one who notices what others miss," as he slipped the card between pages, writing of a truth that hides in plain sight and how some puzzles are solved by simply noticing the things that never moved.

For Patty, he let the ink move quickly, steadily, noting three mornings she had made survivable through sheer will. He tucked the card into her book with, "For the days you carried more than you let on."

For Brian, he wrote with quick strokes, a few words and a margin note about the squeaky stair—his script casual, but his care plain.

For Amanda, he underlined a poem about bravery that wore no costume, no spotlight, and simply called it by name.

For Ms. Wallace, his words were neat, deliberate, unadorned. His final sentence was steady, leaving no room for apology or excess.

For his father, he pressed the note between cartoon panels, smiling to himself.

Each placement felt reverent, a small benediction.

As he looked at the stack, he couldn't help but feel what was missing. He pulled a blank piece of paper from his desk drawer, resting the nib of the pen down for just a moment, allowing the ink to bleed into the page before beginning with a flourish.

WE USED TO SAY ONLY A FEW WORDS TO EACH OTHER, BUT THE WORDS TURNED INTO CONVERSATIONS. MINUTES TURNED INTO HOURS. NOW I'M NOT SURE THERE'S ENOUGH TIME TO SAY EVERYTHING THAT NEEDS TO BE SAID, BUT I'LL START WITH THIS—

YOU NEVER ASKED TO BE MY TEACHER, AND I NEVER ASKED TO BE TAUGHT. YET YOU STAYED, STEADY, INSISTENT, GENTLE AS RAIN ON A CLOSED WINDOW. YOU POINTED OUT DOORS I HADN'T SEEN, PATHS I MIGHT'VE IGNORED. I THOUGHT I WAS ONLY KEEPING COMPANY, BUT YOU WERE SHOWING ME HOW TO NOTICE, HOW TO REMAIN, HOW TO HOLD STILL LONG ENOUGH TO SEE WHAT OTHERS PASS BY. WHAT I CARRY NOW IS SHAPED BY YOUR PATIENCE AND YOUR PERSISTENCE. IF DISTANCE COMES BETWEEN US, KNOW THAT I LEAVE WITH THOSE LESSONS, AND THAT THEY'LL KEEP UNFOLDING WHEREVER I GO. THANK YOU FOR STANDING RESOLUTELY, EVEN WHEN I TRIED PUSHING YOU AWAY.

He folded the improvised note and set it on top of the stack of books. The click of the capped pen was like a lock sliding into place, the permanence of his intent echoing the acceptance letter downstairs. The pages would travel on. And so, soon, would he.

23

ENDINGS AND ECHOES

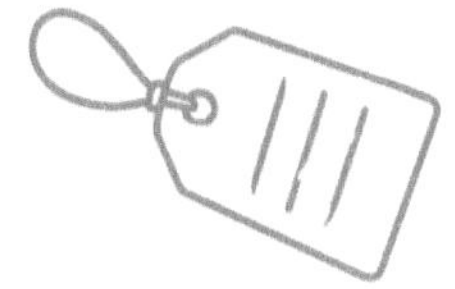

The morning felt different before he even opened his eyes. The air had a looseness to it, like a held note finally allowed to fade. Jonah lay there for a moment, listening—to the faint hum of the fridge downstairs, to the house easing against its frame. He couldn't remember the last time he'd slept this well. No dreams, no churn of half-formed thoughts. Just quiet.

He sat up slowly, the bedsheet creasing at his waist, and looked around his room. Nothing had changed—the stack of books by the wall, the flannel folded on the chair—but it all seemed newly legible, as if each object had been waiting for him to see it clearly one last time. He pressed a hand against the window glass. The pane was cool, the world beyond faintly blue with early light.

Downstairs, a chair scraped against tile.

He dressed, pulling on his worn gray shirt and clean jeans. He paused, his fingers brushing over a small, neat patch on the knee—a repair from last winter. Then he made his way to the kitchen.

The smell of coffee clung to the air—bitter, grounding, familiar. His father was already at the table, newspaper half-folded beside a small plate of toast.

Jonah took a clean mug from the rack and gave it a quick rinse in the sink. The water ran cold against his palms, sharp enough to wake him fully. He dried the mug, filled it from the pot, and slid into the chair across from his father. Neither of them spoke. They rarely needed to.

His father looked up from reading the paper. "You're up early."

"Couldn't sleep late," Jonah said. "Didn't feel right."

A nod. "Big day?"

Jonah hesitated. He hadn't planned a speech, just the truth, plain and measured. "I told Ms. Wallace I'd come in early. I need to talk to everyone today."

His father folded the newspaper completely now, setting it aside. "You've made your decision, then."

"Yeah," Jonah said. "The residency accepted me. I'm going to go."

For a moment, the only sound was the low tick of the kitchen clock. His father's eyes held steady, unreadable in that way

Jonah had come to recognize as careful thinking rather than distance. Then he exhaled, a sound almost like relief.

"Good," he said simply. "It's time."

Jonah looked at him—searching for more, maybe expecting it—and accepted that he'd found everything he needed in the tone. No hesitation, no lament. Just quiet agreement, the kind that made things real.

His father reached for the coffee pot and poured a little more into Jonah's mug. "Eat something before you go," he said, already standing. He opened the breadbox, found a small heel of bread still wrapped in its paper sleeve, and set it in front of him with a butter knife. No fanfare. Just presence.

Jonah tore the heel in half, spread the butter while it was still cold and stiff. "You'll be okay here?"

"I've been okay before," his father said, the faintest smile tugging at the edge of his mouth. Then, softer: "You'll be sure to write?"

"Yeah," Jonah said. "I will."

They finished in companionable silence, two men sharing a table between endings and beginnings. When Jonah stood to leave, his father didn't rise. He only reached across the table, his hand resting briefly over Jonah's wrist—rough, warm, steady.

"That's enough," he said. It was.

Jonah lingered in the doorway long enough to feel the draft from outside, the smell of damp earth carried on it. He didn't look back when he stepped through. Some things you honor by moving forward.

The streets were still damp when Jonah set out, the early light catching in the shallow puddles that gathered along the curb. The air was cool and clean, touched with the faint scent of wet stone. Somewhere down the block, a delivery truck coughed to life, its engine settling into a steady idle.

He walked with his hands in his pockets, boots clicking softly against the uneven walk. The town moved in slow motion at this hour—doors unlocking, windows fogged with the breath of new light. A shopkeeper swept his threshold, bristles scratching the wet pavement. A curtain shifted in an upstairs window.

When the Grind & Bind came into view, Jonah slowed. From across the street, it looked unchanged: the chalkboard sign smudged with ghosted lettering, the fern in the window bending toward the pale sun. But the quiet felt too even, as if the building itself were waiting for someone to speak first.

He crossed over and unlocked the door. The bell gave its small, uncertain chime. Inside, the familiar scent met him—coffee grounds, paper, and the faint citrus of cleaner that never quite left the counter.

He set his bag behind the register, rolled up his sleeves, and began the motions that had built his mornings for years. Wipe the counter. Check the pastry case. Switch on the overheads. The hum of the cooler came back, followed by the soft click of the lights.

He worked without hurry, as though re-creating a memory rather than performing a task.

Patty's clipboard sat where it always did, a pen looped through the ring. The schedule beneath her sharp handwriting read like any other week—columns of names and shifts—but he felt the weight of how few there would be left.

He started the grinder. The low burr filled the air, steady and rhythmic. Steam hissed from the coffee machine, spreading a thin warmth through the room.

The bell chimed again. Ms. Wallace stepped in, her coat dotted with rain.

"Morning, Jonah," she said, locking the door behind her.

He blinked. "Good morning. I wasn't expecting you until later."

"I wanted to talk before the others arrive." She set her umbrella by the shelf, then joined him at the counter. "But you look like you've got something you want to discuss?"

"I did. I do." He hesitated. "But it seems like you do, too."

A small, knowing pause. "Let's sit."

She took a stool beside him, smoothing her sleeves as if aligning her thoughts. The window light broke across the countertop in narrow bands.

"I won't take long," she said. "I've decided to close the shop at the end of the month."

The words settled in the air without an echo. The grinder finished its cycle, leaving a hush so complete he could hear the faint drip from the percolating coffee.

Jonah nodded once. "I thought that might be it."

Ms. Wallace studied him. "You did?"

"Things have been leaning that way," he said. "You've seemed... lighter."

Her mouth curved slightly. "That's one word to describe it, I suppose. Though I'm still not sure how I feel about it all. Not loss, and certainly not regret."

They sat in the silence of people who had already shared too much life to fill it with noise.

"Completion," she finally said. "If I had to fit a single word to it."

"Acceptance," he replied. "The residency, that Redwood program... they accepted me."

Her eyes softened. "Jonah, that's wonderful."

"I wanted you to know first."

"I'm glad you did." She folded her hands. "You've done good work here. More than work, really. You've looked after this place, made it more than it was. Kept things working long after they should've broken down."

He looked down at the counter, tracing a faint coffee ring with his thumb. "Guess I can stop trying to hold it together now."

She smiled gently. "You gave it what it needed. The rest was never yours to fix."

They stayed like that, the light shifting across the floorboards. Outside, a bird landed on the sill and tapped once against the glass.

"I'll be in the office if you need anything." She stood, adjusting her sleeve as though to anchor the moment. "You are, of course, welcome to share your news. But I'd like to tell everyone about the shop together, so they hear it directly from me."

He nodded. "This afternoon?"

"I'd appreciate your discretion until then." She didn't wait for his reply—just crossed to the back, hung her coat, and disappeared into the office. The door shut softly, not final, but firm.

Jonah moved through the space like he always did—quiet, methodical. He checked the grinder level, polished a streak off the counter, and aligned a stack of paper cups near the machine. The motions didn't feel like distraction. They felt like something he could still hold.

Outside, the light had changed. Pale warmth filtered through the front windows, catching in the brushed metal of the pastry case. The street beyond remained mostly still—just a woman with a tote bag crossing diagonally, her shoes scuffing against the wet concrete.

The bell chimed.

Brian stepped in with a gust of colder air, his hoodie zipped high, headphones still hanging around his neck.

"Hey," he said, giving a small wave. "You're early."

"So are you."

"Not by choice. The water heater quit halfway through my shower, so I figured I'd come freeze here instead." He dropped his bag by the hook and tugged on his apron. "Thought I'd beat the espresso machine to the warm-up, but clearly, you already won."

Jonah offered a faint smile. "It's ready if you want a cup."

Brian moved to the machine, shaking his hair out a little like a wet dog. "You already did the inventory? Restocked the cups?"

"Mostly."

He poured a cup and took a sip, then leaned against the counter. "I don't know how you function this early. It's unnatural."

Jonah didn't answer, just set the portafilter back with a soft clink.

Brian glanced around the room. "It's weirdly quiet."

"It's still early."

"Yeah, but—like, even for us." He looked back toward the front door. "Think it's gonna be one of those weirdly slow Thursdays where everyone in town got the same mysterious cold?"

Jonah gave a small shrug. "Could be."

Brian accepted the silence after that. He reached for a towel and started wiping down the front counter, picking up the rhythm without needing direction.

The bell gave its muted chime again—two early regulars stepping in with the quiet assurance of people who didn't need to glance at a menu. One settled near the window, peeling off gloves. The other hovered by the pastry case with a familiar squint, deciding between the same two items as every morning.

Jonah began pulling a double while Brian prepped two cups—one with sugar stirred in before the coffee, the other with cream on the side.

"Left side's the cappuccino," Jonah said under his breath.

Brian nodded, already reaching for the milk pitcher. "Got it."

They moved in a rhythm they didn't have to discuss—passing behind one another with just enough space, pivoting at the same time, hands finding what they needed without looking. The kind of ease that came from repetition, but also from trust.

"I really do want to learn how to fix that water heater," Brian said, watching the steam wand hiss. "It's old, but I think it's just the element. Or the thermostat. Or... something vaguely internal and broken."

Jonah passed him a cup. "Is it electric or gas?"

Brian blinked. "Uh... it has a plug. No flame noises. So—electric?"

Jonah nodded, already reaching for the grinder. "Start with the breaker. Make sure it didn't trip. If that's fine, check the high-limit reset—little red button behind the upper panel."

Brian squinted like he was trying to picture it. "And if that doesn't do it?"

"Then test the thermostat. After that, maybe the element. But start with what's easy."

Brian gave a short laugh. "You say that like any of it's easy."

Jonah shrugged. "If you end up replacing the element, you'll understand just how simple checking the breakers was. You just need a multimeter to test continuity and resistance."

Brian paused. "Right. Totally. I'll just... fetch my multimeter."

Jonah glanced at him. "You don't have one?"

"I have... enthusiasm."

Jonah smirked. "You can borrow mine. I'll show you how to use it."

They slid the completed drinks onto the pickup counter just as one of the regulars approached, pulling a crumpled five from a coat pocket.

Jonah rang up the order while Brian handed off the biscotti—one of the last from yesterday's batch. No fuss, no small talk. Just a nod and a quiet thanks.

The bell chimed again. Two more came in. The shop didn't grow louder, just fuller. Coats unzipped. Chairs eased back. A book opened with the soft crack of a worn spine.

Brian reached for the milk pitcher again. "So if it's not the element?"

Jonah leveled the grounds in the portafilter. "Could be sediment buildup."

Brian sighed. "Cool. So, science."

"More like patience," Jonah said.

Brian bumped his shoulder lightly as he passed. "You say that like I won't accidentally flood my hallway."

"You might."

"Well," Brian said, snapping a lid into place, "at least I'll learn something on the way down."

The bell above the door jangled—sharper this time, more insistent.

Patty stepped in like a weather front, cold air curling in behind her before the door swung shut. She scanned the room quickly: two customers at the window, the pastry case still mostly full, Brian mid-laugh behind the espresso machine. Her eyes landed on Jonah and paused.

She gave a short nod. "Place looks decent." She shrugged off her coat and hung it on the back hook with a thud that felt more like punctuation than noise. "Brian, the display fridge is humming again. Something's off."

Brian's smile flickered. "I'll check it." He disappeared into the back before she could say anything else.

Patty tied her apron, the strings snapping into place with practiced efficiency. She moved behind the counter like someone claiming familiar ground. Checked the till. Ran her finger along the countertop edge. She nodded once more, this time to herself.

Then she looked at Jonah. Her gaze was steady, unblinking.

"You didn't start the ovens," she said.
    "No," Jonah replied. "The morning got away from me."

Patty didn't question it—not directly. She just studied him, her expression unreadable but not unkind.

"Something on your mind?" she asked.
    Jonah nodded, slowly. "Yeah. I've got something to tell you. Both of you."

Brian reappeared just in time to catch the shift in tone. He paused, wiping his hands on a towel, then joined them behind the counter.

Jonah set the cloth in his hands aside.

"The residency accepted me," he said. "Redwood. I'm going."
    Brian blinked, then grinned. "Wait—really? That's huge."

Patty nodded once, quietly. "Didn't doubt it."

Jonah gave a faint smile. "Thanks."

"You planning to stay through the month?" she asked.

"Yeah," Jonah said. "Unless something changes."

"Good." She reached for the clipboard and flipped to the inventory sheet. "Gives us time to figure out how to keep the place upright without you."

Brian leaned in. "We'll manage. Mostly. Probably. With only minor structural damage."

Patty didn't look up. "If I ever cause structural damage, it'll be on purpose."

That pulled a breath of laughter from Jonah, brief but genuine.

Patty turned back to him, her gaze softer now.

"I'm proud of you," she said. "Not just for getting in. For saying yes."

Jonah met her eyes. "That was the hard part."

She gave a small nod, then let the silence close gently between them. After a beat, she picked up a cloth and began wiping down the already-clean espresso bar.

"Well," she said, her tone returning to something steadier, "don't just stand there. These mugs aren't going to restock themselves."

It was the same thing she said most mornings, but today it landed differently. Not a command. An anchor. A promise that, for now, the ritual remained. There was still work to be done.

Jonah slipped into the back with a small stack of returns under one arm. The morning rush had leveled out, giving him just enough of a lull to work the shelves.

The bookstore was quiet—not silent, but settled. The kind of quiet that invited thought but didn't require it.

He moved through the aisles with practiced ease, sliding a poetry collection back into place, pausing a beat to straighten a leaning spine in the next row.

Near the far shelf, Herb stood on the small wooden step stool, reorganizing a run of mystery paperbacks by author, muttering something under his breath.

He didn't look over when Jonah stepped into the aisle. "You know half these customers can't alphabetize."

Jonah smiled faintly. "That's why we have you."

Herb grunted. "Damn right it is."

They worked in tandem for a few minutes—Jonah reshelving returns, Herb consolidating titles into a wire basket that had once held classics but now housed whatever needed wrangling.

The silence between them was easy. Familiar. It had always been like this. Herb wasn't one for conversation, and Jonah had never needed him to be. He slid another book into place and glanced over—Herb was still muttering, the sleeves of his cardigan pushed halfway to his elbows. A small stack teetered near the end of the cart, but Herb didn't seem worried.

Jonah reached out instinctively, steadying it with a palm.

Herb gave a grunt of acknowledgment—not thanks, not annoyance. Just... noted.

"I reshelved the LeCarres," Jonah said after a moment, quieter now. "They'd drifted."

"Yeah," Herb muttered, not turning. "I saw."

Jonah waited for something else, but it didn't come. Just the sound of covers sliding, shelves breathing.

He didn't say it—what was coming, what he knew Herb would learn soon enough. It didn't feel right to say it here, in the middle of all this order, all this care.

Instead, he reached down and straightened the last book on the bottom shelf, fingers lingering a beat too long.

Herb finally looked over.

"Cart's empty," he said.
Jonah nodded. "Yeah."

Herb stepped down from the stool, knees popping just loud enough to complain. He handed Jonah the clipboard from the cart's top, his hand steady, expression unreadable.

"You shelve quietly," he said.
Jonah met his eyes. "I try."
Herb nodded once. "That's the right way."

That was all. He turned and wheeled the cart back toward the backroom, muttering again.

Jonah stayed behind for a moment, his hand still on the shelf.

Then, as Herb turned the cart, he spoke—not loudly, but clearly.

"I'm leaving."

Herb took a few more steps before he stopped. He turned halfway back.

"Leaving the shift?"

Jonah shook his head. "The shop."

That hung there a second.

Herb set the cart brake with his foot. "You get drafted or something?"

"Artist residency," Jonah said. "I leave in a few weeks."

Herb let out a short breath that might've been a laugh. Or just air.

"Who the hell's gonna make my coffee?"

Jonah shrugged. "Brian's getting better."

Herb scoffed. "Better's a low bar."

He turned back toward the cart, then paused again.

"You always got the closest," he said. "Still wasn't right—but closest."

Jonah smiled. "I'll take that."

Herb nodded once, then started rolling the cart forward again.

"The best of the worst," he added over his shoulder. "Don't let it go to your head."

Jonah watched him disappear around the shelves, the familiar creak of the cart wheels fading behind him.

Jonah stepped back onto the café floor just as the bell above the front door gave its softest version of a chime—a late arrival slipping in quietly, already pulling off his gloves.

The tables had filled while he was shelving books. Familiar faces. Regular rhythms. A chair squeaked. A spoon tapped ceramic. The hum of the espresso machine picked up again as Brian pulled another shot.

Patty glanced over from the pastry case. "Good timing. She's coming."

Jonah followed her gaze toward the back office.

Ms. Wallace emerged, her pace unhurried but unmistakably intentional. She paused near the counter and gave a small nod.

"Do you have a moment?" she asked, loud enough for the team to hear but soft enough not to disturb the room.

Patty wiped her hands on a towel and moved to the far end of the counter. Brian looked up from the steaming wand and raised his eyebrows in question.

Jonah nodded once.

Brian glanced down, finished pouring the drink in front of him, and slid the lid on with care. He handed it across the counter to the waiting customer—a young woman with headphones and a half-zipped backpack.

"There you go," he said gently. "Careful, it's hot."

She offered a quiet thanks and dropped a few coins in the tip jar.

Brian watched her go, then untied his apron and dropped it onto the back hook before stepping in beside the others.

A moment later, a soft muttering signaled Herb's arrival from the book side. He didn't say anything to anyone in particular —just folded his arms across his chest and joined the small semi-circle forming near the back counter.

Ms. Wallace waited until they were all within arm's reach—tucked behind the prep counter, near the end of the espresso bar, close enough to hear each other over the low hum of the shop.

She folded her hands, fingers interlaced.

"Thank you for coming together," she began. "I'll keep this brief."

Brian leaned slightly against the back counter. Patty stood still, eyes steady on Ms. Wallace. Jonah didn't move. Herb, off to the side, watched without blinking.

"I've made the decision to close the shop at the end of the month," she said. No buildup. No soft landing. Just the truth, plainly stated.

No one spoke for a moment. The café buzzed on, oblivious.

Brian shifted first, slowly straightening. "Wait—like... for good?"

Ms. Wallace nodded. "Yes. The lease ends in three weeks. I've chosen not to renew it."

Brian looked to Jonah, then to Patty before he let out a long breath. "Wow."

Ms. Wallace's voice remained even. "This wasn't an easy decision. But I believe it's the right one. I didn't want to tell you all in fragments. You've each carried this place, and you deserve to hear it together."

Patty crossed her arms, more out of thought than defiance. "You're sure?"

"I am," Ms. Wallace said. "And I'm grateful to all of you for what we've built here."

From the side, Herb cleared his throat. "Any chance we're faking this for morale?" he asked, deadpan.

Ms. Wallace gave the faintest smile. "No."

Herb nodded once. "Alright then." And with that, he turned and walked back toward the stacks, already adjusting the tilt of a display as he passed. Unbothered, or simply unwilling to show otherwise.

The group lingered in silence for another beat.

Ms. Wallace gave a small nod to the group—almost like a bow—and turned without another word, retreating toward the hallway. The office door clicked shut a few seconds later.

Patty finally exhaled, soft but audible. She looked to Brian. "You okay?"

Brian rubbed a hand across the back of his neck. "Yeah. I just..."

He trailed off, and for once, didn't fill the pause with sarcasm. Patty didn't rush him. Just rested her hand lightly on his arm.

"We'll talk," she said. "Come with me."
    Brian nodded, blinking faster than usual. "Yeah. Okay."
    Patty turned to Jonah. "You've got the counter?"
    Jonah nodded. "Yeah."

She gave him a look that wasn't quite a smile, but wasn't neutral either. Then she turned back toward the hallway, clipboard already in hand, steps steady as ever.

Brian lingered for a moment, then followed her, shoulders a little lower than usual.

Jonah stayed where he was. In the silence after the announcement, his eyes fell on the spider plant on the counter, it's cascade of babies spilling over the edge. "It's outgrown its pot," he thought. The simplicity of the problem was a relief.

A customer approached the register—a man with a folded newspaper and an order he didn't need to repeat. Jonah rang him up without comment, slid the coffee across the counter, and nodded once.

The man tipped his head in return. "Thanks."

Jonah reset the till, wiped a faint ring from the counter, and caught a glimpse of Patty and Brian near the doorway to the back, voices too low to hear. Patty was talking, eyes steady. Brian was listening—really listening. He wasn't smiling, but he wasn't falling apart either.

Jonah looked away before they noticed him watching. A woman approached, asking about a refill. A child with a chocolate muffin pointed out the loose napkins on the edge of the table. Someone waved gently from the window to ask for more sugar.

And Jonah moved between them all—quiet, steady. Still holding the center. At least for now.

The bell above the door jingled again as Amanda stepped in with a breeze at her heels and paint smudged across one knuckle. She glanced around, took in the mood immediately, and slowed just a fraction before heading toward the counter.

Jonah was already there, wiping down a clean surface for the third time.

"Hey," she said, her voice quieter than usual. "Everything okay?"

He nodded. "Yeah. We just... had a team meeting."

"Serious faces all around," she said, eyeing Patty, who was

just returning from the back hallway, clipboard under her arm. "Something happen?"

Patty stepped behind the register and pulled a clean cup from the stack. "You want your usual?"

Amanda blinked at the change of subject, then nodded. "Yeah. Please."

Patty started the drink, her motions steady. She didn't look up as she spoke.

"The shop's closing at the end of the month."

Amanda froze. "Wait—what?"

Patty looked at her now. Not apologetic. Just honest. "Ms. Wallace told us this afternoon. She's not renewing the lease."

"Oh." Amanda's eyes widened, flicked around the shop—like she was trying to memorize it in fast-forward. "Wow."

Patty slid the cup across the counter, lid already in place. "We're still open for now."

Amanda reached for it but didn't move right away.

Jonah stepped around the counter, wiping his hands on a towel as he came. "You headed out?"

"Yeah," she said. "Just needed a warm-up before rehearsal."

He nodded toward the door. "Mind if I walk with you?"

Amanda gave him a longer look then—searching, maybe —but said only, "Sure."

He pulled on his jacket. Patty didn't say anything, just gave him the briefest glance—*You okay?*—and a half-nod when he met her eyes.

Amanda held the door, and the bell gave one last chime as they stepped out into the late afternoon light.

The air outside was cooler now, the sky softening at the edges. They walked in silence for half a block, the sound of their footsteps a quiet counterpoint to the thoughts neither voiced. Amanda held her cup with both hands, not drinking, just absorbing its warmth.

Jonah spoke first, his voice even. "I accepted the residency."

Amanda looked over, her expression unreadable at first—then something settled in her eyes. Not surprise. Just the truth taking its shape.

"When do you go?" she asked.
    "Soon. A couple of weeks."

She nodded once, small and sure, and they walked a little farther before she spoke again.

"So," she said finally, her voice low. "The residency... and the shop. It's all happening at once."

"Yeah," Jonah said. "It is."

"Are you okay?"

He considered the question, really considered it, as they passed the hardware store, the library, the park entrance. The town felt different now, as if he were already seeing it from a slight distance.

"I will be," he said. And for the first time, he knew it was true.

Amanda nodded, accepting that. At the corner where she would turn toward the school, she stopped.

"It's not an ending, you know," she said, echoing his own unspoken thought. "It's a... reassembly."

He smiled, a real, unguarded smile. "Reassembly. I like that."

"I know," she said, smiling back. Then, with a final squeeze of his arm, she turned and walked away, not looking back.

Jonah stood on the corner for a long moment, watching her go. The sun was low now, casting the street in long, golden shadows. He could feel the weight of the day settling in his bones, not as a burden, but as a fact. A completed thing.

He turned—and instead of heading home, his steps carried him back toward the shop. The bell above the door offered a soft chime as he stepped inside once more.

The air inside the Grind & Bind felt dimmer now, touched by the angle of the light and the hush of approaching close. Chairs were tucked against tables. The last few customers lingered over mugs, their conversations low and unrushed.

Near the counter, Ms. Wallace and Patty stood in a quiet pocket of focus, clipboards in hand. A half-packed box sat open between them, tissue paper crinkled like fallen leaves. A row of items waited beside it—small framed signs, a stack of well-worn menus, the bell that used to hang above the side door.

Jonah paused just inside the threshold. The scene felt intimate, unguarded, like catching a glimpse of something before it was meant to be seen.

"You're back," Patty said, not looking up.

He stepped closer, shedding his coat. "Seemed like there might still be work to do."

Ms. Wallace's mouth curved slightly. "There always is."

He joined them at the counter and reached for a folded stack of old bookmarks. "You cataloging or triaging?"

"Both," Patty said. "Trying to decide what's worth storing,

what can be donated, and what's just accumulated sentiment disguised as utility."

Jonah thumbed through the bookmarks, some still dusted faintly with glitter from a long-ago school event. "What if we auctioned some of it off?"

That earned him two looks—one skeptical, one intrigued.

"Not for profit," he added quickly. "Just… for the customers. For the people who care about this place. Might mean more to them than it does boxed up somewhere."

Patty tapped her pen against the clipboard. "You mean let 'em bid on the wobbly table and the mug with the hairline crack?"

"If that's what they want," Jonah said. "People remember things. Even the imperfections."

Ms. Wallace was quiet a moment. Then: "We'd need a system. Tags, descriptions, maybe a silent bid sheet."

"We've got enough Sharpies," Patty murmured, but her voice was already warmer, edging toward possibility.

Brian wandered in from the back, arms smudged faintly with dust. "Are we giving away the squeaky chair? Because that one should come with a liability waiver and a heartfelt apology."

Herb, passing by with a stack of flattened boxes, snorted. "Only sell the books to people who know how to shelve 'em."

"Maybe we hang a sign," Jonah said, smiling faintly. "Warning: objects may be more meaningful than they appear."

There was a pause—just long enough for the laughter to settle into something steadier.

Ms. Wallace nodded once, then twice, as if confirming something unspoken. "Alright then. If we're going to say goodbye... let's do it properly."

Patty marked a note in the margin of her sheet. "We'll need a table near the window. Blank tags, some string. And someone with legible handwriting."

Jonah raised his hand. "I've been told I qualify."

Brian leaned over the counter. "I call dibs on writing the one for the coffee machine. 'Still mostly functional, especially if you believe in it.'"

Laughter rose again—gentler this time, edged with something softer. Not grief. Not yet. Just the beginning of a long, careful farewell.

24

LIGHT AND LEAVING

The next two weeks passed in pieces. Small, folded moments. Not linear, but layered—like the scent of dust and citrus that never quite left the wood. Each day felt both shorter and longer than it should have, time stretching around the edges of goodbye.

The air held a kind of expectancy, the quiet after rain, when the world waits to dry.

The "CLOSING SOON" sign in the front window wasn't large or loud. Just a plain sheet of paper in Jonah's neat handwriting, taped beside the bell. The ink had started to fade a little from sunlight, the paper curling at the corners—a quiet metaphor if anyone had wanted one.

Most customers paused at the door when they saw it. A few turned right around. Others stepped inside anyway— tentative, like interrupting something private.

Some offered condolences in the form of awkward jokes. Others brought pastries, or flowers in mugs. A few asked how much the reading chairs would cost.

One woman, wrapped in a bright scarf, touched the edge of the checkout counter with a reverent kind of sadness. "I got engaged here," she said quietly, eyes not quite meeting Jonah's.

He didn't have an answer, only a nod, and the offer of a paper-wrapped book she'd once asked about but never bought. She left with tears in her eyes and a faint smile. When the door closed behind her, the little bell seemed softer than usual, as if even it understood.

They set the auction up with index cards and string. Each item got a tag: a short description, a starting bid, and space for names and numbers. The air filled with the rustle of paper and the quiet scrape of pen against cardboard, the small sounds of letting go.

Brian made signs using leftover cardstock from the Valentine's Day display. He labeled the shelves with things like Mug #17:

chipped but charming and Lamp, Probably Haunted. Patty didn't stop him.

Customers left scribbled notes along with their bids. A few even signed only with initials, as if anonymity made sentiment easier.

This chair saved my back during finals.

We had our first kiss in this booth.

Please let me know if no one else wants it—I'll take it either way.

Books that weren't auctioned went into large donation boxes, sorted by age range and genre. Ms. Curlee from the library came by twice, her little hatchback filling and emptying with quiet diligence. Each trip felt like a slow redistribution of memory—chapters carried out into new hands.

They packed things slowly—not with hesitation, but with care. Tins from behind the bar, mugs with long-forgotten origins, cookbooks with pages dog-eared by years of flour and spill. The smell of cardboard mixed with lemon cleaner and the faint, sweet ghost of coffee that had soaked into the wood long ago.

Patty organized the back storage by decade, muttering to herself about expired teas and unknown syrups. Brian found three unopened puzzles in the Lost & Found bin and declared them artifacts.

"It's like unearthing a civilization," he said, holding up a single glove and a cracked CD case. "I think this belonged to the Early Caffeinic Period."

Jonah just smiled and kept folding boxes. Every sound—the tape's tear, the thud of a closing lid—felt heavier than it should have. It wasn't sorrowful, exactly. Just full.

On Thursday, Brian burst in with damp hair and an apologetic look, a familiar notebook clutched under one arm. "Okay, okay—I know I'm late, but I have a really good excuse this time."

Patty arched an eyebrow but said nothing, arms folded.

"I fixed the water heater," Brian announced, tugging off his jacket. "Like actually fixed it. Replaced the thermostat and everything. No more cold showers. No hallway flooding. No electrocution."

Jonah paused mid-pour, then gave a small nod. "It was the thermostat?"

"Yeah! One of them was stuck, so when the other switched on it was pulling too much current. Found this old wiring diagram online, did a continuity test, swapped it out, flipped the breaker back on—bam. Hot water." Brian beamed as he reached for his apron.

Patty handed him a towel, her tone dry but not unkind. "Glad you lived to tell the tale."

Brian grinned as he tied on his apron. "I mean, luck was involved. But there were diagrams. And tools. And possibly even some mild cursing."

Jonah smirked, checking the milk temp. "So you're ready for Fielding's full-time?"

Brian nodded, serious now. "Yeah. I think I am. When he offered before, I wasn't sure. It felt like... a maybe. But after today? I think I could actually be good at it. Like, really belong there and be helpful."

There was no fanfare to Jonah's smile—just quiet pride. "You'll definitely bring something good with you."

Brian bumped Jonah's shoulder gently as he passed behind him to grab a stack of lids. "Trying to live up to your legacy, old man."

"Not that old," Jonah said, deadpan.

They fell into rhythm without missing a step. Steam hissed. Cups clinked. The quiet hum of the shop folded around them as they worked, customers moving in and out, unaware of the quiet milestones behind the counter. It felt almost like any other day, which somehow made it matter more.

The last morning came with a gray sky and a hush over the town.

Ms. Wallace arrived early, a box tucked under one arm. She didn't say much, just set her coat in the back and helped pull chairs away from the windows. There was a steadiness to her movements, a grace that came only from someone who had loved a thing long enough to let it go properly.

Patty brought coffee from home—no ceremony, just habit. It tasted slightly different from the shop's blend, darker and smokier, but no one minded.

Herb rearranged the front display one last time, though half the shelves were empty. "You can't just not face the covers," he said, exasperated. "Even ghosts deserve decent shelving."

Amanda arrived mid-morning, windblown and bright-eyed. She held up a poster board covered in bold, uneven letters outlined in silver ink. Final Day. "Figured it deserved a little flourish," she said.

Patty smiled, eyes softening. "It does. Looks perfect."

Amanda taped it neatly beside the door, smoothing the corners. The sunlight caught the edges of the ink and made it shimmer faintly, like something breathing.

No music played. The regulars came and went in respectful silence. A few stayed. Most didn't.

Jonah handed out the last of the biscotti, brewed one final pot in the old machine. He didn't try to memorize anything. He just noticed.

The hiss of steam. The scent of lemon polish. The light sliding across the counter as the day bent toward afternoon. All of it ordinary. All of it sacred.

When the last customer left, they gathered by the counter without a word. Jonah set a small stack of brown paper parcels beside the register—each neatly wrapped, each with a note tucked beneath the string. The air held that mingled scent of paper, ink, and old coffee grounds, faint and comforting.

He handed the first to Brian. "For the man driven by curiosity."

Brian peeled back the paper and thumbed through the book. He blinked, his jaw tight.

"Whoever owned it before you had opinions," Jonah said.

Brian flipped through a few pages, pausing at a passage where someone had underlined: The only thing that makes life possible is permanent, intolerable uncertainty. He laughed. "Guess I found my people. You know this means I have to argue with a stranger now, right?"

Jonah smiled. "That's the hope."

Next, he turned to Herb. "For the man who solved every riddle that mattered."

Herb's expression softened as he took the pair of books. "You sap," he muttered as he carefully tore open the paper. He let out a single, surprised laugh. "A mystery and a diva. You really do know your audience."

Amanda received hers next. She held it reverently, tracing the embossed title with her fingertip.

"These are poems?" she asked.
　　Jonah nodded. "They're meant to be spoken."
　　Amanda smiled faintly. "Then I'll make sure they are."

Her voice softened as she turned it over in her hands, as if even holding it was a kind of performance.

She pressed it to her chest, eyes bright. "You really are the worst at pretending not to care," she said, her voice catching. Then she hugged him, tight and awkward and true. Her perfume smelled faintly of orange peel and pencil shavings.

Patty's came next. Jonah handed it over wordlessly.

She snorted at the title, flipping it open, her thumb brushing the page edges. "Short stories," she said, approvingly. "Dangerous territory. It means I'll start one before lunch and forget to eat."

"That's a risk," Jonah said.

Patty nodded, closing it with a small smile. "Guess that's your way of saying goodbye?"

"Not quite," Jonah said. "More like—thank you."

"Don't get sentimental on me," she said, though her voice softened. "I'll actually miss you, Ashford."

Jonah caught the flicker of emotion behind her eyes, the way she looked away almost immediately—because staying composed was how she said she cared.

Finally, Jonah reached for the last book. It was slim, deliberate, its cover pale gray—the kind that asked you to read slowly. He handed it to Ms. Wallace.

Her gaze lingered on the title before opening it. "You have a knack for irony," she said.

"It's the precision you'll like," Jonah replied. "Every silence counts."

She looked up, studying him for a long moment. "You always paid attention, didn't you?"

He hesitated, then smiled. "I tried."

Ms. Wallace closed the book carefully, her thumb resting in the middle as if to hold the place. "Then you'll do fine wherever you go."

The air felt still afterward, like the pause between heartbeats—each of them quietly holding the weight of what had been.

The final walk-through took longer than expected. Jonah moved from room to room, switching off lights, checking outlets, brushing his hand over doorframes. The air felt different without the steady hum of the espresso machine—a hollow quiet that seemed to gather in the corners.

He paused near the counter. The wood still held the faint outline of a coffee ring. One last receipt scrap lay under the register—blank except for a single smudge of ink. A thin circle of dust outlined where the tip jar had sat, and the patch of floor behind the counter was faintly lighter where his feet had never quite reached.

In the reading nook, the carpet showed the outlines of vanished chairs—pale squares against the deeper wear. A ring of sunlight lay across the wall where a framed print had hung. The room smelled faintly of citrus polish and something warmer—maybe cinnamon, maybe dust, maybe the memory of roasted beans that would never again be ground here.

He could almost hear the ghosts of old sounds—the hiss of milk steaming, the soft clatter of cups, Patty's sharp laugh cutting through Brian's running commentary. The silence wasn't sterile; it was textured, shaped by what had once filled it.

When he turned, the others were waiting by the door. Ms. Wallace's hand rested on the keys. Patty had one of the small pothos plants cradled in her arm, its vines brushing her sleeve; Amanda carried a fern that seemed to tremble in the draft; and Herb balanced the tiny cactus Jonah had given him on top of his stack of books, one careful hand steadying the spines so it wouldn't tip.

No one said who should do it. Ms. Wallace looked at Jonah, and he nodded.

Together, they stepped outside. The bell gave one last chime as she locked the door.

The sound hung in the air for a heartbeat before fading into the quiet street.

For a moment, none of them moved. Behind the glass, the shop's interior looked dimmer, the reflections swallowing what little remained. The bare tables, the faint scuffs, the hollow outlines where light no longer touched—everything still and waiting, like breath held after the final word of a story.

The sign in the window caught the afternoon light, the ink deep and shimmering.

Thank you for everything.

The air outside felt heavier than it had an hour ago, touched by the faint sweetness of spent coffee grounds and rain that hadn't yet fallen. The street was hushed, holding the kind of quiet that comes after a song ends.

They lingered for a moment beneath the awning, none of them quite ready to be the first to go. Patty tucked the small pothos against her chest and gave a short nod toward the others. Amanda stood beside her, the fern balanced carefully in her arms. Brian adjusted the strap of his backpack, the edge of a book peeking out, and gave a half-smile that didn't reach his eyes.

"Guess that's that," he said quietly.

Patty reached over, squeezed his shoulder. "For now."

Herb started down the sidewalk first, moving slowly, the cactus still perched on his stack of books. Patty and Amanda followed, Amanda keeping one hand steady on the fern to keep its soil from spilling. Brian fell into step beside Jonah for a few paces before stopping at the corner.

"I'll see you around," Brian said.

Jonah nodded. "You will."

Brian lingered just long enough to watch Jonah turn the opposite way, then crossed the street toward the hardware store, his figure folding into the slow rhythm of town life.

Ms. Wallace stood beneath the awning a little longer than the rest, keys in hand. She watched each of them go, her expression unreadable but softened by the weight of pride and fatigue. When the street finally grew still again, she turned once more toward the shop window, pressing her palm lightly to the glass. Then she adjusted the strap of her bag, took a quiet breath, and walked away.

Jonah walked alone after that. The air had cooled, the breeze carrying a faint tang of cut grass and exhaust. Sounds drifted from down the street, the hum of an air conditioner, the faint clink of a wind chime, the low roll of a train somewhere past the hills. The sound of his shoes on the uneven pavement was steady, small, but enough.

He found Mr. Beverly on the porch, the same as always.

"You look like a man who's just finished something important," the old man said, looking up from his crossword.

Jonah sat in the other chair. "It was important."

They sat for a while. A breeze rustled the hedge. Somewhere down the street, a screen door clapped shut.

Mr. Beverly turned a page, the paper's soft rasp filling the quiet between them. "Strange thing about endings," he said finally. "They never feel like they happen all at once. More like a tide going out. You don't notice until your feet aren't in the water anymore."

Jonah nodded slowly. "It's quieter than I thought it would be."

"Quiet doesn't mean empty," Mr. Beverly said. "Sometimes it just means it's your turn to listen."

They sat in that quiet for another moment, the high, insistent peeping chorus of spring frogs threading through the air. A car passed somewhere beyond the curve of the street, its tires whispering against the asphalt. Jonah leaned back, eyes tracing the slow drift of a cloud across the reflected glass of a neighbor's window. For the first time in a long while, he didn't feel restless—only steady.

After a moment, he reached into his coat and handed over the folded letter. "I've been meaning to give you this."

Mr. Beverly opened it slowly. Read each line with care. When he reached the middle, he let out a low chuckle.

"That's the thing you were trying to say, isn't it?"

Jonah nodded.

Mr. Beverly folded the letter and tucked it into his pocket without another word. "A season doesn't fail because it ends. It succeeds because it was. This town will have other seasons. So will you."

Jonah didn't reply. He didn't need to.

They sat until the sun shifted low and long across the porch. Then Jonah stood.

Mr. Beverly didn't rise. He just nodded once, like he'd been expecting this for a long time. His eyes softened, though, a quiet pride resting behind the lines of his face. "Keep your hands busy, your heart honest. The rest tends to follow."

Jonah stepped off the porch. The street stretched out in both directions—familiar, but no longer confining.

He walked away, not from something, but with it.

THE ROAD AND THE RIVER

Morning came quietly, the light soft and diffused, as if the house itself were reluctant to let it in. Jonah stood at the kitchen counter, the smell of toast and coffee mingling with the faint chill of dawn. His duffel was already packed and waiting near the door. His father moved slowly between the stove and the table, each motion deliberate—as though giving time itself a chance to stretch.

He cracked one last egg into the pan, folded it onto a slice of bread, and wrapped it in wax paper. When he set it on the table, he only said, "For the road."

Jonah nodded, accepting the simple offering as something heavier than words. He sat across from his father, both of them chewing in companionable silence. The clock above the sink ticked, steady and loud. His father refilled his own mug, then Jonah's, though neither needed more coffee. The scrape of the chair legs, the soft clatter of the spoon—each sound seemed to linger longer than it should, as if neither of them wanted to be the one to end it.

When Jonah finally stood, his father did too. The older man reached out, just a hand on his shoulder, firm, steady. No speech, no advice. Just that small, anchoring gesture.

Jonah gave a faint smile. "I'll call when I get there."

His father grunted in agreement, eyes fixed on the mug between them. Then, almost as an afterthought, he said quietly, "Drive safe."

It was the kind of phrase he'd said a hundred times before, but this time it caught in the air, heavier, as if both knew it was carrying something larger beneath it.

Jonah nodded once more, then stepped toward the door. He hesitated with his hand on the knob, half expecting to hear his father add something else. When he didn't, Jonah just breathed in—the smell of coffee, the faint heat of the stove— and opened the door.

Outside, the air held that pale smell of early light, clean and cold. When the door shut behind him, the house seemed to acknowledge.

He was tightening the last strap on his bag when he heard quick footsteps slapping the pavement. Amanda came running up the sidewalk, wind catching her hair, breath coming in uneven bursts.

"I thought I missed you," she said, laughing between breaths.

Jonah leaned against the car. "Almost."

She bent forward, hands on her knees, trying to catch her breath. "You didn't think you were getting away without saying goodbye, did you?"

"I wasn't sure you'd want to."

Her expression flickered—not fast enough to mask the look of hurt—then settled into resolve. "I didn't. But I needed to."

The space between them filled with the small sounds of morning: a distant dog, the hum of a passing truck, the soft rattle of leaves.

She reached into her coat and pulled out a notebook, wrapped in brown paper and tied with a thin strand of twine. "It's blank for now," she said. "You don't have to write to me, just write. But if you ever do, I'll be here, reading whatever you choose to send. It'll be like sharing a cup of coffee again."

Jonah took it carefully, as if it were something fragile. "You'll make wherever you go feel like it matters."

Her lip quivered into a smile. "Don't make me cry. I practiced being composed."

"Seems like it's going well."

She let out a small, choked laugh, wiping her cheek. Then, as she started to step back, something in her broke loose. She crossed the distance in two quick strides and threw her arms around him, holding tight, face pressed against his shoulder. He returned the hug, surprised but steady, the kind of embrace that said everything words couldn't. When she finally pulled away, her eyes were wet but shining.

"Don't forget us," she said, voice trembling but brave.
Jonah raised a hand. "Wouldn't know how."

She nodded once, then turned and jogged a few steps backward, waving with both hands, laughing through tears before spinning around and running back the way she came.

The miles unspooled easily beneath the tires. The hum of the engine became a kind of steady company, a low note beneath the shifting rhythm of the wind.
He didn't play music. He didn't need to. The road had its own quiet song.

The land began to open before him, with towns thinning, fields widening into low gold and gray. The sky was a deeper blue here, the kind that seemed to expand as you looked at it.

Light spilled across the pavement like cream, pooling at the edges of each curve. Wind caught the cuff of his sleeve, tugging lightly.

He passed a sign for a river he couldn't see; another for a town he wouldn't stop in. Each mile felt less like departure and more like translation—his life shifting languages, still the same words underneath.

By midday, he pulled into a rest stop with simple amenities: a picnic table, a vending machine that hummed faintly in the sun. He unwrapped the sandwich his father had made. The bread had gone soft, but it was still warm in the center.

When he finished eating, he took out the notebook Amanda had given him. The pages smelled faintly of paper and glue— unwritten air. He opened to the first one and stared for a while before beginning to write.

DEAR—
THE HILLS HERE LOOK LIKE THEY'RE EXHALING. THE AIR SMELLS NEW BUT FAMILIAR. MAYBE THAT'S WHAT CHANGE REALLY IS—FAMILIAR THINGS SEEN FROM ANOTHER ROAD.

He paused, then closed the book, resting his hand on it for a moment before slipping it back into his bag. The light shifted through the cottonwoods, dappling the hood of his car.

The residency was smaller than he'd imagined. A handful of cabins scattered near a river bend, all wood and windows, quiet except for the rustle of the water against stone.

Inside the small welcome office, a woman with short gray hair looked up from her clipboard and smiled. "Jonah Ashford, right? We're glad you're here. You've made it just in time."

"I guess I did."

She slid a folded paper toward him—a hand-drawn map. As she spoke, she circled each location in pencil, the marks faint but sure. "You're in the west cabin here. Meals are at the mess hall—this building—and gatherings happen in the group space over by the trees. Orientation's tomorrow morning."

"Got it," Jonah said, studying the map.

"Welcome, Jonah," she added. "If you find that you need anything, there's usually someone at this desk from eight to six, but the other residents are also really helpful."

"Yeah, thanks," he replied as she turned back to her notes.

He stepped outside, gravel crunching beneath his shoes. The air smelled faintly of cedar and damp earth. He followed the path toward his cabin, passing a common room with wide windows that faced the river.

Through the glass, he noticed an open sketchbook left on one of the tables, its pencil lines forming the outline of a hillside and a narrow bridge. He slowed, recognition immediate. The soft graphite smudges were unmistakably familiar.

When he reached his cabin, he opened the door and there she was, standing in the hallway a few paces in front of him, paused between rooms. Her recognition was immediate.

"You made it," Genesis said.

He nodded. "Yeah."

Her smile was small but certain. "Good."

She lingered a moment, then stepped back down the corridor, leaving the door half-open behind her.

He stood there for a while, allowing the silence to settle—not heavy or hollow. Present.

That evening, he boiled water on the small stovetop. The kettle's whistle rose and faded as he poured the tea, watching the steam twist and vanish into the chill air.

He sat at the desk, the notebook open again to a blank page. Outside, the river murmured low and steady, carrying its own memory of distance.

He let the sound wash through him, not trying to name it or hold it. The silence that followed felt alive—no longer the sound of an ending, but of something forming.

He lifted the pen, poised above the page.

And in the quiet, he began.

ABOUT THE AUTHOR

MATTHEW DYER writes about the quiet intersections of ordinary lives—the pauses, gestures, and small acts of care that reveal what words often leave unsaid. His work explores how people endure and connect through change, and how meaning lingers in the spaces between.

He lives with an appreciation for slow mornings, good coffee, and the kind of stillness that allows stories to surface.